Praise for *When the Wa*

When the Waters Came by Candice Sue Patterson is a beautiful story of love and faith triumphing over the worst of circumstances. Patterson adeptly drops wonderfully believable fictional characters into history and takes the reader on an unforgettable journey from tragedy to happily ever after.
–Kathleen Y'Barbo, *Publishers Weekly* bestselling author of
New Leash on Life and the Bayou Nouvelle Brides

Crises always highlight the contrast between good and evil, and *When the Waters Came* shines a brave spotlight upon both. Human bravery and depravity are on full display in the aftermath of the Johnstown flood, and readers are taken on a swirling, heart-wrenching journey as characters wrestle with issues of faith, fault, and forgiveness. This compelling story kept me awake at night.
–Rhonda Dragomir, award-winning author of
historical romance, including *When the Flames Ravaged*

Amazingly detailed and powerfully written, *When the Waters Came* will flood your heart with emotions—sorrow for the tragedy the people of Johnstown endured when the dam broke, admiration for those who labored to administer healing and justice, and tenderness for how God brings blessings out of disasters. Devastated by the ordeal he's endured, Monty struggles to hold onto his faith and minister to his congregation, even while he hides his ties to those responsible. Annamae arrives with the Red Cross, armed with zeal for social justice. But she just might need healing more than those she nurses. Love blooms amid devastation, offering a foundation for a stronger future if Monty and Annamae are willing to overcome their pasts. *When the Waters Came* sets the bar high for a series that highlights one of life's deepest mysteries, how God brings triumph out of tragedy.
–Denise Weimer, multi-published author of *When Hope*
Sank and The Scouts of the Georgia Frontier Series

A DAY TO REMEMBER

When the Waters Came

CANDICE SUE PATTERSON

BARBOUR
PUBLISHING

When the Waters Came ©2024 by Candice Sue Patterson

Print ISBN 978–1-63609–758-9
Adobe Digital Edition (.epub) 978–1-63609–759-6

All scripture quotations, unless otherwise noted, are taken from the King James Version of the Bible.

This book is a work of fiction. Names, characters, places, and incidents are either products of the author's imagination or used fictitiously. Any similarity to actual people, organizations, and/or events is purely coincidental.

Cover design by Faceout Studio

Published by Barbour Publishing, Inc., 1810 Barbour Drive, Uhrichsville, Ohio 44683, www.barbourbooks.com

Our mission is to inspire the world with the life-changing message of the Bible.

 Member of the
Evangelical Christian
Publishers Association

Printed in the United States of America.

DEDICATION

*For the courageous residents of Johnstown, Pennsylvania,
who endured that tragic day. No matter your end, may
your lives and your stories never be forgotten.*

FRIDAY, MAY 31ST, 1889

*"Record that awful date in characters of funeral hue.
It was a dark and stormy day, and amid the darkness
and the storm the angel of death spread his wings
over the fated valley, unseen, unknown."*

~Illustrated *History of the Johnstown Flood*
by Willis Fletcher Johnson

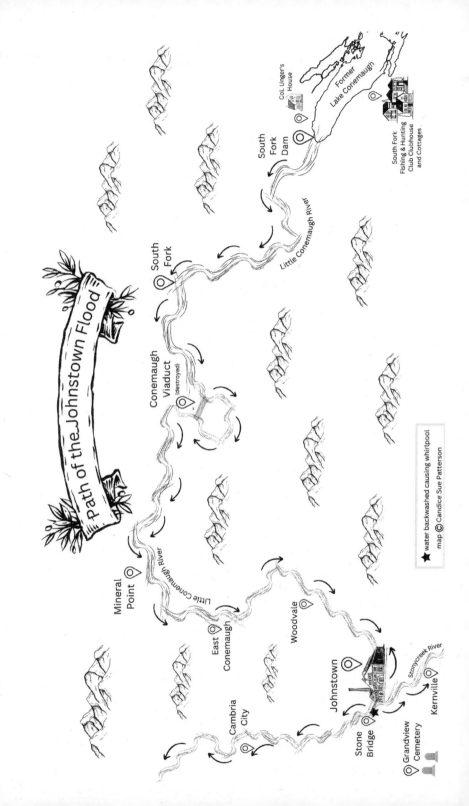

Path of the Johnstown Flood

Col. Unger's House

Former Lake Conemaugh

South Fork Dam

South Fork Fishing & Hunting Club Clubhouse and Cottages

Little Conemaugh River

South Fork

Conemaugh Viaduct (destroyed)

Mineral Point

Little Conemaugh River

East Conemaugh

Woodvale

Johnstown

Stonycreek River

Kernville

Cambria City

Stone Bridge

Grandview Cemetery

★ water backwashed causing whirlpool

map © Candice Sue Patterson

Chapter One

～⌒

*"The morning was delightful, the city was in its gayest mood
with flags, banners, and flowers everywhere. . . . We could
see almost everything of interest from our porch. The streets
were more crowded than we had ever seen before."*

~Reverend H.L. Chapman, Johnstown Methodist Church

JOHNSTOWN, PENNSYLVANIA
MEMORIAL DAY, THURSDAY, MAY 30, 1889

Fog suspended from hemlock and spruce in a ghostly blanket that whispered along the peaks of decorated headstones, and the mourners gathered round. Boots sinking in the spongy earth, Pastor Montgomery Childs stood on the hillside and offered words of comfort and scriptures of hope to mothers who'd lost sons, to wives who'd lost husbands, and to veterans who'd lost comrades, limbs, and pieces of their hearts in the War of the Union. Would that this united land never consume such a number of souls so hastily again.

The Grand Army Veterans and Sons of Veterans stood erect on each side of Monty as darkening clouds moved overhead. The fire department stood at the back of the crowd as well as the Hornerstown Drum Corps. Visitors joined them from towns as far as Somerset and Altoona.

A drop of rain hit the end of Monty's nose as a trumpet's doleful tone sliced the air. Would the rain never cease for more than a few hours? Though his residence in Johnstown was a meager two years, the native populace declared this the wettest spring in decades. Happy little creeks that bubbled and foamed through the Alleghenies were now rushing torrents emptying into the swollen Little Conemaugh River. The pickerel and bass needn't exhaust any effort since the current carried them along. The ground was so saturated, even the violets and geraniums that crowned the forest floor bent in merciful prayer.

Monty rather enjoyed a rainy day. It cleansed, it healed, it sustained life. But this much rain was preposterous.

The American flag, held erect by Benedict Covington, hung limp as the sky unleashed. As Colonel Elwood's last trumpet note faded away, Monty said, "That concludes our ceremony."

He'd planned to say much more about the men who'd sacrificed their lives to give others freedom, but no words, no matter how eloquently spoken, meant anything when water puddled ankle high. Some attendees had traveled a long way to pay their respects and needed to board their trains before they floated away.

As the crowd dispersed down the curving path that led back to Johnstown, Monty opened his umbrella, tucked his Bible inside his coat, and followed behind the mass of spectators. At two thirty, the parade had started at the end of Main Street, marched through town, taken a right on Bedford, and then turned south to Sandyvale where Grandview Cemetery was spread out on the highest, flattest ground in the area.

It was beautiful property, stretching green in every direction. A wall of trees hindered any view of Johnstown lying in the bowl-like valley below, protecting visitors from the loud noises of the mills and the acrid stench of the smokestacks. The air here was the purest for miles around.

Complaints ensued from members of the Austrian Music Society about the rain bathing their instruments. By the time the attendees reached their destination, they'd all suffer a good drenching. Yesterday's *Tribune* predicted more rainstorms this evening and into tomorrow. What they needed was sunshine after the long, dreary winter.

In town, Monty picked up his pace toward home. He passed several businesses, closed until six so the proprietors and their families could join the festivities. With school out for the holiday, children scrambled about, playing in puddles and helping with chores. The town was in a cheerful mood, shouts of celebration and music replacing the clank and rumble of the mills. Men and women dashed about, undeterred by the weather. Residents were used to spring rain and spring floods, and little hindered them from their activities.

The Hulbert House brimmed with guests flowing in and out of the hotel, the first in Johnstown with an elevator. Drops of rain pinged off the No VACANCY shingle. Business everywhere was booming, especially this week with all the out-of-town guests exchanging currency.

Unfortunately, that meant the forty saloons open today benefited as well. There were a hundred and twenty-three across the valley, including establishments like Lizzie Thompson's Place at the end of Locust Street, offering soiled doves at a fair price. Monty's stomach turned each time he thought of it. He was the one those folks came to when they needed help or a way out of their debauchery. Some situations were just too complicated to repair.

He ducked under the opera house's overhang that announced *Zozo the Magic Queen* and *Uncle Tom's Cabin* playing at five and seven thirty. Once the streetcar passed, he dashed across the road and alongside dwellings and businesses to his home on Macedonia Street, east of the Stonycreek River. He was fortunate to live by the church a short distance from downtown and not nearer one of the mills where the homes were shacks or tenements sloppily built to house immigrant workers.

Johnstown was rough and bustling and growing. And yet, Monty felt more at home here among these people than he ever had with his family in the luxury of Pittsburgh's East End.

As he stepped onto his front porch, he gazed up the mountain where the South Fork Fishing and Hunting Club roosted on the bank of Lake Conemaugh. He couldn't see the exorbitant clubhouse from fourteen miles away, of course, but the landscape materialized in his mind's eye. Trees reflecting off the glassy surface of the water, sailboats slicing across the lake, couples strolling arm in arm down the boardwalk. The perfumed women dressed in white, with pink in their cheeks from the sunlight. The scent of brandy and imported cigars that clung to the finely tailored suits of the male guests after dinner.

Members, like his uncle, were rough and worldly in a different way from the Johnstown immigrants—and ten times greedier. Most folks in Johnstown were poor, while the men who owned the mills and factories where they worked ate lavish dinners in their servant-filled homes in Philadelphia and Pittsburgh and enjoyed extended weekends of pleasure at the lake.

After laboring sixteen hours a day, seven days a week, for wages which would never come close to providing for their families, the millworkers' reward was the stench of the foundries clinging to their hair, clothes, and skin no matter how much soap they used or how many times they washed. Monty was honored to call such hardworking folks his brothers and sisters in Christ. They certainly had more integrity than most of the men who ran in his uncle's social circle. Still, he prayed fervently for the souls of those men who were too wealthy to see their need for God—even if a camel walking through the eye of a needle was more likely than their humbling themselves to pray for salvation.

For the rest of the afternoon, Monty sat at his kitchen table studying the Bible for his Sunday sermon, eating the leftover trout he'd caught in Stonycreek yesterday, and writing a letter to his friend from seminary who'd recently taken a church near the Adirondack Mountains.

The rain stopped at five, just in time for the streetlamps to light up the town. Johnstown was low in the valley with the Alleghenies brushing the surrounding sky, and residents were lucky to see seven hours of sunlight per day.

During evening prayers, Monty asked the Lord for this to be the end of the rain.

Long after he'd fallen asleep, he awoke to a deluge beating on his roof. Monty rolled over, afraid the force with which it fell from the sky would send the downpour crashing through the shingles. He lay, drowsy in the dark, and waited. For what he didn't know, but an ominous weight settled over him. After a while, the downpour lessened, and the pattering rhythm lulled him back to sleep.

Chapter Two

~

"River twenty feet and rising, higher than ever before; water in first floor. Have moved to second. River gauges carried away. Rainfall, two and three-tenth inches."

~Telegraph sent to Pittsburgh at eleven o'clock by Mrs. H.M. Ogle, Signal Service representative and Western Union manager in Johnstown

FRIDAY, MAY 31

Monty awoke to two inches of water covering his lawn. He stood on his porch and measured it by the reflection in the streetlight. The rain had poured throughout the night and had yet to cease. By the time dawn crested the mountains at a quarter till ten, that number had grown to three.

Spring flooding had arrived.

It happened every year when the snow melted off the mountains and the rains came, swelling the tributaries that rolled through Johnstown. The Little Conemaugh River intersected with Stonycreek at the Stone Bridge, where it flowed southeast and eventually released into the Atlantic. Though Monty still had much to learn about the valley and its inhabitants, he'd learned after his first spring to invest in a good pair of boots.

He jammed his feet into them and raised the collar of his slicker high on his neck. The trek to Heiser's General Store might be miserable, but it was better than going hungry like he had the year prior when the rising water held him hostage for two days straight.

The butcher shop was not open due to "flooding at home," the sign read. Ruffed grouse and wild turkey hung from hooks in the window. Across the street, Mrs. Lowe and her son stepped out of the library and huddled together beneath an umbrella to protect their borrowed materials. The library was funded by the Cambria Iron Works and had recently started holding night classes for anyone in the community who wished to strengthen their education.

A hand slapped Monty's shoulder, splashing water against his ears. He almost lost his footing in the mud where he'd stepped off the boardwalk to allow a group of ladies a clear path to the cafe. Everett McDonough steadied him by the arm. "What're we to do with all this rain, Pastor?"

Monty squinted into the stormy sky. "Build an ark, I suppose."

Everett chuckled. "May have to. Heard tell Cambria Iron Works sent their men home early to care for their families. Flooded tenements. The Little C is rising faster than folks can carry their belongings to the second floor. The telegraph office is closed for the day too. First floor filling up with water. Hettie's working the wire from the second."

Flooded tenements were nothing new. Poorly built in lower areas of the valley, some balanced on nothing but the runoff from the mill that had hardened like stone. The occupants were accustomed to securing their belongings higher during the rain. The telegraph office flooding was altogether different.

A crackle of thunder sounded above, and the rain gained in intensity. Monty had planned to make his purchases at Heiser's since he needed to speak with George about Founder's Day anyway; but if the monsoon continued at this pace, everything he bought would be ruined by the time he got home. James Quinn's dry goods store was closer. Monty could survive off salt pork, rice, and beans for a few days.

They waded across the flooded street, now four inches and rising, and ducked beneath the overhang of the dry goods store where a patron exited with his purchase. In the next instant, the door slammed and locked. Mr. Quinn squinted through the glass pane. Monty knocked, unsure what he would do if the man didn't allow him inside.

Mr. Quinn's stern frown accentuated his stylish Vandyke beard, threaded with as much gray as brown. He looked at his pocket watch then yanked the door open. "Five minutes, Pastor Childs. Then I'm going home to gather my family and get them to higher ground."

The fear in the man's voice thrummed a chord of unease in Monty's gut.

"Thank you, Mr. Quinn." Monty went straight to work gathering supplies while Everett waited on the porch.

As Mr. Quinn tallied Monty's bill, he said, "You ever get a feeling deep inside, one so nagging and clear you know it must be God speaking to you?"

"I do. Trust His voice, Mr. Quinn. It'll never steer you wrong."

Monty helped the man slip his purchases into cloth bags he promised to bring back when the weather cleared.

"Rosina's in Kansas visiting family. Little Marie's had the measles. She's recovering but weak. Hate to take her out in this cold rain, don't want the daylight to bother her eyes, but I might just go home and gather Aunt Abbie and the kids and slip on out for a few days. I'm terrified that dam is going to break."

The man's hand trembled as he slid the bags across the counter.

"Thank you again for letting me inside. I'll be praying it doesn't. And for your family."

Monty left the store and returned to the wet outdoors. There was something different in the air now. A foreboding from Mr. Quinn's words that sat heavy against his chest. He wasn't one to let other people's fears poke at him, but this wasn't a normal spring flood. And the dam that held back Lake Conemaugh at the South Fork Fishing and Hunting Club wasn't safe.

Thunder rolled across the valley.

Everett reached for a bag to lighten Monty's load. "Heard tell the railroad officials sent a telegram warning folks to evacuate. Something about a bridge washed out two miles east and they expect more to follow. It's also rumored the lake's spilling over and the dam might break."

"That rumor spreads through town every time it rains." Monty faced the mountain, where a lake almost three miles long and a mile and a half wide hovered above them like the angel of death on Judgment Day.

James Quinn was known for being an anxious individual, and talk of the dam collapsing had been passed down through the generations until it had become folklore. If those warnings from the railroad officials held merit, few would take them seriously.

Folks had tried to convince the South Fork Fishing and Hunting Club to reinforce the dam for years. They'd ignored the pleas.

If the dam failed, it would decimate Johnstown.

Even without a collapse, if the rain continued, the two adjoining rivers that ran through Johnstown would swell large enough to put everyone in trouble. James Quinn was right in moving his family to higher ground.

"Something 'bout this is different, Pastor."

The unease in Everett's voice echoed Monty's thoughts. "Heard tell of anything else I need to know?"

"Nah. Stay safe, Pastor. I'm off to see that the Mrs. and children stay dry. May not be in church on Sunday. If it rains through the night, we'll be leaving on the morning train to visit my mother in Philadelphia until this weather changes course."

"Godspeed, Everett." Monty stuck out his hand.

With a firm grip, Everett grasped it. "Godspeed."

He handed Monty the bag then stepped into the deluge. Monty remained under the porch's covering, watching life move around him. Horse hooves navigated through the flooded streets. Five inches, if he gauged correctly. The barber, the bank, and Miss Millie's Cookhouse seemed to conduct business as usual. Bodies raced toward the train station. Monty sent up a silent prayer for the protection of every soul before racing for home.

As he passed the Quinns' large brick home, he spotted a little girl around the age of six sitting on the front porch step, barefoot and splashing in the water pooled in the yard. Ducklings swam around her ankles. Monty wasn't familiar with the Quinn children, but he recognized Vincent, the girl's nearly grown brother, assisting those traversing nearby. A moment later, James Quinn raced past Monty and into his yard, snatched the little girl up, and scolded her all the way indoors.

The cloth bags did little to protect Monty's purchases, and by the time he stepped through his front door, he and his once-dry goods were soaked through. He slipped off his boots and hung his slicker on a wall hook. Rain dripped onto the rug he'd purchased from Mrs. Callen when he'd first moved to town. The home was drafty and plain, but it was his.

Shivering, he stoked the fire in the cookstove, added two logs, and peeled off his wet shirt. Rain pelted the windows, sending the chill deeper into his bones. He'd continue studying for his sermon and maybe read a few chapters of *Great Expectations*, a popular novel from his childhood he'd yet to indulge in. His cousin, Whitney Whitcomb, had recently mailed it to him as a cruel nod to his orphan upbringing. He'd accept the gift by reading it, writing his full critique of the novel, and sending it to her.

She'd taken as much offense at his announcement denouncing the family business and enrollment in seminary as his uncle. They'd once been as close as siblings, but Whitney had allowed the poison of her father to seep into her blood, and she sank her teeth into Monty every chance the distance between them allowed.

After donning fresh clothes and dry shoes, he put away the items he'd bought at Quinn's Dry Goods and removed the salt-cured ham Widow Mason had delivered to him yesterday morning in appreciation for him repairing her broken stair railing. Ham slices sizzled and popped in the pan, joined by another sound he didn't recognize. He leaned his head to the side and waited. There it was again, louder.

Was someone yelling?

He went to the front door and opened it just enough to determine if the sound came from town. A man raced down the road on horseback, panic contorting his features. His poor beast foamed at the mouth. "To the hills, for God's sake!" It was the scream of a madman. "To the hills for your lives!"

Monty's neighbors had opened their doors to witness the commotion as well. They exchanged uncertain glances across the street, unsure what to make of it all. The man flew past them, water splashing around his horse's ankles, screaming his warning like Paul Revere on the cusp of British attack.

A roar unlike anything Monty had ever witnessed started and grew louder with each passing second. He looked in the direction the man had come from, and fear pierced his heart. Black mist rolled into the air. Then Monty saw a wall of water as tall as any building, devouring everything in its path.

The dam had broken.

"Save yourselves!" Monty yelled, and slammed his door.

He ran toward the stairs. His foot slapped the first step when his worst nightmare turned frighteningly real.

Chapter Three

"*Dam broken. Flood coming. Tell—*"
~Telegraph sent to Pittsburgh at 3:10 by Mrs. H.M. Ogle, Signal
Service representative and Western Union manager in Johnstown,
moments before the flood washed the telegraph office away

Monty's front door exploded off its hinges, splintering the thick slab and sending shards across the room. Water poured through the opening, and his house shook from the force. His mind refused to accept the horror playing before his eyes. Legs pumping of their own volition, he vaulted up the stairs as dark, foamy water swallowed the parlor floor. Like the worst kind of beast, it groaned and expanded, filling the room and swiping at his feet on the steps.

High ground.

Fast.

When he reached the top step, the house shifted. Furniture tumbled, and the sound of breaking glass filled the air. He pitched into the wall. Pain radiated through his head and shoulder, but he couldn't stop now. The water was rising.

Listing to the side, he leaped over a small table that had fallen from the bedroom into the hallway. Daguerreotypes of his parents and siblings hung crooked on their nails. He struggled to reach the door leading to the attic. The roar of water deafened his ears. His heart slammed against his chest. He twisted the knob, but the door held fast. *Oh, God, I can't perish like this. Not like this.*

Water breached the stairs and rushed into the rooms on his right. He yanked again. The tilting house had pinched the frame against the door. Even if he had to scratch a hole with his fingernails, he was getting to that attic.

The house shook again. He braced himself, palms flat against the wall. Something had crashed against the structure. He could sense it. He was fortunate it still stood on the foundation at all. With the roar of a mighty warrior, Monty kicked the attic door several times. Each blow weakened the wood until it finally split. Pain pulsed up his leg, but the water pooling around his boots gave him a supernatural determination. One last kick, and the center of the door split apart.

Monty punched a hole large enough to slip his body through. Water swirled around his ankles. Fists bleeding, he lifted a wet foot and shoved it through the opening. Wood clawed his back as he squeezed through the narrow opening and freed his other leg.

The dim light of the attic made it hard to navigate. He felt for the stairs using his hands and crawled as fast as he could. A loud crack shocked his eardrums. The room shifted. His house was floating. He groped for the stair railing. He had to keep moving. For an instant, he felt like a bobber in a pond, and then the house smashed into something, sending him tumbling into a stack of old trunks.

Agony ripped through his head. His body ached. Tears pushed into his eyes. He shut them tight, if only to block out the reality of this nightmare. He had to get as high as he could. The water was coming for him. Yes, heaven awaited, but Monty wasn't ready to inhabit it today.

A shaft of pale light above caught his attention, and he glanced at the rafters. Rain fell from a hole in the roof.

Air.

That meant the giant wall of water hadn't swallowed his entire house yet. If he could climb the joists and reach the hole, he could try to make it large enough to fit through. If the water continued to rise in the attic, he would have air.

He jumped and attempted to grip a beam, but his fingertips, slick with blood, only skimmed the wood. He wiped his fingers on his pant leg and tried again. Though he made progress, it wasn't enough. Water began seeping over the top step of the attic. He grasped the handle of a trunk and dragged it beneath the joist as best as he could on the slanting floor. Oh, why had he insisted on bringing his book collection from home? The hefty weight could be the deciding factor between life and death.

Getting as close as he could, he hopped onto the trunk and lunged for the joist. A solid grip. The trunk slid from under his feet and crashed against the wall. This was his last chance. He swung his legs to gain momentum and then kicked high enough to lock his ankles around the beam. Chest heaving, sweat dripped from his temples. Or was it blood?

Lord, give me strength.

He worked his burning muscles until he sat upright on the beam. The wood's angles bit into his thighs. He bowed his head and prayed. Splashing drowned his thoughts. Water bubbled over the attic stairs.

God, don't let me drown. Please.

He scooted along the joist until he reached the hole.

A thud sounded above him. Footsteps?

Cries for help blended with the roar of water, rending his heart. Was this how Noah felt after God sealed the ark and the waters came—helpless, tortured, frail? Monty could no more help them than he could help himself. Bile rose in his throat. Pushing past the fear threatening to hold him stationary, he braced between the joist and the rafter on shaky legs and began punching the roof shingles around the hole with his fist.

Blood poured down his arm as more skin scraped and peeled from his knuckles. A face appeared on the other side of the opening, startling Monty so fiercely he almost lost his grip. "There's someone in here," the man yelled.

Hands gripped the edges of the hole and began ripping wood and shingles.

"You got any rope in that attic?" A man with a nasty gash on his forehead shoved his face inside. "People are rushing past in the water. We need to save as many as we can."

Rope. Did he have rope? No.

Looking below at the attic's contents not devoured by water, he spied an old bed sheet covering a floor-to-ceiling mirror the previous owners had left behind. Half of it was underwater. "Will a sheet do?"

"Anything is worth a try," the man replied. "Can you reach it?"

Monty was losing steam as fast as the water was rising. "I think so."

Stepping from joist to joist, he traveled at a downward slope. His brain screamed at him to retreat to the hole and save himself, but the Lord had called him to help save others' lives. He needed to at least try.

On the last joist, he bent and reached for the sheet. The fabric was weighty and half soaked through, making it harder to carry. He worked his way back to the roof hole and shoved the bedsheet through. The drenched part of the sheet rubbed against him as hands tugged it through. Now he was bloody and wet.

Two arms reached down for him. While he'd retrieved the sheet, the men had worked on making the hole large enough for him to squeeze through.

He reached up and clutched their wrists. They hoisted him through the hole, and a roofing nail ripped his thigh, but at least he had air. He collapsed onto the roof, hands and gashed leg throbbing, and let the cold rain pelt his body. His limbs shook from exertion. Nausea rising, he rolled onto his side and pushed himself to sitting.

Monty wasn't prepared for what he saw. Water surrounded every rooftop as far as he could see, but many buildings had washed away completely. His house no longer stood on its foundation and was now wedged against the side of the church. The two structures held fast to each other, the old structure bracing the newer one.

A stream of human bodies swept through what was once Locust Street. Some attempted to grab anything they could find, while others let the current sweep them away. For the ones floating face down, it was too late.

Possessions of every kind littered the dark water—teacups, dishes, furniture, a dollhouse, animal carcasses, farming tools, books, rolls of barbed wire, machinery, wagons. A boxcar moved in the distance. Mr. Graves's new draft horse, Lancelot, bellowed as it passed, bobbing in the waves like a rocking horse.

"There!" one man on Monty's roof shouted. A fellow balanced on top of the boxcar, riding the wave as if it were a boat. If the car turned sideways and smacked into Monty's house, they'd all go for a swim.

The man with the gash on his forehead shouted toward the boxcar. "Grab this!"

Monty saw that one of them had tied a knot in the sheet. With precise movements, the man tossed the sheet at the boxcar while the other man braced for the weight. The man from the boxcar caught it, but it slipped through his fingertips, and he continued down the river.

For what felt like hours, though was likely only minutes, Monty and the two men attempted to save all they could. But their efforts were to no avail. When the sky grew even darker with the oncoming night and the rush of bodies headed downstream appeared to have already gone to Jesus, they huddled together and watched the water rise higher.

"Look there." One of the men pointed up ahead. He crawled to the edge of the roof, squinting. "It's Max McCachren. He has a little girl."

Sure enough, the large man came at them, floating on a mattress with a small child clinging to his neck. Seeing them, Max kicked, attempting to move the raft closer to the house. He wasn't gaining ground. He was still a good fifteen feet away, and if Monty didn't do something soon, Max and the little girl would be gone to them forever.

"Throw the baby!" Monty yelled.

"Do you think you can catch her?" Max called back.

"We can try." Monty stretched out his arms. The water had risen to just three feet below his roofline, but the church held his house firmly.

Max extricated the girl's arms from around his neck. She screamed in protest and fought against him. With a battle-like cry, Max pitched the child through the air. Catching her by one arm and the fabric of her clothes, Monty hoisted her securely onto the roof.

Max floated past. His smile of triumph was quickly dashed by the fate that surely awaited him.

The girl, much older than he'd guessed, gripped Monty's neck tightly enough he feared she'd strangle him. Closer to the age of six, the poor thing wore nothing but her underclothes. One man unknotted the sheet, and they cocooned her inside it. It was wet and cold, but if they took turns holding her, maybe their body heat would keep her from freezing to death.

She snuggled against Monty's chest, burrowing in the sheet so it covered her head. The rain eased, but it was little comfort at this point. After a while, the rush of water slowed its pace around them, and the guttural cries of survivors sounded over the gush of water. Monty rested his cheek against the top of the girl's head and wept.

Chapter Four

"I have lost everything on earth now but my life, and I will return to my old Virginia home and lay me down for my last great sleep."

~Mrs. Fenn, after losing her husband and seven children in the flood

Monty jerked awake when the shivers racking his body grew too intense to allow him to doze. He was fighting shock and exhaustion. The rain was nothing but a sprinkle now, but their wet state, coupled with the cool evening, could easily send them into hypothermia. He prayed the heat of his body, if he had any left, would keep the girl in his lap from freezing.

The devastation was worse farther downtown. Their vantage point on the roof allowed them a view of the wall of water building at the stone bridge, likely from debris clogging the arches. The water appeared to switch courses, creating a whirlpool. If anyone managed to survive the ride down, it would take a miracle to survive the churning destruction. The buildings on the northwest end of town that had survived the first wave rose into the air with the water's force then smashed into a thousand pieces, one by one.

Monty's home and church were on the southeast side of town, higher up the slope. The elevation was likely the only thing that saved them. Mr. Miller's red barn had been swept from its stone foundation at the southern tip of Woodvale and now sat on top of the Beyers' new home on what used to be Magnolia Street. Houses and buildings, splintered like toothpicks, lay at every conceivable angle, many impaled with uprooted trees.

Telegraph poles bent at odd angles, the wires nothing but a jumble. Balls of barbed wire, steel manufacturing equipment, merchandise from stores with the tags attached, and personal possessions of every kind bobbed in the torrent.

Johnstown was decimated.

He wondered how the other towns that lay below the dam fared.

The mountains were dark and moving, filled with survivors watching and wailing for their lost loved ones. His head pounded from it all. It was too much for mind and heart to bear.

Mr. Sherman from Woodvale, one of the men who'd pulled Monty from the attic, slept against the saturated shingles. He'd floated down the wave on a tabletop then jumped from his makeshift raft onto the roof of a house near Miller Street. Sometime later, his perch became unsteady, forcing him to leap to other rooftops and over debris until he found a stable structure. Mr. Sherman didn't know what had hit his head to create the wound, but the filthy water was a concern for infection.

The other man was new to Johnstown. Mr. Ramey, as he'd introduced himself, had moved from Ohio last October with his wife and children to work in the flour mill. He hadn't spoken a word since he'd told Monty that information. Simply stared ahead, unblinking, shock making him more a ghostly corpse than alive.

Like Ramey, Monty was numb inside, unsure how to process the horrors he'd seen and heard. How he wished he could perform miracles so he could utter "Peace, be still," and the raging water would cease. God was above them, witnessing the tragedy unfold. Monty wasn't sure how to process that either.

He turned and remembered the wave had thrown his home against the church. The steeple bearing a small cross caused the back of his eyes to burn. He had to hold himself together. Had to keep breathing, keep going. The Lord would need Monty in this place when this was over.

He scooted closer to Ramey, causing the girl to clutch his shirt and whimper. "If we're going to survive the night, we need to get as warm as we can with what we have available. I say we walk to the roof of the church, force the steeple over, and lower into the attic. We'll have to move quickly to use the last of daylight. It'll be a tight fit, but it'll be dry and warmer than out here."

The man didn't react or in any way let Monty know he heard. Monty nudged him. "The church?"

Ramey's hollow eyes fastened on Monty. "I tried to save them. I tried to hang on to them, but the force was too strong." He swallowed. "My wife was the first to let go. Then, one by one, my children slipped away from me. There was nothing I could do."

The man's voice broke, and tears poured down his cheeks. Monty had never seen a life so broken. Nothing he could say or do would ease Ramey's pain, so he prayed for the man. Or tried to through the fog in his brain. They were more thoughts than prayers.

Monty left him to cry and passed the girl to Mr. Sherman. She screamed and reached for Monty then latched onto Mr. Sherman and disappeared back inside her cocoon.

Leaping over the transition in roof grades, Monty steadied his balance then dropped to his knees and crawled up the steep slope to the steeple. Pain seared his hands that resembled butchered meat more than appendages. His busted, swollen knuckles looked twice their normal size. Even so, he was getting into that church attic.

Monty pushed, heaved, kicked, and slammed into the steeple, only managing to make a large dent in the metal the width of his side. He'd loosened the screws, but it wasn't enough. The noise roused Ramey, who blinked and pressed a palm to his head before standing to help. When he reached Monty's side, Monty explained what he was doing, and Ramey added his strength.

Darkness swallowed the desolate valley. Moans lifted from the injured. Pleading and wailing echoed through the air.

Then a loud blast startled Monty, and his foot slipped on the steep pitch. Ramey caught his arm. Sherman joined them with the little girl, and they all watched in horror as the debris piled at the viaduct across town burst into flames as tall as the wave had been.

Oh, God.

The screams grew louder. Monty's blood froze. The water continued its swirl, its reflection clear in the firelight. A fate worse than drowning.

The horrid stench of burning flesh carried on the breeze as angry flames of red and orange built toward the heavens.

Monty turned his head and gagged.

Ramey patted his shoulder. "Let's finish this."

Understanding, Monty forced himself to continue demolishing the steeple. A few minutes later, they'd leaned it on its side, exposing the square hole in the roof. Light flickered off Ramey as he lowered inside. Monty reached for the little girl, who went to him without complaint, and Sherman went in next, the tears tracking his cheeks glittering in the flames. Monty went last, passing the child to Sherman before climbing down. Why wasn't the flood itself torture enough? He couldn't let such devilish thoughts overtake him. He had to be strong.

Monty ducked into the attic space that was barely large enough for an eight-year-old to stand. It had a solid floor and was at least ten degrees warmer than it was outside. Sitting with his back against the wall where the roof peaked, he reached for the child and curled her against his chest. She pressed her hands over her ears and whimpered. Monty wished he could escape the screaming so easily.

Instead of pining for what would never come, Monty clamped his eyes shut and silently begged God for answers.

Chapter Five

"During all this solemn Sunday, Johnstown has been drenched
with the tears of stricken mortals, and the air is filled with
sobs and sighs that come from breaking hearts."
~City Solicitor Keuhn, when asked to estimate the damage of Johnstown

WASHINGTON, D.C.
SATURDAY, JUNE 1, 1889

Annamae woke to glorious sunshine streaming through her bedroom window. Eyelids fluttering against the brightness, she smiled, relishing the warmth bathing her face. It had rained for a week straight, oppressing not only the land but her spirit. People needed sunshine. It lifted spirits, provided nutrients, helped the sickly to—

She jerked upright. Sunlight. She'd overslept!

After throwing the blankets aside, she wiggled her legs free of her tangled nightdress and crossed the room to the bureau for her timepiece. She groaned. Her internal clock normally wouldn't let her sleep past sunrise. In all her years of nursing, she'd never reported late.

Her stomach soured at the scolding that was sure to come if Miss

Barton discovered Annamae's indiscretion. One did not want to disappoint Clara Barton. Especially when she'd been chosen over dozens of other nurses who'd applied to assist the Red Cross as a first responder during an emergency.

As fast as she could, she dressed, brushed and pinned her hair, tied a white apron over her brown dress, added her matching cap, and secured her shoes. Always tidy to a fault, she ignored her messy bed, slipped her coin purse into her pocket, and locked the door behind her. Though she enjoyed walking the mile to the hospital on sunny days, she'd take the streetcar this morning.

She raced down the two flights of stairs, threw open the door, and jolted to a stop. A sparkling lake covered D Street and most of the Washington Monument grounds. On Ohio Avenue, the water was almost as high as the first-story windows on the buildings. She'd seen the Potomac flood many times but never high enough to reach the monument.

To the west, children splashed in water that touched their knees. Laughter bounced off the brick structures. The water wasn't as high on her end of D Street, but upon closer inspection, she discovered it contained bits of muck and debris floating in it. If the smell was any indication, the sewers had filled with river water and the contents were leeching up into the streets. She wished people were more concerned about situations that could cause contamination and infection. She'd like to give the parents of those children an earful for allowing them to play in such impure conditions.

Someday, perhaps, the medical field would create a medication that could battle the diseases caused by such bacteria. For now, cleanliness and avoidance were key.

She sighed. Unless they were patients in her hospital, she could no more tell those parents how to care for their children than she could tell President Harrison how to run the country. What she could do was find a way to the hospital for her shift. Doctor Martin was expecting her.

A horse and wagon plodded down 13th Street, sending sprays of water into the air with each step. The water wasn't higher than the mare's pastern, but it was too deep for Annamae to walk through. She didn't know who the man was or where he was going, but maybe he'd allow her to ride along. She held out her arm and waved to gain the driver's attention. At first glance, he turned away. Then his gaze swiveled to her again, and he nudged the horse closer to the street's edge.

"Whoa," he commanded the beast.

Annamae raised her skirt and skittered to avoid the tide soaking into her boots and uniform.

"Can I help you, ma'am?" His gray mustache was unkempt and touched the inside of his nose.

"I'm a nurse at Jericho Square Hospital. They're expecting me, and I have no way of traveling through this water to get there. I know it's a lot to ask of a stranger, but for the good of those poor souls awaiting my services, would you be so kind as to drive me?"

The portly man took off his hat, scratched his nearly balding head, and plopped it back on. "Well now, I suppose I can drive you as far as I can, but the streets south of here are under four feet of water, as well as most of Pennsylvania Avenue. The Potomac spilled into the Government Fishpond, and now fish are swimming all over this city. A carp two feet long was caught in the ladies' waiting room at the Baltimore and Potomac station."

"Oh my." She could hardly imagine it. Annamae lifted her hand so he could assist her into the wagon, unsure if he was in earnest or an amazing storyteller. She perched on the bench beside him. "As close as you can get will do. Thank you, Mr. . . ."

"Elijah Kesbernan. And you are?"

Late for work. "Miss Annamae Worthington."

He tipped his hat and set the horse into motion. "Well now, Miss Worthington, I'm not sure what you're going to do once we reach the crossroads. Are you a good swimmer?"

He chuckled, and she smiled out of politeness. Of course she could swim, but that was out of the question.

Folks went about their business despite the situation, mostly men. The few women who had ventured out either held their hems indecently high to avoid saturation or let their skirts soak the water clear up to their thighs. Annamae was determined to report to her shift and do so spotlessly, if it was the last thing she did.

Two blocks south, the water had grown as high as the mare's knees, and Mr. Kesbernan slowed to a stop. "Sorry I can't get you farther, Miss Worthington, but the high water is carrying all kinds of debris, and I can't chance injuring my horse."

"I understand." She looked around for a patch of dry ground on which to disembark. Boards and small items of all kinds floated in the water, but there was no place for her to land. "I wonder where all this debris came from."

"The Potomac is rushing so forcefully, it's knocked down every shanty on the river's edge. The mills and the fertilizing works are half underwater too. All kinds of things are washing up."

The river was always so calm, she could hardly believe it. "Has it really rained that much?"

His head tipped to the side. "Didn't you hear? The South Fork Dam at Lake Conemaugh burst and destroyed what was Johnstown, Pennsylvania."

"What *was?*"

"The whole city is gone. This morning's paper estimates the deceased to be in the thousands."

Annamae's heart sank. "That must be at least a hundred miles from here. All this water can't possibly be from that. Can it?"

"More like two hundred. The paper says the telegrams from Pittsburgh reported that when the dam broke, a wall of water close to sixty feet high raced down the mountain. All that flows southeast and combines with our already swollen waters, spelling disaster for us too."

He handed her a folded newspaper he retrieved from his coat pocket. She skimmed the article that reiterated everything he'd just relayed as well as detailing the hundreds of houses and thousands of animal carcasses and human bodies that had traveled the tributaries for miles. All of Johnstown was destroyed in a matter of minutes.

Lord, have mercy.

Reporting to the hospital was vital now. If Johnstown was declared an emergency, and it needed to be, Miss Barton would call for her right away.

Annamae looked for another way to get to the hospital. Finding none, her frustration grew. She would be of no use to anyone if she arrived wet and filthy with nothing clean and dry to change into.

Movement caught her attention at the intersection of C Street and Louisiana Avenue. A rowboat floated down the usually crowded street. Both passengers cradled fishing poles. Annamae stood in the stationary wagon and waved her arms. "Hello there. Please, help me."

She turned to Mr. Kesbernan. "Would you be willing to go just a little farther? I believe them to be my only hope of getting to the hospital."

Mr. Kesbernan worked his lips beneath his mustache. The end of his red nose twitched. "Well now, I suppose I can. Best have a seat though."

She obeyed, and he inched the horse and wagon forward while the men paddled their direction. At their approach, Annamae realized there were more than two men in the boat. A little girl, about age four, Annamae guessed, sat directly behind the lead man, clutching her doll. Upon closer inspection, the other adult passenger wasn't a man at all but a woman in a dark brown dress tucked around her legs to reveal their shape. No hat. The woman's hair was pulled so severely into a bun it tugged the skin around her eyes.

"Is everything all right, ma'am?" This gentleman had a mustache as well, but it was coal black. His blue eyes assessed Mr. Kesbernan as if looking for injury or danger.

"Could I trouble you for a ride to Jericho Square Hospital?" Annamae asked. "I'll gladly pay you what I'd planned to spend on the streetcar."

A deep wrinkle formed between the man's eyebrows as his gaze raked over her cap and apron. "Jah, come aboard."

He and Mr. Kesbernan assisted her into the boat. She bit back a squeal as her weight caused it to teeter. The girl giggled. The woman scooted over, making room for Annamae.

Mr. Kesbernan refused her offer of payment, wished them all a good day, and tugged on the reins. He turned his horse around and continued the way they'd come. The man guiding the boat swiveled to her and said, "Is it the hospital on 6th and Pennsylvania?"

"Yes, that's it. Thank you, sir." Annamae smiled at the little girl and engaged the woman in conversation as they rowed through the city. For a moment, she felt as if she were a character in *The Merchant of Venice*, enjoying a gondola ride through the watery streets. Such a thing was too bizarre for the capital city, and the moment didn't last.

The woman had a thick German accent. From what Annamae could understand, the family had been fishing for their supper since the markets were closed from the flooding. Annamae explained about the sewers leeching into the streets and how important it was to make sure the fish was cleaned and cooked entirely through before consuming. She figured there would be many cases of bacteria and infection at the hospital over the next few days.

Twenty minutes later, the man stopped in front of the hospital. Annamae pulled coins from her purse and held them out to him. He reached out to accept, but his wife slapped his outstretched hand and glowered. The corners of his lips turned down. "Jah. My pleasure to be good citizen."

Annamae smiled and returned the coins to her purse. "Thank you, both."

She waved goodbye to the little girl, stood, and rocked the boat. She sat back down and gripped the sides.

A man wearing a blue and gray postal uniform with a bulging sack over his shoulder chuckled as he waded by. He offered to assist her, and, with his help, she stood again. Annamae frowned at the murky water. The hospital steps were too far away, and her shoes would be soaked through by the time she reached them. Maybe she could find dry stockings and an extra pair of shoes somewhere inside.

She yelped in surprise when the postal worker swept his arms beneath her and carried her to the steps. Annamae secured her hold around his neck. She'd never been carried by a man before. She'd helped carry plenty of men, however. Invalids. Her face heated as he lowered her to the first dry step.

"Special delivery." The postal worker touched the brim of his cap and laughed as he continued wading along Pennsylvania Avenue.

With a chuckle, Annamae lifted her skirt, which was damp at the hem, and hurried inside the hospital.

She rushed down the hall and past the other nurses coming and going. When Doctor Martin stepped from a patient's bedside, she caught him before he moved to the next.

"I apologize for my tardiness, Doctor." She had difficulty catching her breath. "The streets are flooded, and I had trouble getting here without the streetcar."

Doctor Martin smiled. Then he touched her elbow and led her to a vacant corner in the room. "I wasn't sure you'd be able to make it at all. I'm glad you're safe."

The handsome widower was always tender with her. They'd worked together for the past couple of years, and a month ago he'd expressed interest in wanting to become more than her superior. The prospect had both thrilled her and cloaked her with dread. She wanted a companion to journey beside in this life, but if they ever married, he would expect her to give up nursing to create a home—and she wasn't sure she was ready to do that yet.

"You've got a telegram in my office," he said. "Have you seen the papers? Johnstown, Pennsylvania has been destroyed. Miss Clara Barton is leaving with a crew right away. She wants you to report to headquarters immediately."

Her heart raced. This was it. After all those months of apprenticing under Miss Barton and earning her place within the Red Cross, the chance to use her skills and serve others had come. She went to fetch the telegram, but Doctor Martin caught her apron strings. She spun back around, her face filling with another round of heat. He chuckled while she sputtered and retied her bow.

"Don't worry, no one was looking."

"It isn't funny."

"Lighten up, Annamae." His whispered scold was gentle. "Life is too short to be so serious all the time."

His gaze wandered to some faraway place behind her. He was thinking of his wife, no doubt.

Her temper cooled.

"You just startled me is all." When his attention swiveled back to her, she smiled her apology.

"I'm hoping I have time to escort you to dinner before you leave. If

Johnstown is as bad as they say, I may not see you for a very long time."

Will you miss me? The foolish words were on the tip of her tongue, but she swallowed them down. "You'll have Martha to keep you in line."

He rolled his eyes, eliciting a giggle from her. Martha was the oldest nurse at the hospital and the most scatterbrained. The staff spent as much time monitoring her as they did the patients. Even so, Martha's job was secure since she was the older sister of the hospital's director.

"Doctor Martin," Nurse Bennett whisper-shouted from the other side of the room. She gestured to a lump completely covered with a sheet.

A patient gone to Jesus.

He held up a finger.

"The telegram is on my desk. If there's time, Annamae, any time at all, please allow me to see you before you leave."

She nodded and watched him walk away.

The delicate way he said her first name when no one else was around to hear was romantic enough to make her feel like a schoolgirl with a crush. But adult relationships had very lasting consequences, and she wanted to be absolutely certain of her feelings for him before she led him any further. She enjoyed his company and their easy friendship and didn't want to break his heart. Matthew had already suffered enough.

Walking at a fast clip, she went into his office and retrieved the telegram delivered at six o'clock this morning. She glanced at her timepiece. Ten thirty. She had to hurry to catch Miss Barton before the first responders left.

Annamae scribbled a quick note she left on Doctor Martin's desk and exited the hospital, only to be reminded of the waterlogged streets. Well, there was nothing she could do other than remove her shoes, wad up her skirt, and walk. No matter the risk, she was not missing this opportunity with the Red Cross. Curious onlookers watched her as she prepared for her venture out.

The water was chilly, and she prayed she didn't step on anything that would pierce her feet. Thankfully, at the end of the block, the water receded, and 8th Street was dry. She lowered her skirt but kept hold of her shoes. Dirt and grime stuck to the bottom of her stockings. No matter. Miss Barton would have a Red Cross uniform for her to change into anyway.

The streetcar was still running north on 9th Street. She waited, and when the next car arrived, she hopped on and paid the fare, ignoring the scandalized looks of the other passengers at her traveling without shoes. Three quarters of an hour later, she stepped off at the corner of 9th and I Street and hurried to the Red Cross Headquarters.

The building was abuzz with telegraph machines clicking and workers gathering and stacking supplies. Annamae found Miss Barton on the second floor, issuing orders to the porter regarding the delivery of her trunks to the train station.

The petite woman frowned at the shoes in Annamae's grip and at her stockinged toes peeking out from the bottom of her skirt. Creases of disapproval appeared around her eyes and mouth. "Miss Worthington, there you are. I was about to send Jeffries to the hospital to fetch you."

Annamae apologized and started into the story of why she was late and not wearing shoes, but Miss Barton held up her palm. "We haven't time for excuses. However, there's always time for propriety. Haven't we discussed not allowing your passion to overshadow your good sense before? The Red Cross must maintain professionalism."

"Yes, ma'am." Annamae studied the floor.

Miss Barton relayed the details of Johnstown to Annamae. The devastation was as bad as the paper had described. "I need you packed and your trunk at the station by four. Bring only one. We're meeting Doctor Hubbard and traveling as close to Johnstown as we can get. I've already alerted the Pittsburgh Red Cross to meet us there with supplies. The rest of the team will follow us in a few days. We must hurry, Miss Worthington. The survivors of Johnstown desperately need our help."

Chapter Six

"That is my child. There lies my family.
Go on and get the rest of them."

~Mr. Gilmore, who lost his wife and five children;
their bodies were identifiable only by their clothing

JOHNSTOWN, PENNSYLVANIA
SUNDAY, JUNE 2

Monty had never been more grateful for daylight. He, Mr. Sherman, Mr. Ramey, and the little girl had been trapped in the church attic for over twenty-four hours. Day dawned over the mountains around nine Saturday morning but hadn't shed enough light on the valley to make traveling safe. The air was chilly, and the sky continued crying as if mourning the lives that once made the town thrive. They'd emerged through the hole where the steeple once stood proud and gazed over the destruction below, unable to leave their post for the swell of water. Hungry, thirsty, and battered, they had been forced by the darkness to spend another night in the cramped attic where, just after midnight, Ramey turned mad.

His maniacal rage echoed across the entire valley. Monty had done his best to shelter the child, who had yet to utter a single word. Sherman had comforted Ramey when he shook, pinned him to the floor when he raved, and dozed when Ramey had run out of steam.

Monty was getting off this roof with this child today if it meant he had to jump into the water and take his chances.

With barely a sliver of energy remaining, Monty crawled out of the hole, holding the sleeping child, and peered across town. A large crowd gathered at the stone bridge. Smoke rose into the air from Friday night's explosion. The debris was so thick and saturated with flammable materials, it might burn for days. Hundreds of moving bodies lined the high hills, fortunate to have escaped yet forced to watch their neighbors, friends, and family carried downstream.

The water had finally receded enough for travel. Relief filled him. He needed to find food, if any were to be had. The child had soiled her underclothes and the sheet wrapped around her. She needed a bath, fresh clothes, and warmth, if any existed in Johnstown anymore.

Something putrid carried on the breeze, an ungodly smell unlike anything he'd ever experienced. His stomach flipped, and food dropped to the end of his priority list. Months of work lay ahead in sifting through the debris, clearing roadways and rail lines, resetting telegraph poles, rebuilding homes and businesses, and finding and burying the dead. Where would any of them find the strength?

Or would everyone leave and start afresh somewhere else?

Guilt poked him for leaving Sherman and Ramey asleep in the church, but if he didn't set his feet on earthen ground soon, he'd be the next to turn crazy.

He roused the girl from sleep. She blinked a few times before her memory kicked in and her eyes grew wide. The way she clutched at him in unabashed fear broke his heart. "It's all right, sweetheart. We need to get off this roof so I can help you find your family. I'll need you to walk on your own and listen to my instructions. I'll be with you the entire way. There's nothing to fear."

Except having no family, no home, and no possessions to return to, if that were the case.

Her unsteady legs made it difficult for her to balance on the steep pitch of the roof, but they got down it and then leaped across to the roof of his house. His hands throbbed from the punishment he'd given them attempting to survive.

He lowered into the attic by way of the hole he'd escaped through two days earlier. Then, bracing on a joist, he helped her onto him piggy-back style. Her thin arms nearly choked him as he leaped to the attic floor and staggered down the tilted narrow steps to the second story where every possession he owned was broken, upended, or waterlogged.

Not trusting his weight on the soft plank boards since this part of the home had been underwater much longer than the attic, he carefully descended to the first floor. The force had pushed his cookstove across the room, impaling the wall. A wagon sat in his kitchen. One of its wheels had detached and sat askew in his fireplace. All the windows were busted, and a nasty sludge coated everything. A flash of blue fabric underneath the wagon snagged his attention. He started to bend and inspect it when a hand, its flesh the gray pallor of death, caught his attention. The room swayed, and Monty fought back dry heaves. He needed to get the girl out of here before she noticed the corpse. Heaven only knew what horrors she'd see over the coming days, and if he could spare her this, he would.

The insides of his cheeks stuck to his teeth, and he craved water like he craved air, yet he didn't want to see water again for the rest of his life. *Why, Lord?* The question circled his brain like a runaway carousel. *Why did this happen?*

A cold sweat broke out along his forehead. Now that they were on solid ground, he loosened the girl's hold around his throat and moved her to one hip, like one might carry a toddler. Without hesitation, she wrapped legs so filthy they were almost black around his waist and locked her ankles together. She looped her arms around his neck, this time putting pressure on the side of his neck and not his Adam's apple.

He hobbled to where his front door once opened onto a bustling street filled with commerce. Now it was packed with mud and debris. With the meager amount of strength he possessed, he kicked the few boards and broken possessions out of the way and climbed out. Chunks of houses, broken timbers, mud, metal, animals, and bodies formed a road where

Macedonia Street used to run west to the stone bridge. Every inch of the landscape was changed.

Careful of stepping on nails and the deceased, he walked toward higher ground. There was no way to shelter the girl from this. His weak legs carried him past homes splintered beyond recognition, conjoined and piled upon one another like a stack of children's blocks knocked over. Survivors combed the wreckage, looking for signs of loved ones. Of their former lives. Monty's heart ached as much as his stomach, both numb yet throbbing with pain. He asked each person they passed if they recognized the little girl, but no one did.

Monty had been taught that God would never give a person more than they could bear. Whoever said that had obviously never listened to the screams and wailings from souls about to drown. Or burn. Had never heard the guttural cries from those who'd lost every member of their family and were truly all alone now. Had never reached out to save someone, only for them to be swept downstream.

The passage in First Corinthians was often misquoted, as it promised that God would not suffer his children to be *tempted* above what they could handle without making a way of escape. This was no temptation. But he wished it held an escape route all the same. It was truly more than he could bear.

The destruction grew worse the closer they got to the bridge. Nothing here was recognizable. Sections that had once divided commerce and quaint streets were now acres of splintered debris. All except for the grand piano resting on a pile of timber, not a key broken. The instrument sat proud and erect, as if waiting for someone to come by and make it sing again—not understanding the family it had once belonged to was most likely in the next world.

They passed soul after grieving soul. Everyone remaining, desperate and destitute. Monty had never seen anything like it. In his aureate upbringing, he'd experienced nothing even close to it. Intense emotion swirled inside him until he feared he'd burst from his skin. The greatest of his feelings was hunger.

On the highest point of what was once Franklin Street sat a three-story building, unscathed. Smoke curled from one of the two chimneys. The scent of something cooking turned his feet in that direction until he stood on the front porch, huffing from the exertion. An elderly lady met him in the doorway.

He coaxed the girl onto her own feet. "Ma'am, do you recognize this child?"

His voice sounded nothing like his own.

She shuffled onto the porch, lifted the bit of sheet that hid the girl's face, and frowned. Dirt smeared the woman's wrinkled cheeks. "Hmm, can't say as I do. Where'd you find her?"

"Saved from the water, ma'am."

The woman pushed the sheet completely off the girl's head. "You look old enough to talk. Tell us your name, child."

The girl buried her face in Monty's leg, which caused shooting pain where the roofing nail had sliced him.

"Who are your parents?" The woman tried again.

Nothing.

Monty and Mr. Sherman had already asked those questions and more, trying to cajole the child into giving them a clue they could use to help locate her family.

"This poor, freezing child." The woman reached for her. "I'm Mrs. Lanney. Y'ins come on in and eat a bite. I've salt pork and beans cooking."

The girl fussed when Mrs. Lanney reached for her hand but then clung to the older woman who hollered into the house, "Elizabeth, fill a bucket with warm water and get this child cleaned up. Anna, you go fetch her some warm flannels from a trunk. Then we'll get her fed and warmed by the fire."

The salt pork and beans tasted as good as the rack of lamb his uncle's chef used to serve at Clayton. Monty could honestly say he'd never been more grateful for a meal, even if his swollen hands could hardly hold the spoon. There were many in the house to feed with more survivors straggling in, and his limited portion left him wanting.

But he was grateful.

Cleaned and dressed in clothes that didn't match, the girl plopped herself onto Monty's lap by the fireplace. Her shoes, one too big and one too small, poked out from beneath her dress. The more questions folks asked her, the tighter she clamped her lips. Monty hated that she was soiling her fresh clothing by clinging to his grimy frame.

Three elderly women everyone called "the Bowser sisters" sat across from Monty, attempting to place which family the child belonged to. After going through most every family in Johnstown, the sister with eyebrows as gray as her hair slapped her knee and sat forward in her chair. "Aren't you little Gertrude Quinn?"

Monty watched the girl for signs of recognition, but she only blinked at the woman. He searched his memory for the moments he'd spoken to James Quinn at the dry goods store right before the dam burst. Could this be the child he'd seen on his way home, splashing in the yard with the ducklings?

Yes, it well could be.

Struggling to a stand, that Bowser sister walked to the front door and yelled into the yard, "Mrs. Foster, come see if you recognize this child. She might be your niece, Gertrude Quinn."

In no time, a middle-aged woman with blond hair burst into the room and knelt in front of Monty, studying the child. Leaping from his cross-legged position, the girl flew at the woman and wrapped her in a hug. Tears streaked down Mrs. Foster's cheeks. "Thank God, it's little Gertrude." She yanked a small stick from the nest of hair at the girl's nape, laughing. "You barely look human, but you're alive. Oh, you sweet girl."

Monty's eyes burned with emotion. At least Gertrude had someone to care for her now.

Snapping to attention, Mrs. Foster pushed the girl at arm's length and onto Monty's lap. "Your father. I must fetch him. He thinks—oh, he'll be so thrilled."

She ran from the room and, twenty minutes later, returned with a man who looked like a shadow of James Quinn. Trembling and crying like a child himself, he swayed with Gertrude in his arms. "The house— I saw it go down, chimney and all. How are you here?"

Another child, five or so years older than Gertrude, ran to Mr. Quinn's side and threw her arms around them both. "My poor little sister. I'll never let you out of my sight again."

Monty's head filled with an odd pressure he couldn't describe. So much loss, so much grief, so much joy in so short a time made it hard for him to process any one thing that had happened. Little Gertrude was safe with her family now. Praise be to God. It was time for him to let the family reunite.

He stood and moved to the door in a dense, invisible fog that seemed to weigh his every step. Time crawled, and he had no idea where he was going. He just knew he had to keep moving or perish.

When the debris beneath his feet turned brittle and the surface sprinkled with ashes, Monty walked west toward the woods. He could no longer look into his fellow man's faces. Could no more stomach what he saw in their eyes. He simply passed by as if he were a ghost of no significance. A part of him almost wished he were.

He stepped over fallen trees but kept progressing up the incline, boots sinking in the muddy earth. The searing pain in his leg muscles matched the burning in his heart. Breaths sounded loud in his ears. His vision grew fuzzy at the edges. Sweat rolled down the sides of his face.

Someone clamped a hand on his shoulder.

Monty jerked from his stupor.

"Pastor?" Ernie Dickenson's hand shook against Monty's suspender. Eyes and nose red from crying or lack of drink was anyone's guess. Monty had spent many an hour trying to help the immigrant man. Ernie wanted to escape his vice, but not enough to relinquish his hold on the bottle.

Ernie's voice broke, and spittle leaked onto his chin. "You've always told me that the Lord would care for me. Will He look after me now?"

Would He? Monty was no longer certain of anything. For the first time since giving his life to Christ, God felt far out of reach.

All Monty could do was stare into Ernie's sad, hope-filled eyes and nod. Then, without a word, he turned and continued his trek up the mountain. His feet ground pieces of porcelain tea sets into the earth. China dishes littered the grass, and a ripped silken tablecloth, presumably from one of the luxurious Pullman cars that had graced the station on that fateful afternoon, pooled against the base of a tree. The thought of anyone being trapped alive in one of those cars when the wave hit made his stomach hitch.

An open trunk half-buried in the hillside revealed the contents once neatly packed inside—lace handkerchiefs, a buttonhook, a petticoat, and the photograph of a man—that were now stained from water. Had the woman who owned this trunk survived?

He continued walking. Continued breathing. It was all he could do.

Unsure how long he'd wandered, he dropped onto a wilted patch of asparagus ferns. Hot tears rolled down his cheeks. He almost wished he'd perished in the waters. The mourning, the hunger, the cold, the uncertainty—it was all too much. Uncontrollable sobs came, unbidden.

A cat meowed beside him.

Monty swallowed and turned his blurry, puffy eyes to the feline rubbing against his leg. It was cut in several places, and its wet fur stuck out at all angles. Monty reached to comfort the creature—and himself—when it raised its head. One eye socket was void.

The cat crawled onto Monty's lap, rubbed its face against his chest, and purred. After all this poor thing had gone through, it found solace in a stranger.

Snuggling the cat close, he wiped his own eyes with the back of his hand and winced as the action stung his raw knuckles. The forest was cold, and the gray clouds promised even more rain. Shock and hunger played tricks with his body temperature. He should have stayed next to the fire and the Bowser sisters, but the haven couldn't hold everyone who'd survived, and others would be more in need than he was.

He stood, cradled the cat, and returned to the open trunk. He rummaged through the feminine belongings before finally yanking out the petticoat, rebuking himself the entire way to the fern patch. Lowering onto the pile of flora, he settled the cat on his lap and slipped the petticoat with its mounds of thick warm fabric over his shoulders. The feline purred beneath the mass and kneaded its front paws on his thigh. Monty gazed in every direction. Hordes of people wandered the mountainside. Homeless. Starving.

One thing was certain—he wasn't suffering alone.

Chapter Seven

~⁓

"When such a calamitous visitation falls upon any section of our country, we can do no more than to put about the dark picture the golden border of love and charity. It is in such fires as these that the brotherhood of man is welded."

~President Harrison, at Willard's Hall, appealing for financial assistance for the Johnstown survivors

JOHNSTOWN, PENNSYLVANIA
TUESDAY, JUNE 4

Annamae gaped at the devastation below. Johnstown was in a bowl surrounded by the Allegheny Mountains. All across the valley, houses and businesses were splintered into toothpicks, some piled atop one another. Machinery, railcars, and furniture lay strewn like dice thrown onto a table. A smoky haze rose and swirled around church steeples and other scant structures remaining on their foundations. The wave had raced down the mountain so violently, it had redirected the river, leaving parts of the old riverbed standing with stagnant water. The very place where she stood had been scalped of soil, making her feet ache against the uneven bedrock.

She looked to Miss Barton for direction. The woman's initial dismay turned to calculated thought with a twist of her lips. Annamae had apprenticed under her long enough to recognize her mental process. In a few minutes, she would tell them exactly where to go, what to do, and whom to help first. Annamae was glad Miss Barton was in charge. She herself could never guess where to begin in all the ruination.

The air was mild, and the breeze lent a blessed coolness across her sweaty brow. With it came the stench of contaminated water and death, eliciting a gag she covered with a cough. Five miles was the closest they could get to Johnstown with the washed-out tracks. A kind farmer had brought them closer in his wagon until the incline grew too steep for the horses to pull the heavy load of luggage and passengers. They'd packed themselves like mules and walked the rest of the way down the incline. A good mile and three quarters, Annamae guessed. She refused to give thought to her overworked muscles or her parched mouth. The people of Johnstown needed far more attention than she.

General Hastings, Pennsylvania's adjutant general, dropped a pack at his feet and sighed. He swiped his fingers over his sweaty brow then rubbed them down his pants legs. His grim expression deepened the lines on his aging face. He glanced up at the heavy clouds sweeping across the sky. More water was the last thing these people needed.

"How are we to assist you, Miss Barton?" he asked.

The Red Cross warrior raised her small stature, lifting her chin with enough confidence to match the general's six-foot frame. Miss Barton's raven hair, free of a single strand of gray for her sixty-eight years, glistened from her exertion. "You misunderstand, General Hastings. We've no need of assistance. We've come to assist. I have already notified the Red Cross of Philadelphia that their services will be needed. Their group is composed mostly of medical men. I've also asked them to bring as many tents as they can gather. If they are not already here, they should arrive shortly."

General Hastings's mouth quirked in amusement. They'd found the general soon after stepping off the train. He told them he'd arrived in Johnstown on Sunday and had gone to the nearest station early this morning to send a telegram for more men. Looters had begun scouring the grounds, stealing jewelry off the deceased and valuable belongings from the debris. So many were wreaking havoc, the local militia the general had mustered wasn't enough to keep order.

The thought made Annamae's stomach cramp.

Miss Barton turned to their stenographer, Sylvester Ward. "Mr. Ward, prepare to intercept the first dispatches of any description to enter this desolate city. The accounts that make their way to Washington must be accurate. I'm tired of pompous newspapermen embellishing facts to sell papers."

The general pressed his lips together.

"Yes, ma'am." Mr. Ward nodded.

"The first thing we'll do"—Miss Barton addressed the group—"is establish a place to settle our tents. Then Dr. Hubbell, Miss Worthington, and I will immediately begin addressing the most pressing medical needs. General Hastings, continue establishing order. While such disasters can bring out the best in humankind, they can also bring out the worst. Beatrice, see about food. We'll be working round-the-clock for the next few weeks at least. Might as well start with a good meal."

Beatrice, Miss Barton's lady's maid, dipped her head in acquiescence.

"You'll be hard-pressed to find a full meal down there," General Hastings said. "Dry goods, restaurants, even the livestock have been destroyed. Captain Bill Jones arrived this morning with a small group and as much food as they could bring, but there are a lot of bellies to fill, and it'll go fast. You're welcome to eat beans and biscuits with my militia."

"Thank you, General." Miss Barton adjusted the load she carried and continued their journey.

Bracing for the horrors below, Annamae followed the group into the barren valley, the mud and muck threatening to steal the boots from her feet as she walked. The river lapped the shoreline, rocking back and forth. Hundreds of people, dazed and weeping, dug in the muddy banks. Annamae's tears joined those poor souls who unearthed a loved one. She moved along, following Miss Barton around bent rails and climbing over broken locomotives and strands of stray barbed wire.

They passed thousands who had nowhere proper to sleep. Many rested atop random debris, curled in the fetal position and wrapped in filthy, ratty blankets or shawls. Most hadn't enough clothing on to ward off the chilly temperature, no doubt having been caught unawares in the need to flee for their lives.

The hunger. It was visible in their sunken cheeks and pale faces. Many onlookers watched them with curiosity, their uniforms and supply bags announcing they'd arrived from elsewhere to help. Though the American Red Cross had been established for seven years, most of the nation had yet to become familiar with their services. Miss Barton had long argued the Red Cross was meant for such emergencies, and now she would prove it to the nation.

When ideal grounds could not be found for camp, they set up temporary headquarters inside an abandoned railroad car that had been pushed off the mangled tracks. Miss Barton instructed Mr. Ward to set up an old crate she'd found as a desk. Two soldiers erected the tents they'd brought on each side of headquarters. While the rest of their group ate with General Hastings' men, Miss Barton stayed at the railcar with Mr. Ward to compile a list of specific supplies needed. Annamae promised to bring them food when she returned.

The Philadelphia Red Cross Society had arrived and was setting up additional tents by the time Annamae arrived back at headquarters. Thick drizzle made everything slick, and it was proving difficult to keep the supplies dry. Some tents would house the workers while others would protect the sick and injured. Another set of tents would become a hospital for surgeries or extreme cases.

Bodies moved like hummingbirds to establish the area for relief while General Hastings' men publicized their arrival and location. Members of the Philadelphia Red Cross spread out and started assessing which survivors needed immediate medical attention. At barely five in the evening, daylight was fading, and victims flowed into their tents with hypothermia, pneumonia, and broken bones.

Two men delivered a man consumed with fever, his leg twisted at an unnatural angle. They'd rescued him from the water but could not extricate the barbed wire embedded into the skin. Dr. Hubbell called for an immediate amputation to isolate the infection and, hopefully, save the man's life. Annamae had assisted in amputations before but always within a sterile hospital room with a full staff and plenty of supplies. Never had she worked in such a crude environment. Miss Barton must have sensed her trepidation and volunteered to assist the doctor while Annamae assisted elsewhere.

Through the halo of lantern light, Annamae worked long into the night, talking to and comforting patients while she cleaned and disinfected their wounds. Small fires burned throughout the remainder of town. From what General Hastings said, survivors were not only using them to stay warm but had abandoned the hillsides to congregate around the light and avoid confrontation with looters. She'd overheard two reporters discussing the onslaught of greedy Hungarians and Slavs as they'd walked by. It struck both fear and fury inside Annamae. To think anyone could do something as despicable as cutting off appendages from the dead for their possessions or violating innocent women who were merely trying to find traces of their husbands and children in the rubble.

May God have mercy on them all.

At midnight, Miss Barton approached Annamae's station, covering a yawn with her hand. "Get some rest, Miss Worthington. More nurses and supplies have arrived from Washington. They slept on the train, so they'll take over the night hours."

Annamae didn't feel right sleeping when so many needed medical attention. "How are we to help them all?"

"Oh, this is nothing, my dear," Clara said. "So long as we have no bullets flying around us. See you at sunrise."

A yawn of her own bubbled up, and Annamae gave into it, knowing if Miss Barton had succeeded in the Civil War, she would succeed here too.

Annamae hadn't noticed how tired she was until Miss Barton mentioned sleeping. Now her feet lumbered like steel blocks. In the women's tent, she slipped out of her shoes and dirty apron and crawled onto her cot. The pillow was flat, and the wool blanket was scratchy, but Annamae didn't remember falling asleep until her weighty eyelids cracked open the next morning.

Stiff and sore, she stretched to limber her muscles. Nurses entered and exited the tent while others slept. Annamae splashed cold water on her face and neck, put on a fresh apron and her shoes, brushed her hair and plaited it as best she could without a mirror, then donned her cap. Outside, the sunrise bathed the mountain in beautiful gold. How she wished those rays would shine healing over the land as well, but the angry clouds in the distance sprinting closer promised more rain.

Annamae rubbed her arms for warmth as she walked to the medical tents. She smiled at a little girl standing on a chair that was half buried in the mud. Her scarf was knotted beneath her chin, stockings and shoes caked with mud. She overheard the girl's father asking Doctor Hubbell why his little Gertrude would no longer speak.

Poor thing. Shock did that to people sometimes.

Miss Barton stood outside headquarters, directing two men carrying crates. She motioned Annamae closer while issuing orders to Mr. Rochester, the workman who'd accompanied them to Johnstown. "Lumber is coming from Pittsburgh. I want six buildings, exactly one hundred feet by fifty, built as quickly as you can. Use as many able-bodied survivors as possible. Let them know these will serve as hotels to house displaced residents and distribute supplies—all at no cost to them. I guarantee you'll have plenty of men ready to put their hands to work."

"Right away, ma'am." Mr. Rochester acknowledged Annamae with a nod then exited the tent.

It always entertained Annamae to see men bow to Clara Barton's demands. Gentle and regal as a queen, Miss Barton's character commanded respect, and men seemed perfectly happy to support her in any way they could.

"Good morning, Miss Barton." Annamae clasped her hands in front of her and waited for instructions.

"Miss Worthington, we're going to be working closely with one another over the next few months at least. I think it's time you called me Clara."

"Yes, Miss...Clara."

"Very well. Please assist Dr. Hubbell this morning. Several have requested medical services, and they're lined up for a city block. Supplies will arrive at headquarters throughout the day. I'm off to dictate another telegram to Mr. Ward and delegate some paperwork to Beatrice."

Annamae always marveled at the feats the woman could accomplish given time and people to delegate to.

Before Doctor Hubbell could see the next patient, Annamae informed him she was to assist him for the rest of her shift. He pulled her aside, his face hard as granite, and spoke in low tones. "Doctor Rose is working with a team to clear debris and set up tents about a quarter mile from here. Once they're finished, make up as many sickbeds as you can. We may need to send patients there for isolated care. If so, that station will be quarantined."

"What is it?" she whispered.

Dismay was clear in the grim lines of his mouth. "There isn't a drop of clean water in which to bathe or drink within miles of this town. What's here is contaminated with corpses, oil, open plumbing, and a number of other things. Do you understand what I'm saying?"

Annamae swallowed, knowing the dangers that lurked in unclean water. "Yes, sir."

"Keep yourself as clean as you can, especially before eating. I'm hoping we won't need those sick beds, but odds are we won't have enough. You are young and strong and capable. That's why I'm asking you to help me with this."

Despite the concern for her own health snaking down her spine, she'd taken an oath as a Red Cross nurse to assist where needed, no matter what. Her spirit wilted as Doctor Hubbell turned to his next patient. As if the residents of Johnstown hadn't suffered enough, now they were vulnerable to typhoid fever.

Chapter Eight

"No one has any idea of the feelings of a man who acts as undertaker, gravedigger, and pallbearer for his own family."

~William Gaffney, Johnstown insurance agent who lost fourteen family members, including his wife and children

WEDNESDAY, JUNE 5

"I now pronounce you man and wife." Monty tried to conjure some measure of lightness to his words, but his voice remained monotone. He'd helped lay the bride's and groom's families to rest moments before they'd asked him to officiate their union. A marriage not for love but for necessity. Comfort. Companionship.

Monty had never felt more alone than he did right now, but he was also grateful he'd had no spouse or children to lose.

"You may kiss the bride." Monty closed the soggy tome written by Mark Twain in his scabbed hands.

The couple shifted awkwardly and met each other's melancholy gaze. Monty had never officiated a ceremony without his Bible before, but his had not survived the waters, and pretending the novel in his hands was the Good Book brought him a small measure of comfort.

Liam Linkletter inched toward his new bride and brushed a chaste kiss along her cheek. A tear escaped Myrna's right eye.

Monty looked away. Five days had passed since the great flood stole their lives, and yet life marched on. Babies had been delivered in the shells of former homes, atop piles of debris, or in the woods. New marriages were forged. Families reunited. Loved ones buried. Neighbor greeting neighbor.

Through it all, Monty had wandered the ruins aimlessly. Numb? Angry? He didn't know how he felt. He'd ask God for answers if he could. He would cry out for wisdom if he thought his words would penetrate past the treetops. Everything Monty had perceived about God and faith and life confused him now. He couldn't sleep. Could barely choke down the rice and potatoes they served at the relief stations. He could never unsee the masses of people perishing before his eyes, never silence the pleas for help as they took their last breath.

The experience had changed him. And not just his actions or his mindset, but his very core. The Montgomery Childs of the past twenty-four years would be entirely different for the rest of his days.

Ignoring his stomach's plea for nourishment, he left the burial field and walked by Prospect Hill to see what all the banging was about. Dizziness made his steps falter, but he caught himself. The strange sensation lasted only a few moments, and then his brain cleared. Blinking hard, he felt confident enough to continue.

A woman ran out of a nearby shack and dashed in front of him, inches from colliding. Her smile neutralized the stench of her filthy dress. She raised her palms to the sky and sang, joy in her face beaming brighter than the sun above them. When she caught sight of the old depot station converted into a temporary morgue, she grew somber. Two men neared, carrying a body stretched out on a door.

An unseen force broke inside her, and wails filled the air. She beat her fists on her forehead until Monty feared she'd damage her brain. He commanded her to stop, but she turned her fury to her dress, ripping the tattered garment into rags. "Ma'am, stop this," he said. "Stop it now."

Eyes crazed, she grabbed his arms and pressed her face close to his.

The ligaments in her neck bulged. "I shall go crazy if they don't find his body," she screamed. She shook like an autumn leaf in a windstorm. "He was a good man. I loved him, and he loved me."

She fell into his chest and sobbed. "Where is he?" she wailed over and over.

She repeated the sentence so many times Monty feared he would go mad himself.

Then, with a jolt, she flung herself away and snarled, "Where is he? You must help me find him!"

Monty had thought his heart couldn't break any more. He was wrong. He wasn't capable of helping anyone, especially reuniting this once youthful woman with a man who was likely dead.

Before he could react, she sped toward the river. "I must find him."

She jumped into the still turbulent water. Her skirts bubbled up around her. Dirty water saturated the fabric, and she sank. Two men witnessing the scene went in after her. She struggled and flailed as they dragged her ashore. Moments later, she fainted.

The entire hillside had gone eerily quiet. Even the banging Monty came to investigate had stopped. The spectators waited for the men to lift her—heavy skirts and all—and take her away before resuming their business. In some strange way, they seemed to understand the poor woman's inner turmoil. They understood the weight of her burden.

Slowly, work ensued. Monty walked in the noise's direction—he now recognized it as hammers nailing wood—surprised to see construction this soon since supplies were hindered by the broken rail lines. All around him, folks sifted through debris, tossing boards and items that needed to be burned into piles and anything salvageable into wagons. Monty hadn't been back to his home since he escaped the church attic. He wasn't ready to see it again. Wasn't ready to disassemble the wagon that had crashed into his kitchen or to attempt to identify the once-vibrant life.

He knew he needed to go back out of respect for that soul and for the sake of the person's family. For the sake of joining the rest of the community in restoring their town. He knew this, and yet all he could do was watch the happenings around him and feel utterly helpless.

What was wrong with him? He was always first in line to serve. He sought ways to serve. Every living creature, man or beast, needed help right now, and all he could do was let the seconds of each day pass while he tried to keep hold of his faculties.

As he approached the construction, he recognized Benedict Covington in the crowd of men carrying, holding, and nailing lumber. Had it really been just six days ago that the young man held their country's flag at the cemetery in memory of those who'd gone on before?

Ben lifted boards onto his shoulder and noticed Monty. He carried the boards to the men framing the walls then jogged to him. "Hey, Pastor."

"I'm glad to see you, Ben. Your family"—he swallowed—"are they well?"

Ben's posture wilted, and the end of his nose turned red. "Joanna, she's safe. The schoolmaster sent the kids home early because of the rain, but she stayed to clean the slates. As she left the schoolhouse, she heard a man yell that the dam had broken and for everyone to run to the hills. She barely escaped before the wave swept past. But Momma and Daddy. . ." His voice broke. "They went down."

Monty put a hand on the lad's shoulder and squeezed. So many souls had "gone down." Words like *died* or *drowned* or *killed* were too harsh to speak aloud. Instead, everyone referred to "going down," and everyone understood.

"We found them encased in mud, clinging to one another." Ben's voice broke, but a moment later he lifted his chin, determined to be brave. Moisture dripped beneath his nose, and he wiped it away with the back of his dirty hand.

Monty had no more tears to cry. The Covingtons were the best of people. They'd be sorely missed.

"What's going on here?" Monty pointed at the construction.

"Miss Clara Barton from Washington is here. Brought the Red Cross with her. She's commissioned six large buildings to be built in cleared and level areas throughout town. Her workman called them hotels. Anyone who's displaced from their homes will have a room with a bed, three hot meals a day, a place to wash up, and anything they need provided by donations."

Monty had read about the Red Cross but wasn't familiar with their purpose. Was it possible for one organization to care for so many? It would cost thousands to rebuild and house the survivors. And what of the men responsible for this ruination? What were they doing to help?

A seam of anger split his desolate spirit.

He'd overheard talk of the whys over the past few days. This had been no judgment day or act of God. Not in the biblical sense. The truth was that this had happened from the selfishness and indifference of the industrial kings who ran the country and spent summers recreating at the top of the mountain. But proving it would be no easy task.

The dizziness returned.

"Pastor?"

Monty shook his head to clear the heavy fog that suddenly coated his thoughts. Wrong move. Ben kept him upright, and within a few seconds, he was fine again. "Sorry."

"Are you feeling all right, Pastor? You're not looking good."

"I'm perfectly fine. Now, what were you saying?"

"I. . .was gonna say we can use your help. The more men we have, and the faster these hotels go up, the sooner we can get folks cared for."

Monty nodded. "Have you seen Elder?"

"Who, sir?"

Monty shook his head to unscramble his tangled thoughts. "Cyrus Elder, attorney for the Cambria Iron Works, council for the Johnstown waterworks, solicitor for the Savings Bank. . ."

"Um." Ben stepped away, and Monty realized he'd been gripping the young man's arms. He must look as crazy as the woman who'd run into the river. "I've heard of him, Pastor, but I wouldn't know him if I saw him. I'm sorry."

Monty fought to remain calm. "It's fine. You're doing great work here, Ben. I'll try to join you soon. I need to discover the fate of Elder and speak to him about an important matter if he's still with us."

"Pastor, wait." Ben caught his wrist. He assessed Monty's appearance. "Have you eaten? Volunteers from Pittsburgh have set up a commissary near the depot. They might offer you a warm meal and clean clothes."

That wasn't such a bad idea. His trousers and once-white shirt were covered in grime, the soles of his shoes were cracked and rubbing blisters on his feet. The rank odor in the air could very well be him.

"Thank you, Ben." He shook the young man's hand.

The tension in Ben's face relaxed, and he went back to his work.

Travel was difficult, as the landscape was barely recognizable save for the stone bridge still piled with debris, the spire of the Methodist church, and a few other buildings that stayed on their foundations, but it was enough to give Monty a general direction of where he needed to go.

It took him an hour to navigate the wreckage and find the commissary. Supplies were few, but he got a bowl of pork and beans, a chunk of stale bread, clean clothes, and boots. Washing was another matter. Small tents erected on each end of the commissary were used for bathhouses, one for men and one for women. There were bowls, pitchers, cakes of soap, and barrels of water, but none of it was clean. He did his best to wash thoroughly and then wrestled the new clothes onto his wet body.

The trousers were too long and the shirt a size too small, but he was grateful all the same. His spirit was already a little lighter.

Monty stepped from the tent and tossed his old clothes and shoes into a large metal ring where an attendant monitored the fire burning items no longer of use. The sound of crinkling pages drew his head around. A list nailed to the side of the commissary flapped in the afternoon breeze. Curious, Monty glanced it over. It was a list of those known to have survived.

"Add your name, if you haven't already." A middle-aged woman—a volunteer, he presumed by her pristine condition—pointed to a pencil tied to a thin rope and nailed beside the papers. "They're putting them up at every station so those who don't find their loved ones on the lists know to check the morgues. The Red Cross stations have them as well. They're documenting the names of patients along with the status of their health."

She folded a baby blanket over one arm. The barrel behind her was full of them. Sadly, a necessity not as sought after, since most infants had not survived. In fact, from the reports he'd heard, three-quarters of the town's children had gone to Jesus.

"Are you missing anyone?" she asked.

"No."

The woman offered a wan smile. "If you need anything else, sir, please visit us again. We'll do what we can."

"Thank you."

She disappeared back into the commissary to assist the line gathering out front. A strangeness settled over Monty, but he ignored it and searched the list for church members and any other names he recognized. Mr. and Mrs. Stevenson had survived, as well as Charlie Dick. Reverend Beale, Willard Bantley, Abram Dillar, Louis Murr. Monty knew about the Bowser sisters and little Gertrude, all alive and well. Victor Heiser, Reverend H.L. Chapman, and Mrs. Brinker. With every relieved breath that someone had survived, he knew there'd be more full of grief in the coming days.

The white tents of the Red Cross were closer than the other commissaries, so he'd search their survivor list for Cyrus Elder. To Monty's knowledge, Elder was the only Johnstown resident who was also a member of the South Fork Fishing and Hunting Club, and Monty wanted answers to why their dam had broken.

Halfway to the Red Cross tents, confusion settled over Monty. Where was he going? What was his intent once he got there?

His eyes had difficulty focusing on the white flag with a red cross flapping in the breeze. He stayed fixed on it, like a sailor fixed on the horizon, and with each step, his world returned to normal. More residents seemed to be gathered at the tents than at the relief stations. Nurses and doctors in white coats and aprons moved like worker bees among the dirty and forlorn faces. A few patients had visible wounds, but many waited for less obvious reasons. One man stood to the side and retched into a chamber pot.

The pork and beans gurgled in Monty's stomach. Were they in danger of disease?

So many people. So many needs. Would their troubles never cease?

Chapter Nine

⁓

"A profound melancholia associated with an almost absolute disregard of the future—a peculiar intonation of words, the persons speaking mechanically."

~Correspondent for the *Medical News of Philadelphia* regarding a surprising number of cases of prolonged shock from the flood victims

Annamae pressed her fingertips into the muscles in her neck to work out the ache. She'd never experienced aiding this many necessities at once. She'd never seen anything like it, not even during the scarlet fever epidemic two years ago when hundreds of people had flooded the capital's hospitals. Many had been turned away for lack of treatment space. She'd worked dawn to dusk for days, quarantined within the walls of the building. It had been hard work—long and tedious and sometimes heartbreaking—but nothing like this.

Arching her back, she felt her spine crack, relieving the pressure. She exited the side flap of the tent for fresh air and a few moments of respite. In every direction, people worked on crews removing debris, transporting the deceased to the morgues for identification and burial, distributing supplies, building new construction, and compiling information for those who'd lost someone.

It reminded Annamae of the time Rufus Ellington destroyed a large anthill behind their schoolhouse when she was six. Though she'd begged him not to, he'd scattered the mountain of dirt, laughing at her distress. Immediately, hundreds of ants spilled to the surface, and each did its part, rebuilding what had taken them weeks to create.

The brisk air made her shiver, but the unusually cool temperature for a June day was a blessing. It helped to slow the decomposition process and made for a more comfortable workday. Thunderheads drifted across the sky, promising another dousing. The Red Cross team going door-to-door assessing needs would endure an even more arduous task if cleanup was delayed.

To her right, a man sidled between the tents, hands in his pockets. His shirt fit him tightly, like a glove, leaving nothing about his muscular form to the imagination. The extra-wide cuff of his pants compensated for too long an inseam. He wore no suspenders or hat, but that was normal in the current circumstances. Things like proper etiquette and hats were the least of anyone's concerns.

His rich brown hair was longer on top than the rest, and it flopped to one side in a large wave, appearing damp. The lethargic speed of his stride and the glaze in his eyes struck her as a man in shock. Appearing not much older than her twenty-one years, he seemed lost. Dazed. A flood victim, certainly. Wearing clothes from the meager donations that had made it into the valley, she guessed, by their clean appearance.

She'd seen this disoriented behavior before, and she'd heard Miss Barton—Clara—describe it many times when telling stories of the war.

Annamae moved to intercept him. "Sir? Is everything all right?"

He stopped and blinked at her.

"Are you in need of medical attention?" She crossed her arms over her middle to ward off the chill, amazed at how much warmer it was inside the tents.

"No." His head tipped to the side.

Serious eyes the color of her daddy's old dungarees seemed to brighten as he took her in. His hard square jaw and muscular build were intimidating, but the softness of his demeanor and the boyish twinkle in his gaze heightened her nurturing instincts.

How could a man look ridiculous and glorious at the same time?

"Are you searching for someone?" she asked.

"Um." He frowned in thought. A few moments passed before he said, "Yes."

His slow, one-word answers told her enough.

"You're peaked. I'm a nurse with the Red Cross, and I'm here to help. May I examine you, Mr. . . . ?"

"Monty." The name scraped along his vocal cords as if his throat was parched.

"Several are complaining of feeling ill—nausea, aching limbs, severe fatigue. Are you feeling any of those symptoms, Mr. Monty?"

His thick eyebrows furrowed again. "Monty is my given name."

Oh. She always addressed patients by their surname. It kept things professional and her emotions distant.

"May I?" She didn't wait for his reply but pressed her cool fingers to his forehead. Then to his cheek.

"Fever. Only a touch though. Do you have any injuries, cuts, bruises? It—"

He caught her lowering hand and pressed her palm against his cheek. His stubble poked her skin.

She stiffened, ready to fight him off if needed.

Instead of manhandling her, his eyelids closed. Then he sighed. "Your hand feels nice."

Clara certainly hadn't taught her about this during her apprenticeship. His liberties should offend her, and she should scold him back into his rightful place. She'd done it many times when male patients attempted to flirt with her. But she could tell this Monty fellow's actions weren't menacing. If anything, they were oddly childlike. He simply needed the comfort of human touch after all he'd gone through.

And ointment on those puckered and scabbed hands.

Annamae searched their surroundings to see if anyone witnessed their exchange. Relieved that no one seemed to have noticed, she said, "Monty, will you please follow me into the medical tent so I can assess your condition?"

At least that way, they'd be on formal grounds.

His eyelids twitched then opened, and he released her. Chagrin made one side of his mouth tick upward, and his face held color now. He nodded and followed her inside.

She gestured to the nearest vacant "bed," which was nothing more than a thick plank topped by thin ticking wrapped in a clean sheet. Two other nurses worked in the room of twelve patients. Monty sat on the bed while she retrieved her bag of instruments.

His knees pressed against the outside of her thighs as she lifted each eyelid. "Are you experiencing stomach cramping, rash, or chills?"

"No."

She reached behind her and tightened the loosening bow of her apron. "Have you regurgitated or had the runs?"

His lips parted, and he reared back. "No, ma'am."

She grinned. "Sickness is nothing to be embarrassed about."

He squirmed and looked down at his lap. "I'm not used to discussing such things with a lady."

"A lady, yes, but I'm also a nurse. It's my job to inquire about *such things* with all patients. I apologize if it makes you uncomfortable."

With all the horrific things the Johnstown residents had experienced and seen the last few days, she was surprised this conversation made a chink in his pride.

She told him to breathe normally and listened to his heartbeat with a stethoscope. Perfect. She reached for the patient list beside her and wrote his first name. "What is your surname, Mr. Monty?"

"Childs. Montgomery Childs."

This seemed to shame him more than her previous question.

"Are you a resident of Johnstown, Mr. Childs?" She could guarantee he was, but Clara had commanded they ask since many volunteers had arrived from the outlying towns. Should the volunteers come to need medical attention as well, this was how they could keep their patients separated on record. Clara prided herself on detailed bookkeeping.

"Yes."

"And what is your occupation, Mr. Childs?"

"I'm a pastor."

Pastor Montgomery Childs. That had a pleasant sound to it. "With the utmost respect to your calling, may I address you simply as Mr. Childs?"

"I prefer you just call me Monty, ma'am."

The more he talked, the more his brain seemed to thaw from its frozen state. She continued asking him random questions in soothing tones while she checked his ears and throat.

Her fingers didn't detect any swollen glands. "Did you lose anyone, Monty?"

"No. My family lives elsewhere, and I'm unmarried."

His Adam's apple bobbed against her fingertips.

A rush of heat flashed through her body. She performed this same routine with dozens of patients daily. Something about his powerful neck peeking through his open collar, her fingers dancing along his flushed skin, and their close proximity made the examination feel intimate. She dropped her hands and put space between them.

Annamae cleared her throat before speaking. "Are you having pain anywhere? If so, I can fetch a doctor to examine you."

Monty covered a yawn with his marred hand. "I'm stiff and sore, and I have a cut on my leg, but nothing that requires a doctor."

"Cuts can turn infectious. How did you hurt your hands?"

Monty held them up and studied both sides as if forgetting he suffered the wounds. "The wave knocked my home off its foundation and into the church. I made it to the attic, but the water was rising. I punched a hole through the roof to escape."

The statement stole the breath from her lungs. She couldn't imagine.

Blinking back tears of compassion, she retrieved salve from the supply table, lifted his hand in hers, and rubbed the thick substance into the skin. "Have you eaten?"

He yawned again. "I ate a bowl of pork and beans from the commissary about an hour ago."

"How long has it been since you've slept?" Her fingers rubbed in small circles, working the salve into every inch of skin.

He shrugged. "A little here and there. I've had some dizzy spells."

"Well, good news then." She placed the lid on the salve and wiped her greasy fingers on her apron. "I believe your condition to be nothing more than exhaustion and your body adjusting to what you've experienced the last several days. I'll have one of the doctors examine your leg, but I'd like for you to rest here a while so we can monitor your symptoms in case your dizziness stems from a more severe condition. Will you do that for me?"

She scribbled his diagnosis on the paper.

He fiddled with a loose string on his pant leg. "I need to find an acquaintance about an important matter."

"I understand, but you need rest and observation more." After witnessing the devastation, she could confidently say his lack of sleep stemmed from having no proper place to rest his head.

She set the paper aside and leaned toward him, softening her voice. "At least stay long enough to get some sleep."

As if his body had decided for him, he yawned again, and his muscles visibly relaxed. He removed his boots, and she guided his head to the small square of a pillow. "After your nap, I'll see what I can do to help you locate your acquaintance."

His eyes closed. She covered him with a wool blanket, tucking it under his feet that hung three inches off the end of the bed. She turned to walk away, but he blindly grabbed her pinky. "You'll be here? In case I need anything?"

His words slurred.

"I'll be here, Mr. Childs."

"Monty," he whispered.

An indescribable movement shifted in her chest. "I'll be here, Monty."

Before she'd finished her sentence, his breathing fell into the slow, deep rhythm of sleep.

She extracted her finger from his grip and left the front of the tent to see about the next patient, her insides quaking over the gentle stranger's touch.

Chapter Ten

"We are creatures of the moment; we live from one little space to another; and only one interest at a time fills these."
~William Dean Howells in *A Hazard of New Fortunes*, 1889

THURSDAY, JUNE 6

Had the woman with the haunted eyes and gentle hands been an ethereal creature or an apparition of his own making?

The low hum of voices and clinking of glass roused him awake. Nurses in white aprons moved about the tent, tending to those stretched on beds. His mind replayed the ghostly woman who'd set his restless spirit at ease. She'd convinced him to sleep, and what a blessed sleep it was. So deep, in fact, he struggled to decipher which of his memories from the past few days were real and which were fiction.

After stretching his stiff muscles, he sat upright with a moan. The orange tabby cat he'd cared for in the woods jumped from its coil at his side and meowed. He hadn't seen it since he'd abandoned the petticoat in the underbrush. It was good to see that it was well.

A man wearing a white coat opened the tent flap to reveal the pink of dawn rising behind the hills. Monty was certain he'd reached these tents in full daylight, which meant he'd been asleep for almost an entire day.

The nurse stocking a crate with small glass bottles turned to him and smiled. She was real after all.

Monty's blood stirred at this, sharpening his senses. She abandoned her task and walked to his bedside, hands in her apron pockets. "How are you feeling, Monty?"

He recalled asking her not to refer to him as Mr. Childs. If anyone here from outside of Johnstown connected his surname to his uncle, it could be downright dangerous.

"Much better now that I've gotten sleep."

Purple shadows marred her skin beneath large brown eyes the color of the imported chocolates his aunt Adelaide used to purchase to spoil her guests at dinner parties. Her mouth opened wide, and she covered it with her fingers. "I'm glad to hear it. Now that you've gotten some rest, I should do the same."

The cat crawled onto his lap, knocking the blanket from his legs, but she caught it before it hit the ground. She placed it at the foot of the bed then lifted the tabby and cradled it against her chest. "He's been keeping vigil by your bedside since four o'clock yesterday. I cleaned him up as best I could and rubbed some medication on his eye. He was lucky to have survived and reunited with his owner."

Monty rubbed his crusted and slightly goopy eyes. He must have slept in a near coma. "He's not mine. We found each other in the woods after the flood and kept each other warm one night."

The cat stuck its nose in the air, purring loudly enough to garner the attention of most in the room. "How long have I been asleep?" he asked.

"Since yesterday, around the noon hour."

"Have you been here this whole time?"

She snuggled the top of the cat's head against her chin then placed him on the ground. She brushed dark, curly tendrils escaping her white cap with a sweep of her hand as if stalling her answer. "I stepped away long enough for meals."

Monty placed a hand on his thigh and studied her closer. "Why have you not rested?"

Bottom lip clenched between her teeth, she reached for the blanket and began folding it. "I promised you I'd be here."

He rocked back, stunned. These tents had dozens of patients. Surely she didn't make individual promises to each one.

It was a comfort to know that amid all this chaos human kindness still existed. Her outward beauty intensified with her beautiful gesture.

"Thank you." His throaty tone had him clearing his throat.

A pretty pink stained her cheeks. She looped the folded blanket across one arm, dark lashes fanning her cheeks. "No new or worsening symptoms?"

"No, ma'am."

"Well then, Monty, you're free to go. A doctor rolled up your pant-leg after you fell asleep yesterday, examined your cut, and cleared you of infection. Promise me you'll come back if you need anything."

He stood, and a splinter of wood jabbed into the arch of his foot. The broken boards they'd laid as a makeshift floor were already sinking into the soggy earth from the weight of traffic. The hem of his too-long pants hugged the ground.

Monty searched for his boots and found them beside the bed. "I will Miss. . .?"

"Annamae." Her voice was quiet. "Since, at your request, we've skipped formalities and gone straight to our given names."

Her nose wrinkled with her grin.

"I hope I haven't offended you."

"Not at all."

Annamae. A harmonious name worthy of a songbird species or the title of a graceful ship. Such romantic thoughts were rare for him in the best of times, but the fact they were hitting him now was, though not unfounded, still quite odd.

Monty bent and laced one boot then the other. "Thank you, Annamae. For everything."

She halted his exit with a touch on his sleeve. "One moment."

Tail in the air, the cat wound between his ankles.

She passed him the folded blanket, returned to the crate she'd been unloading, and scooped up a pile of fabric. "I found these in the supply tent while you slept. They should fit you more comfortably."

Monty thumbed through the tidy stack. "That's very thoughtful, but I don't want to take these if someone else has greater need."

She gestured to his collar. He looked down to find that two buttons he'd secured on the too-small shirt yesterday were missing, exposing the hollow of his neck and a sliver of his chest.

"Oh." Now it was his turn to blush.

She grinned. "I'd say your need is as great as the next. You can always take what you're currently wearing to the commissary later, and they'll wash and mend them for someone else."

"I'll do that."

"Keep the blanket. Donations are pouring in, and we aim to make sure everyone in Johnstown has at least one covering." She reached inside her apron pocket and pulled out a tin of salve. "Your home, your church. Do they remain?"

He accepted the tin. "There's no salvaging my home. The church will need to be gutted and repaired but stands."

"You don't plan to sleep beneath the steeple again, do you?"

"I hope to never step foot inside an attic another day in my life."

"Where will you stay?" Those large, curious eyes blinked up at him, concern written in their weary corners.

"If John the Baptist survived living in the wilderness, I suppose I can too."

He was jesting, but no humor lit her face.

"I would feel better if you'd let me help you find lodging. Can you follow me to headquarters? It's not far."

"You've already been gracious, Miss Annamae. I won't take any more of your time."

"Please? My tent is in that direction anyway. Now that you're awake, I plan to sleep the day away."

What else did he have to do? There'd be no Thursday afternoon Bible study. He had no Bible, no meeting place, and his congregation was either scattered or passed away.

His heart wished to ease her sweet concern for him. "After you."

He gestured to the front of the tent.

She quickly stripped the sheet from the tick mattress and the pillow-case from the paper-thin pillow and stuffed them into a large barrel on the way out. The cat followed beside them.

The destroyed landscape came alive with the breaking of day. People milled about delivering supplies, standing in line for medical help, walking to the commissary, sifting through debris, and any number of things. He was grateful the Red Cross had come to their aid.

Monty slowed his steps on the muddy earth to keep pace beside her.

"Supplies and volunteers are arriving on nearly every train." She gestured to the people rushing about. "I can't believe how quickly folks have rallied together to help."

He was sure her words meant to offer comfort, but none came. All the comforts their lives had afforded were stolen the second the dam collapsed. It would take months to rebuild Johnstown, if not years. Their lives would never be the same.

Not wishing to be rude by remaining silent, he joined the conversation. "How are supplies getting here? The water washed away or mangled the tracks beyond use."

"The trains can get as far as South Fork. That's how we arrived. I've heard that from there, supplies are being taken over a pontoon bridge to a swinging bridge and then brought down into the valley."

The name of South Fork brought acid into his throat. Monty had been to the fishing and hunting club named after the stopover town as his uncle's guest and had witnessed how close the surface of the water was to the crest of the dam during normal weather. After his uncle had commanded the dam be lowered to make the service road from the station to the club wide enough for two carriages to pass, the middle started to sag—an issue his uncle had ignored as easily as one might a gnat at a picnic.

They turned and cut down an aisle between tents. Annamae's brow furrowed as they sidled past patients lying on beds and hanging over chamber pots.

"What is it?" he whispered.

She looked from left to right then pulled him away from any listening ears. "I'm confiding in you as a man of the clergy. We don't wish to start a panic. Do you understand?"

He nodded.

"Every watershed for miles is contaminated. This town is in very real danger of typhoid fever. Some have already been exhibiting signs, though no cases have officially been declared."

Her embarrassing question from yesterday surfaced in his mind. That explained why she was adamant that he stay under her care in case his health grew worse. Typhoid fever was highly contagious. A few cases could turn into an epidemic within days.

She flattened her palm against her stomach. "Miss Clara Barton has sent a telegram to the surgeon general requesting his presence. However, it could be days before he arrives with disinfectants. Clean your hands thoroughly before eating. Be careful using any utensils from the commissary. Be certain they've cleaned them. Don't use any communal cups at water stations. If you come across anyone with symptoms, send them here."

"I will."

She continued into the tent with the Red Cross flag flying at its peak. A woman sat behind a crate she used as a desk. "Hetty, I need to find accommodations for Pastor Childs, please."

The woman looked up from her papers and rubbed her temple. "You're only the hundredth person to ask me to work a miracle in the last hour."

Annamae raised her pert little chin. "I've thoroughly examined the pastor and deemed him healthy. Can you not find room for him in one of the buildings still standing? I heard Miss Barton say they've turned them into havens until the hotels are finished."

The woman sighed. "They're already full. Alma Hall is housing two hundred and forty-nine and informed us there's not room for even one more body." She set her pencil down. "The churches, apartments, and tenement houses that survived are also full. I heard more tents are being erected beside the old woolen mill this morning. Check there."

Monty thanked the woman, and they left.

"I apologize for that outcome," Annamae said. "I hope you're able to find lodging."

The dejection in her words eased the tightness in his chest. She genuinely cared where he laid his head tonight, which made his homeless state a little less bleak.

"I appreciate your efforts, but I believe I'll stay at the church." He ran a hand along the linen shirt packed into a neat square. "The Lord has promised to give the weary rest. What better place than in His house? Besides, I've got to go back and face it sometime."

Though he had to admit he was reluctant to slide his neck into the yoke of cleaning and restoring it all.

Her lips pursed in concentration. "One night when Miss Barton and I were working late, I asked about her time during the war and how—with all the different wounds and lives fading around her—she even knew where to begin and how best to help the soldiers. She answered, 'All a body can do is focus on what can be accomplished each day. Take care physically and spiritually so one can be of service to others. And most importantly, remember who holds the entire world in His hands.'"

Monty swallowed the truth hard, emotions coming fast. "You've been a godsend, Miss Annamae."

Before she could reply, he headed for the church.

The steeple had always been his compass in the booming town, but now it was broken like everything else. Franklin Street, along with many others, was unrecognizable, so he walked in what he hoped was the general direction of Macedonia Street until he spotted the familiar roofline.

His search for Cyrus Elder could take days, if the man was even alive. But find him he would. Everyone in this town deserved answers, and Cyrus was the closest thing they had to the club members at the moment. However, it could wait.

Clutching the bundle to his side, Monty trekked up the incline of rubble. The cat trotted east to the hills, likely searching for a rodent to prey upon. Folks nodded or waved as he passed as if relieved to see another soul they recognized alive. As he neared the church, he saw more men clearing the destruction.

"Pastor!" Kenneth Breslin threw down his saw and jumped out of a fallen tree that had crushed the iron fence behind the church. It surrounded the small cemetery of the town's founders, but many of the granite head-stones were crushed or had been washed away.

At least ten other men in his congregation filed from elsewhere on the grounds to join them. Kenneth's smile almost reached his ears. "Glad to see you alive, Pastor. No one seemed to know if you'd gone down or not. Ernie said he saw you the next day, but no one knew whether to believe him. Showed up to help clean, breath stinking of whisky."

Monty searched the faces. Several yards away, Ernie stumbled from the side of the church where Monty's house had been forced against it, shaky hand gripping a shovel.

"Ernie saw me," Monty said, only for Kenneth's ears. "He might imbibe, but he's not a liar. You all don't give him enough credit." Monty glanced around. "What's the state of everyone's family?"

Kenneth turned his head and spit. "William put his wife and baby on a train as soon as the waters started rising Friday morning. They're safe in Philadelphia. James lost his mother, as she was ailing and couldn't get out of bed to run. Robert's still looking for his two boys. Said he'd be over after he's checked all the morgues again today. Fred's wife was walking to her sister's house higher on the hill when the wave swept her away. And Ernie ain't got nobody."

Likely the reason he drank.

"Any word on damage to the rest of the area?"

"Men from the newspapers arrived almost immediately. They're reporting minor damage to South Fork. The planing mill and viaduct were destroyed. Sixteen died in Mineral Point. The wave took everything away, so there's no telling there was even once a town there. The roundhouse and depot at East Conemaugh are gone, and in Woodvale, it wiped out the Gautier works, the tannery, the streetcar shed, and most every resident."

Good heavens. The water consumed the entire hillside then. Monty ran a hand down his face. "What's everyone doing here?"

Jim Parkes laid a hand on Monty's shoulder. "All our homes are gone except Ted's, and his is barely standing. But we're alive. You've done so much for us, Pastor, we thought we'd start with cleaning your place. And the church. We'll be needing spiritual bread while we rebuild this town and try to make sense of all this."

Hot tears filled Monty's eyes. These men had lost nearly everything, and their first thought after their own families was for him and the church. Shame burned deep in Monty's gut for avoiding his position over the last few days. He didn't know how he would begin ministering to these men in the wake of this disaster, but he owed it to them to try.

He wiped his damp eyes and sniffed. "Thanks, fellas. Let's get to work."

Chapter Eleven

⌒

"CAUSE OF THE CALAMITY. . .THE PITTSBURGH FISHING CLUB CHIEFLY RESPONSIBLE."

~ Headline from the *New York Sun* days after the disaster

SATURDAY, JUNE 8

Sunlight poured through the grimy window of the church and bathed the pew where Monty slept. He was grateful for an enclosed place to rest, but the fern-covered hillside had been softer. He sat up and rubbed the sleep from his eyes, jolting the cat snoozing by his head. "Sorry, buddy," he croaked.

The tabby lowered his arched back then stretched one leg at a time. When his routine ended, he rubbed against Monty's arm and meowed. Bumpy scars brushed Monty's fingertips as he scratched the cat's head. "I know, I'm hungry too."

Monty and the men of his congregation had worked hard the last two days, cleaning the area surrounding the church, cutting the large tree that had fallen into the cemetery, and chopping it into logs for anyone in need of firewood. He'd hoped to clear enough to hold a service tomorrow, but there was still too much work to do.

74

Monty had burned nearly all of his belongings to prevent disease from contamination. His Bible, the one thing he'd carried since the start of seminary, they'd found beneath a foot of sludge in what used to be the road. Some clothes in the smashed bureau were salvageable but required a good scrubbing. The house itself would have to come down. Wedged at a dangerous angle against the church, the structure was too far off its foundation to repair, and some of the foundation itself had washed away.

The church, to everyone's astonishment, remained steadfast despite it bracing his house. Mr. Jensen, a man well skilled in construction, had confirmed it after inspecting the foundation himself. Monty shouldn't have been surprised. Jesus was the chief cornerstone, and nothing was more solid a foundation than that.

Sure, they'd have to strip most of the structure and rebuild, but it was nothing that couldn't be accomplished with serving hands, determination, and sweat. After the church was whole again, he'd see to constructing a modest, one-level home on higher ground and on a taller foundation to protect against the normal spring flooding. Now that Lake Conemaugh was drained and several investigations of the South Fork Fishing and Hunting Club were underway—according to recent news headlines—the danger of the dam's rebuilding and subsequent future threats of such monstrous proportion occurring again shouldn't pose any threat.

Monty folded the blanket Miss Annamae had given him and placed it at the end of the pew. The church stank like mildew, the other pews were upended, and the front door was missing, but he had a place to rest his head.

Like Miss Annamae had graciously reminded him, all a body could do was trust and focus on what could be accomplished that day. And all he could do today was work hard, survive, and accompany Robert Townsend to the morgues to search for his missing boys.

Monty tucked in his shirt and ran his fingers through his hair before stepping outside. He'd visit one of the bathhouses later, but for now, he'd eat breakfast at the commissary and then meet up with Robert. His feline friend trotted in the opposite direction, presumably to fill his belly as well.

Yesterday's afternoon rain had set the town's progress back yet again.

It seemed as if all the earth's ocean water had evaporated into the sky and poured down over Pennsylvania the past month. He had a clearer perception of Noah and his mental anguish now. Though drunkenness was never justified, Monty understood Noah's temptation to escape the screams that never left his mind. But in order to dissuade Ernie from the bottle and the many others seizing alcohol from the trains, Monty must stay sober.

The clank of picks and shovels sounded through the morning air as men worked to clear mud and debris from the former streets. Deep-throated shouts and the echo of timber crashing joined the rhythm of cleanup. As Monty reached the commissary, a long whistle blasted through the hills. Everyone stilled, and an eerie silence fell over the town. The whistle of a train was something they hadn't heard in the week since the wave had demolished the station, sending railcars, twisted rail lines, and trapped passengers into the angry whirlpool at the stone bridge. Replacing the lines was one of the first things the military put into action to make the delivery of supplies more efficient.

Dark puffs of smoke from burning debris piles lifted in the air and mixed with the scent of decay and biscuits and gravy. At the commissary, folks sat at tables and on upturned crates or barrels to eat. Monty greeted Mrs. Benton and her three children, who were eating one last meal in Johnstown before taking the train from Sang Hollow to Pittsburgh, where they'd board another train for Connecticut to live with her sister. Almost everyone had lost someone, and grief weighed every countenance in the valley.

Plate in hand, Monty searched for a place to sit. Everett McDonough rose from a table, tucked a newspaper under his arm, and picked up his empty plate. "Everett," Monty called, lifting his hand in greeting.

The man scoured the surrounding faces, searching for the owner of the voice. Surprise lit his features when he spotted Monty. "Good to see you, Pastor."

They shook hands.

"You as well. Your family?"

Everett's expression grew somber, and he stared at the table, shaking his head.

"I'm sorry, Everett. What can I do?"

The man inhaled through his nose, flaring his nostrils. "There's nothing to do but make sure these men pay."

Everett slapped the newspaper against Monty's chest, eyes flashing with anger. "Everyone in this town needs to provide their account to one of the reporters so they can print every blasted story and gain the attention of someone who can put an end to things like this. We must demand justice for our families."

Monty held the newspaper in place while Everett wiped his watery eyes with a thumb and forefinger. "In the meantime, there's plenty of work to be done on one of the committees." His voice trailed off, and he stared at something behind Monty. "It's all we can do."

Before Monty could agree, Everett snapped back from wherever his memory had disappeared to, gave Monty a hearty slap on the shoulder, and then stalked away, vengeance bolstering his stance.

The newspaper crinkled in Monty's hand. He sat, smoothed the crease from the middle, and then bowed his head to pray. While he ate, he skimmed through the articles, wondering where Everett had gotten this copy. Several headlines pointed fingers at the club members, while others declared it merely to be "a terrible act of God."

Though it certainly felt as if God had unleashed all His fury, Monty knew the event stemmed from several sources, beginning with the state of Pennsylvania selling the western section of the canal decades ago.

He skimmed the next page. The disaster had garnered President Harrison's attention, and he promised funds and supplies to the victims. The last article updated readers on the cleanup efforts. According to an A.R. Whitney, who was reportedly on-site, the folks of Johnstown were being recruited into one of the many relief committees headed by Arthur Moxham, president of the Johnson Steel Company in the nearby town of Moxham, which was named after himself. So far, there was a finance committee; a supplies committee; one for morgues, overseen by Reverend Beale; a removal committee guided by Tom Johnson, Moxham's business partner; a policing committee to oversee security and crime, led by a Captain Hart; and a hospitals committee, entrusted to Miss Clara Barton and the Red Cross.

The image of a dark-haired nurse with pensive eyes took over his thoughts, and he wondered how she fared.

A loud boom sent them all jumping. The few women in the crowd screamed. A crusty-looking man sitting at the other end of Monty's table, never breaking stride with his meal, yelled, "Continue on. It ain't nothing but my men blasting the mess at the stone bridge with dynamite."

"Dynamite?" A volunteer—judging by her southern accent—who was collecting abandoned utensils and trash clutched the collar at her throat.

"Ain't nothing else to use," the stranger said. "The mess is too thick and dangerous for horses. All kinds of stuff tangled up down there. My men are well trained. It's perfectly safe. No more frettin'."

The statement seemed to offer the woman a modicum of ease, and she returned to her task.

Monty hurried to finish his breakfast then walked to the Adams Street schoolhouse, where an emergency morgue had opened. Not finding Robert, he held his shirt against his nose and searched the bodies laid out on anything flat that could be found and read the names written on paper dangling from strings on their toes. A few names and faces he recognized; most he did not. Many were unidentified, with tags that read "unknown." Some had only a description of approximate age, hair color, height, and the clothes they wore written beneath their gender. If the decaying body was distorted and unrecognizable, there was no tag at all.

He checked the morgue at the old train depot and then walked the three miles to Morrellville to search the saloon they'd converted to a morgue. There, Monty found the boys' names written on a list compiled by the committee tasked with recording the information. His heart broke.

Monty returned to the church. Sitting on the pew where Monty had slept, head in hands, Robert wept. Monty's footsteps thunked in the hollow sanctuary. *Sanctuary* was an appropriate word for what they all needed in these dire circumstances.

The pew creaked beneath Monty's weight. He remained silent. Sometimes, words were simply not useful. This being one of those moments, Monty offered strength through his presence and silent prayer.

Several minutes passed before Robert wiped his eyes and leaned back against the pew, staring at the slanted cross dangling on the wall. "Someone found the boys. They'd washed all the way to Sheridan. A farmer dug them out of his field, Tad's hand still clutching Thomas's jacket."

The boys' laughter and mischievous antics would be missed on this earth. No doubt they were enjoying a competitive race down the streets of gold.

Robert gripped his thighs so hard his knuckles paled. "I don't understand why, Pastor. Why did God take my boys and leave me here? The dam has always held. All these years—always. Why fail now?"

Anguish poured from Robert's being.

Monty knew why, but telling Robert the truth wouldn't bring his boys back.

The dam had failed once before. Christmas Day of 1879. The year Monty had lost his family forever, taking his share of his parents' inheritance and gaining his Uncle Henry's secrets.

For the last seven days, Monty thought the experiences of what he'd seen and heard had tortured him. Now, he wondered if it was more those secrets clawing their way through his conscience. Was he just as guilty for this disaster as the men on the club roster? Could he have prevented this by speaking out against the club before that fateful day? His head told him it wouldn't have made a difference, as the most affluent men of Johnstown had been fighting for the dam's restructure for years.

His heart told him the opposite.

Monty opened his mouth to speak words of comfort to Robert when Jim Parkes ran into the church. "Pastor, we need your help. It's Ben. He's been working on one of those Red Cross hotels and started feeling sick last night. Just found him passed out behind the old gaming hall, covered in vomit and. . . We've got to get him to the hospital. Now."

Without another thought for Robert, Monty ran to where Ben Covington lay on a board in the rutted, muddy street. He should have gone back to help Ben's crew on the hotel like he'd said he would. Ernie stood next to Ben, wheezing, his body shaking. "I'll take over from here," Monty said, patting Ernie's arm, knowing the man could never carry the load as far as the hospital, sober or drunk.

Ernie wiped his sweaty forehead, leaving a streak of clean skin behind.

His eyes held the sheen of desire for the devil's drink. "Thank you, Pastor."

Monty wished he held the power to break the chains of addiction from Ernie, but the man had to want it for himself. "You're welcome to stay in the church tonight, Ernie. It'll be better for your soul than Lizzie Thompson's."

War fought in the twitches on Ernie's face.

Monty bent and lifted one end of the board while Jim lifted the other. Dodging ruts and debris, they packed toward the Red Cross flag whipping high in the breeze. The trip was mostly downhill, but the good bit of distance caused sweat to collect on Monty's chest and back. The muscles in his arms were on fire by the time they reached the tent.

A nurse intercepted them. "What's the nature of the injury?"

Jim relayed the few details he knew.

Another nurse, carrying an armful of folded sheets, caught Monty's eye. "Annamae!" he called.

She turned, and her brows furrowed. At the sight of them, she thrust her burden into a passing nurse's arms, lifted her skirt, and ran to them. "What is it?"

"Typhoid," he said in unison with the other nurse.

"This way." Annamae jogged through the group of tents to a set erected away from the others. When the two men entered with Ben, Annamae had already prepared a bed and was gathering supplies. "Transfer him to the bed, please."

They obeyed.

She opened one of Ben's eyes to check the pupil, then the other. "There's a cake of lye soap beside the water barrel outside. Use it to wash your hands and arms thoroughly at least three times. If you can find clean clothing, do so, and then wash with lye again afterward. They should have extra cakes at the commissary. Stay away from others as best as you can for at least twelve hours. If no symptoms occur, you may return to your duties, but must return here immediately if you begin to have symptoms."

Monty helped her remove Ben's soiled boots.

"Go," she commanded.

Eyes wide with fear, Jim obeyed, rushed to the barrel, and began scrubbing.

WHEN THE WATERS CAME

Annamae unbuttoned Ben's shirt. "Now, Monty. Don't risk getting sick."

"I'm not leaving him. I'm already exposed. Let me help."

She studied his face, glanced around at the limited medical staff working the area, and then sighed. "He needs fresh clothing. These and his boots will need burned."

Annamae pointed to an area even farther away from the main tents where a small fire smoldered.

Together, they stripped the young man, and Monty helped her clean him with wet rags before they placed him in a clean nightshirt. The stench of sickness escaping both ends made Monty gag, but he refused to give in before the pretty nurse with a steel nose. He made several trips, carrying the soiled rags, clothing, and boots to the fire. Monty walked backward to the water barrel, watching it burn.

Lord, please let Ben survive.

He joined Annamae at the water barrel and disinfected his hands and arms, scrubbing his shirt sleeves as well. Jim was already heading away from the sick camp.

"I'm guessing this kid is a friend of yours?" One delicate eyebrow lifted as she rolled her sleeves up to her elbows. Small wrists led to slim arms of pale, creamy skin.

"His family were members of the church. He is like a brother to me."

Compassion filled her expression. "You'll have to stay out of the way as we have many patients to care for, but I welcome your help when needed."

"I will."

After shaking the dripping water from her arms, she held them out to air dry as she stalked back to the tent. They spent the rest of the day settling in new patients, making up beds, and stocking supplies. Monty stood vigil, offering Ben small sips of water and broth, applying wet compresses to his burning forehead, and holding the chamber pot when he retched. Annamae moved about the tent, helping other patients as well, but Monty could only focus on and pray for Ben.

As the night shadows took over, the young man faded into unconsciousness, and his breathing grew shallower. Stuffing down his anger, Monty prepared himself for the boy's passing. He gripped Ben's hand, leaned over his weak body, and whispered, "Thanks for being a great friend."

At a quarter to midnight, with the serenade of crickets all around them, Ben joined his parents in heaven. Monty raised the sheet to cover Ben's face, the end of his nose stinging. How was he ever going to tell sweet Joanna that she was the only one in the Covington family left?

A sob escaped, but Monty clamped his lips shut and stuffed it down. A small, feminine hand touched his back. He turned his face away, not wanting to wail in front of an audience. She surprised him by snaking her hand across the entire width of him. The side of Annamae's soft body pressed against his as they both stared at Ben's outline under the sheet. The raw need for human comfort had Monty's arm cradling her in a hard yet controlled squeeze.

"I'm very sorry for your loss," she whispered, gazing up at his face.

Monty pivoted and folded her against his chest, embracing her as tightly as he could without suffocating her. He needed a friend. The connection of human touch. Of knowing he wasn't alone. As the other patients and nurses moved around them, they stood entwined at Ben's bedside and hoped, without words, for a brighter tomorrow.

Chapter Twelve

*"But that is the way we are made: we don't
reason, where we feel; we just feel."*

~ *A Connecticut Yankee in King Arthur's Court* by Mark Twain, 1889

SUNDAY, JUNE 9

Annamae knew holding this man went against all propriety, and yet she did so without fear of consequences. Monty's grief was a palpable energy radiating from his veins and into hers. Healing didn't only consist of the right combination of medicine and methods but of human touch. Kindness. Encouragement. Patience and prayer. Monty had suffered minimal external wounds in surviving the flood, but his lacerations deep inside bled freely.

He sniffed. The hard muscles of his chest rose and fell on a sigh before his arms slipped away. As soon as there was enough space between them for her to recall how closely their bodies had touched, bashfulness overrode her compassion. She tucked stray hairs behind her ears to give her hands something to do. The other nurses moved about the tent acting as if they hadn't noticed their embrace, but Annamae caught their sidelong glances and frowns of disapproval.

Monty wiped a hand down his face. "I apologize for my forward behavior."

"You've done nothing to be ashamed of. Losing a loved one is never easy. We all need consolation from time to time."

Except the condolences she'd offered him left her skin tingling and her arms wanting more.

Matthew's light caresses had certainly never left her wanting. Though he was a good man, a wonderful physician, and would make a fine, honorable husband, his attention always left her confused. She'd never understood why until now.

Monty closed his eyes and gripped Ben's hand.

She lowered her voice. "I'll inform the crew to prepare his body for burial."

"May I go with you? I could use fresh air."

She nodded.

Annamae led them to the water barrel and instructed Monty to scrub with the lye soap while she did the same. The water was as chilly as the early morning air, and a miserable shiver stole through her, making her long for the warmth of Monty's arms again. "How old was Ben, and what's his full name?"

She flung excess water from her hands and arms as he followed her around the maze of tents to the headquarters. Monty slipped his hands into his pockets. For the first time since he'd arrived at the tent, she realized he'd changed into something that better fit his sturdy frame. "Benedict Covington. Seventeen."

The loss of a young life hit much harder than others, it seemed.

Annamae stood in the tent doorway where Hetty Swank sat behind an actual desk in lieu of a crate and recorded the day's notes in a logbook by lantern light. She relayed the news of Ben's passing to Hetty, who asked if Ben had any known living relatives to contact. Annamae looked to Monty for the answer.

"His sister, Joanna, is eleven. She's the only one of their family besides Ben to survive the flood. She's been staying with a friend at Holt House while Ben works."

"Has anyone informed her of his passing?" Hetty asked.

"No, ma'am."

"Someone from the Red Cross will inform her at dawn." Hetty said it cooly, as if Ben were merely a number on the list of deaths and all she was concerned about was being able to write a crisp checkmark beside his name in her book.

"I'm her pastor. It would be best coming from me." Monty rubbed his toe in the dirt, aggravating the shadows made by the lantern.

"That will be fine." Hetty made a notation next to Ben's name and removed her glasses to rub the bridge of her nose. "Do you know if she has any relatives outside of Johnstown?"

"None that I know of," he said.

"I'll inform Reverend Beale to document her with the other orphans for adoption." Hetty replaced her glasses and continued writing.

Annamae wanted to ask Hetty if she had a block of ice for a heart.

"You can't do that. This is her home." Monty withdrew his hands from his pockets and stepped toward Hetty, agony pleading from his features.

Hetty set her pen down. "Do you intend to care for the girl yourself?"

"I..." The defeat leeching from that one tiny word tortured Annamae. "No, ma'am."

Hetty blew out a tired breath. "I understand this situation isn't ideal. None of them are. But there are hundreds of surviving families in Johnstown, and the ones that included children are almost all missing at least one. Some, multiple or all. I hope a nice local family will adopt her, but it's not likely. Those families won't be looking to replace their beloved children. However, there are folks all over Pennsylvania and beyond willing to adopt for many noble reasons. That may be best for Joanna."

Without replying, Monty stalked away, shoulders slumped.

Annamae thanked Hetty and followed him. "I know this is hard to hear, but Hetty is right. Folks are barely surviving as it is. They can't afford to feed another mouth."

"Joanna isn't just a mouth. She's a child who's lost everything and deserves to be loved and cared for."

Annamae lowered her head at the scolding. Apparently, she was no better than Hetty. "I apologize. I didn't mean to sound callous."

Monty ran his fingers through his hair. "It's going to be hard enough to tell her about Ben, but to tell her she's going to be forced to live with strangers is unbearable."

They were halfway to the typhoid tents when he stopped in the middle of the open field. Head tilted toward the sky, he exhaled a loud breath. The full moon cast a silver glow over the sleepy landscape. Crickets chirped around them. Annamae wished she possessed the right words to lighten Monty's burden, but nothing she thought of seemed appropriate. The chilly air seeped into her bones, but she dared not move for fear of disturbing his spirit further.

A curtain of clouds cast a shadow over the moon for several moments then lifted to reveal the orb in all its glory. Annamae crossed her arms around her middle. " 'Truly, the moon shines with a good grace,' " she whispered.

Monty looked at her.

"Shakespeare. When I was a girl, my dad would quote this line every time we'd spread a blanket on the ground and gaze at the stars."

"*A Midsummer Night's Dream.*"

She grinned. "You know it?"

"Why are you so shocked?"

"Well, because—I mean. . .you're a pastor."

His hands, once again, fell into his pockets. "I fail to see your point."

"It's a strange tale of love. Unrefined." Her cheeks heated. "Primitive."

He chuckled low in his throat. "Ah, so because I'm a pastor, I shouldn't read anything other than the Bible?"

She opened her mouth to reply but thought better of it and closed her lips with a click of her teeth.

To her surprise, he laughed harder. "I wasn't always a pastor, you know."

"You weren't born with a tiny Bible in your hand?"

"I was 'born unto trouble, as the sparks fly upward.' " He nudged her elbow with his. "Job five verse seven."

She was glad to have diverted his grief even if but for a short time. "When did you rebel with Shakespeare then?"

"William was required at the university."

She tipped her head. "You didn't go to seminary?"

"I did. After I graduated from the university and grew brave enough to defy my family's wishes to follow God's calling."

"I see. May I ask what your family wished for you?"

He rolled his tongue inside his cheek. "They wanted to include me in the family business."

His tone said he'd spoken all he was willing to on the matter, though she was curious to know every detail. "And you? Tell me more about the man who quoted the unsuitable-for-pastors Shakespeare to his young daughter under the stars."

Alone in this field beneath the moon, the conversation felt intimate. If she wasn't about to freeze, she'd want to stay in this spot all night long and learn everything she could about Monty Childs.

"My mother died when I was five, so it was just me and Papa." She smiled. "Papa was a dreamer. After a long day working at the mill, he'd come home and wash up, and then we'd eat dinner and spend nigh to half an hour stargazing. We'd talk about the places we wanted to travel, the things we wanted to do. We'd make outrageous plans for the future, like going on safari in Africa, seeing the Taj Mahal, climbing an Egyptian pyramid. My favorite was hunting for pirate treasure in Tortuga."

"Treasure hunting? I'm stunned. Since you're a nurse, I assumed you were born with rolled bandages in one hand and a thermometer in the other."

She giggled at the thought. "He also used to tell me that during the first crescent moon of the month, if I took all my spare coins out of one pocket and put them in the other, I'd have good luck until the next crescent moon."

"That's ridiculous."

Tears sprang to her eyes as her father's loving face materialized in her memory. "It was. We both knew there weren't any spare coins to carry in our pockets."

Having a normal conversation in a rugged field that days ago had been under several feet of churning water was surreal. And nice. For a few minutes, he could ignore the utter misery of the past week and pretend they were simply a man and a woman getting to know each other.

Ahead, two men exited a tent, carrying a body on a stretcher. Monty turned his back, not wanting to accept that Ben was really gone. He wanted to stay in the previous moment, pretending. "What happened to your father?"

Annamae picked at her fingernail. "He was a puddler at the Edgar Thomson Steel Mill in Braddock. For twelve hours a day, he stirred spikes of pure iron into the churning slag. His skin was tough as leather from the heat exposed to it year after year."

Monty instantly regretted thinking this would be a normal conversation. He knew well what a puddler was. Coke and steel were how his uncle had amassed their family's wealth.

Her hands dropped to her sides. "The Amalgamated Association of Iron and Steel Workers had been pushing Andrew Carnegie and his men to implement safety measures for their workers, but they refused. My father provided the association with insider information on working conditions while the association encouraged the workers to strike. I came home from school one day and was told by his supervisor that the brackets on the platform above the smelting pot where my father stirred had popped loose, and he'd fallen into the molten iron."

Monty's stomach roiled, and he flinched.

"I'm sorry," she said. "I was supposed to be distracting you from death, and I've brought it around full circle."

He stared at the moon. "Unfortunately, death is part of life."

And he'd seen more in the past week than he ever cared to see again.

"And what of your nursing?" he asked. "Where does that fall into your story?"

"I refused to believe his death was happenstance. Falling into that molten iron was his greatest fear. He told me how checking the security of the platform was the first thing he did every day. I wanted to fight the company in court, but I couldn't prove my theory that someone sabotaged the platform so he'd cease informing the association. None of the witnesses would confess what they'd seen, fearing for their own lives and those of their family. I was sixteen. I had no money to hire a lawyer as we barely made enough to pay rent and eat.

"The company's idea of proper condolences was three hundred dollars and an eviction notice to leave the tenement within three days. I wasn't at liberty to stay since my father was no longer an employee. I put that money to use by learning a skill I could use to help the poor, abandoned, wounded, and forgotten."

No doubt his uncle was the one who'd decided three hundred dollars was worth a man's life. Carnegie had soft places in his heart and loose pockets. The idea of a young woman orphaned and homeless from an incident in his mill would have kept him up at night. That was why Carnegie had hired Henry Clay Frick to manage his mills. Uncle Henry was as hard as the steel rolling off the presses. He made sure jobs got done, no matter how unconventional the method. Carnegie didn't ask questions. That way, his conscience remained clean.

Monty rubbed the back of his neck. "I'm sorry for what you've endured, but I'm glad you're here. Although Tortuga would've been a greater adventure."

She grinned. "My father taught me how to navigate the stars so I could always find my way home. Keep your gaze fixed upon the One who created those stars, Monty. He'll guide you home."

Warmth split the middle of Monty's chest. He'd needed that simple reminder.

Annamae craned her neck to see around him and pointed. "They've gone now. If you don't start with any symptoms through the night, and you wash and change your clothes, you should be safe to find Ben's sister after daybreak."

"I appreciate you doing all you could to save Ben."

"I wish I could've done more." She shivered.

"You need to get warm. I won't keep you any longer."

"Wait."

He shifted to face her.

"Unfortunately, Ben won't be the last casualty of typhoid. Until the disinfectants arrive and are used, this is going to get much worse. I know you have your own responsibilities with the church, but we could use a chaplain to help ease people's transition."

Monty was called to lead, guide, and comfort others, even into the next life. But he didn't think the humanity in him could bear any more death.

"I'll consider it and let you know."

As he walked back to the church alone, guided by the dim light of fires warming the homeless, all his mind would focus on was the panic in Ben's eyes. All he could hear were the screams of those rushing downriver. All he could feel was the loneliness Annamae must have felt standing by her father's grave, dressed in black, alone.

As soon as he visited Joanna, he'd search every inch of the remains of this town for Cyrus Elder. If the man had gone down, then he'd find his way to Pittsburgh and storm the ornate wooden doors of Clayton, his uncle's estate. Someone owed him answers. Not only for the people of Johnstown but for the tender and loving nurse who very well may have saved his life.

Chapter Thirteen

~~~~~~~~~~~~~~~~

"The State Board of Health hereby directs and empowers you
to immediately summon a posse to patrol the Conemaugh
River, tear down the drift heaps and remove the dead bodies,
both human beings and domestic animals. This is absolutely
necessary to protect your county from pestilence."

~Telegram sent by Dr. Benjamin Lee, head of the Pennsylvania Board
of Health, to the four counties between Johnstown and Pittsburgh

MONDAY, JUNE 10

Supplies poured in faster than the Red Cross could sort, catalog, and store
them before the next shipment arrived. As soon as the warehouse was
stocked, supplies were distributed so quickly that inventory ran low until
more cataloguing and stocking were completed. The warehouse made it
easier to protect the supplies from the rain that insisted on covering the
valley. The deceased continued to be found as the precipitation melted dirt
into mud and unearthed bodies both mangled and perfectly preserved.

Annamae lifted her hem and dodged around a group of men with
pickaxes and shovels, all concentrating on what they'd found. She focused

her attention in the opposite direction, not wishing to glimpse their discovery. She should have stayed at her post in the typhoid tent, but more nurses had arrived this morning ready to assist, and she needed to see Monty. His brokenness disrupted her sleep, creating haunting images of him telling Joanna she was all alone.

Annamae knew what it was like to be a girl with no prospects, alone in the world. If she had the means, the temptation of adopting the child herself would be hard to resist. She didn't know what kindness she could offer to the girl, but she knew she had to see with her own eyes that Joanna was okay.

She followed the directions to Holt House that had been given to her by a local man out of work from the woolen mill. He'd told her nigh to half of his life story before answering her question. This side of town was less damaged as the buildings rested on higher ground. She paused and searched for the two-story red colonial but saw nothing of what the man described behind the mass of people milling about. Standing on tiptoe wouldn't do her any good, but maybe that tree stump would offer perspective.

Her first two attempts to climb the stump had her stumbling backward.

"Ma'am, do you need help?" A boy around the age of eight with freckles splayed across his nose and a bag of newspapers slung across his chest blinked up at her with curious eyes.

She supposed she appeared rather ridiculous. "I'm looking for Holt House."

"Did you think you'd find it on that stump?" His head tipped to the side.

"No. I was trying to see over the crowd and rooftops."

"Ah." He beckoned for her to follow him.

Up another block he turned right, and the red colonial came into view. "Thank you, young man."

Annamae hurried to the entrance, wondering if she'd already missed Monty's arrival.

The door was open, allowing those seeking asylum to enter and exit at will. Though the number of beds set up there were occupied, during the day it acted as a commissary to feed the hungry from its large kitchen.

Stepping inside, she blinked her eyes to adjust to the dim light and excused herself through the visitors standing in line for breakfast.

None of the faces were Monty's. She went from room to room on the first floor until she recognized his form in the parlor's corner. His back to her, he knelt before a small girl with reddish hair who clutched a ratty doll to her chest. Annamae stood in the doorway, breathless. Though she couldn't decipher his words, the low rumble of his voice wrapped around her heart and squeezed.

His large hands raised to cradle Joanna's arms. Short, high-pitched sobs escaped the girl's mouth, and tears rushed down her cheeks. Annamae covered her mouth to contain her own emotions. Monty pulled Joanna to him and patted her back, his gentle encouragement stinging Annamae's eyes.

She wanted to run to Joanna, pick up the doll that had dropped to the floor, and tell her everything was going to be okay. The way she'd wished someone would have done for her when her father died. It was like being on the fringes of the past, watching herself as Mr. Nesbit told her that her father had fallen into the molten pit.

All she could do was stand there and watch them, tortured between duty and compassion. Hetty was right. She was an unmarried woman without the means of supporting a child. And saving Joanna wouldn't save herself. Yes, it was hard, but the best thing for Joanna was an adoption into a new family.

Monty inched Joanna away from his shoulder and placed his large hands on the sides of her face. Annamae knew the roughness of those hands well from rubbing in the salve and from his hold on her the night before. He brushed the girl's tears with his thumbs, gentle, tender, and Annamae's heart melted to her toes.

Unfamiliar with the intense attraction that hit her so swiftly, she hastened back to her post at the Red Cross tents. Joanna would be fine. Annamae would pray for her and trust that God would place her in the care of wonderful parents.

No matter how fast she walked, she couldn't shed the strange emotions rolling inside her. Was it sadness? Anger? Hate? Whatever it was, it had started last night with her confession to Monty about her father's passing and grew stronger at the sight of Joanna.

She stuffed the feelings down as she entered the warehouse for clean sheets and lye soap. There was no time to dwell on her grief today when she had beds to make and patients to attend to. Typhoid victims were growing in number, and the next few weeks would be critical and exhausting.

"Annamae."

She turned toward the voice and moved to the end of the aisle. Clara Barton joined her, large skirts brushing against crates as she passed. Worry tightened Annamae's stomach. Had Clara learned she'd abandoned her post?

"The surgeon general will arrive on the evening train." A telegram dangled from Clara's fingertips. "Finish what you're doing and then take a few hours to recuperate. Once he arrives with the disinfectants, I'll need you to help train the others on how to use them properly.

"He will also meet with the various committees and teach them which disinfectants are best to use on which materials and in which areas. He may enlist your help with that as well."

Relief filled Annamae. She was glad to be helping these people. Not that nursing sick patients wasn't helping, but all trained nurses knew how to care for typhoid. Not everyone got the privilege of working in the field with Clara Barton and the surgeon general.

"Yes, ma'am." A sharp pain radiated from the small of Annamae's back up to her shoulder blades. She would not miss standing over a boiling cauldron to stir soiled bed linens.

The thought brought memories of her father close to the surface again, and she imagined him standing on the platform year after year, stirring the iron, heat so intense it changed the texture of his skin. All to provide food and shelter for her. She blinked away tears.

"Is something wrong?" Clara frowned.

"No, ma'am. The heavy amounts of lye soap I've been using for the laundry are bothering my skin and eyes." She raised one of her sleeves. The flesh was dry, bumpy, and pink.

The lines on Clara's forehead relaxed. "Well, you'll get a break soon enough. However, there's something I must speak to you about."

Clara paused as another nurse entered the warehouse for supplies. A few moments later, in came another.

"Let's take a short walk, Miss Worthington."

Annamae's stomach cramped as she followed Clara outside. She should have known she couldn't hide anything from the woman. Clara was practically omniscient. Annamae braced herself for a good scolding.

The sky was a cloudless cerulean blue, the first since before the flood. The hillsides were a vivid green, springing with hope and life. Annamae wanted to take comfort in this, but since she was back to *Miss Worthington*, she found it difficult.

Remaining quiet by Clara's side, Annamae waited until the woman was ready to speak. Each footstep brought another wave of dread coursing through her veins. It wasn't until they'd passed the tents and approached the base of the hill the locals called "the avenue to Grandview Cemetery" did Clara speak.

"I've heard rumors regarding your behavior with a patient last night—embraces, whispering, a moonlit walk."

Oh, that.

Embarrassment filled Annamae, chased by anger. She hadn't done anything wrong. How dare the other nurses stir up trouble when they should concentrate on their own work?

"He's lived through circumstances unimaginable to us who didn't live through the flood. Yesterday, he brought one of his dearest friends to us in hopes we could sustain him of typhoid, only for the young man to die. Needing comfort from the horrors he's experienced the past week, he embraced me. What could I do but bridge the gap from stranger to friend?"

Annamae omitted the part about her touching him first. She hadn't meant to initiate contact, but her heart overpowered her brain sometimes. "He's a pastor. There was nothing untoward in his actions."

The serious lines of Clara's mouth quirked up at the corners. "That's quite a defense for my small statement."

"I hate idle gossip."

"As do I. That's why I came to you directly."

Annamae took a deep breath and instantly regretted it. The air reeked of decay and stagnant water. "We were whispering because it was midnight, and we didn't want to disturb the other patients. The boy's name was Ben, only seventeen years old. Ben has a younger sister, and Monty was upset at having to inform her about her brother's passing and that she would have to join the orphan train."

Clara bent her head. "Poor child."

A robin landed on a nearby tree branch and flicked its wings. For the first time, Annamae noticed how every tree at the base of the hill was charred black, like they'd burned, yet stood strong. Surely, that hadn't resulted from the flood.

"Is that why you disappeared to Holt House this morning?"

Annamae's head whipped around. "I. . .yes. I wanted to check on Monty and Joanna."

"Monty, eh?" Mischief danced in Clara's dark eyes.

"Mr. Childs. I mentioned to him our need of a chaplain with all the other ministers already committed to the morgues and relief committees. He said he'd let me know."

"Very good." Clara's narrowed but playful eyes told Annamae she saw deeper than the surface of her words. "And this moonlit walk?"

Annamae chuckled at the ridiculousness of the rumor. "He went with me to headquarters to report Ben's passing so his body could be transported to the morgue. Then we returned to the tent—under the moon because it was midnight—and then he left to sleep in his church."

"Very well, Annamae." Clara patted her hand. "I wanted to hear your side of the tale. I know how some women like to chatter."

So, she was back to Annamae now.

"I suppose I needn't remind you of our position here." Clara's features turned serious, accentuating the puffiness under her lower eyelashes. "We're here to serve, and we must be aboveboard in all that we do. Even when comforting a patient. You mustn't allow your emotions to override your good sense."

What was she supposed to have done, pushed Monty away? "Yes, ma'am."

"I haven't seen this much desolation, this much need, in many years." Clara craned her neck and gazed in every direction.

Smoke lifted from fires of burning debris. The air was full of the hum of voices, shouts, crashes, booms, and wails. "Our purpose isn't always easy, as nurses or as women."

Annamae studied the fierce warrior who barely reached her chin.

"You can't give a piece of your heart to each patient, or you'll go mad. You must learn to distance your emotions, do what needs to be done, and save the tears for when it's all over."

"Is that how you survived nursing during the war?" Annamae wondered how such a fine and genteel woman could withstand such horrors and still be the lady Clara was today.

A peaceful sense of accomplishment curled Clara's mouth. "Have I ever told you about my brother, David?"

"No, ma'am."

"To me, David was like a hero out of a storybook. Tall and athletic. Courageous. Never one to turn down a dare. He was the one who taught me to ride horses. You see, I used to be dreadfully afraid of them."

Annamae found it hard to believe this woman had ever been afraid of anything.

"David and I were very close, even though we were years apart in age. In the spring of 1832, during a barn raising, he wanted to prove his athleticism by volunteering to nail the high rafters to the ridgepole. Knowing him, there was a lady present he wanted to impress. But a board broke beneath his feet, and he crashed into a pile of heavy timbers. Got a terrible blow to the head. For two years he hovered between life and death, and I refused to leave his side."

"What happened?"

"I was only eleven, and it upset me to watch the doctors apply leeches. Bloodletting is an awful practice—don't ever allow a physician to talk you into doing it."

Annamae nodded.

"I thought they'd drain him dry. Nothing worked. That's when I decided *my* nursing would help him the most. I only left that room for one half day the entire two years. I almost forgot there was an outside world beyond those bedroom walls."

Clara chuckled.

"He'd have terrible fits of anger and nervousness. Clung to me through it all. It wasn't until the steam baths that he finally improved. By that time, I had lost most of my strength. I'd forgotten how to be a child."

"Did David recover?"

"Fully. He became an assistant quartermaster for the Union army."

Annamae's skin pebbled. What an amazing story.

What an amazing lady.

Clara raised her chin. "I shared that with you so you know I'm aware of how a patient can suffer mental scars as well as physical. I also know how hard it is to distance yourself when you have a tender heart. Many a man during the war reminded me of David, lying on a sick bed, crying out for someone to end his misery. I comforted as best I could. Once, I made a pie using the soldier's mother's recipe he carried in his pocket onto the battlefield, of all things. But I always had to guard my heart. Think before I acted. The entry I'd gained on the battlefield to help those men could be snatched away at the slightest impropriety."

Annamae considered the unspoken warning in Clara's advice. "I understand, ma'am."

"You're a good girl. I knew you would." Clara spun toward the tents. "Now, go finish making those beds and then get some sleep until the surgeon general arrives."

Though Clara's words had been nothing but kind, Annamae's pride felt beaten and whipped. She contemplated Clara's words as she tucked clean sheets around the thin, stained ticks and carried the soiled laundry away to the boiling cauldron. This position was all she had now that her father was gone, and she'd worked hard for it. She had to do everything she could to keep it. Even if it meant isolating her heart from the handsome, broken pastor.

Chapter Fourteen

"I told them that the dam would break sometime
and cause just such a disaster as this."

~ John Fulton, manager of Cambria Iron Works

Monty could hardly navigate the mass of bodies traveling through the wreckage, commissaries, cleanup crews, and committee stations. Visitors wearing tailored suits or displaying outlandish beribboned hats and carrying parasols came to gawk at the disaster. His stomach revolted at how many thought nothing of taking a meal from the commissary or of swiping a trinket they found protruding from the ground so they could return home with a souvenir from the Johnstown flood.

This town had made history, and where thousands across the nation scrambled to help, it also generated despicable behavior that made it difficult to live the Bible passages about patience and being slow to wrath. Did these people not care that they were taking food away from those who'd already lost everything?

The noonday sun shone clear and bright above him, a welcome reprieve from the rain. It stirred a hope inside that the folks of Johnstown would prosper again. With all the volunteers and survivors working every daylight hour, he believed it would.

Hammers, picks, axes, and dynamite blasts filled the town, yet one voice around him rose higher than it all. Monty scanned the landscape, searching for the owner. On an embankment by the depot, where General Hastings had set up his headquarters, Reverend David Beale, open Bible in his hands, and another fellow appeared to be holding some kind of church service. A small crowd had gathered round, and as Monty headed that direction, more curious people joined.

Beale stood on a packing box, the back corners sunken into the earth, making it a level and secure platform. "Just yesterday, I overheard a visitor ask one of our small boys how bad things were here in Johnstown. The boy replied, 'If I was the biggest liar on the face of the earth, I could not tell you half.'"

Murmured amens followed. A solemnness settled over the group.

"To tell the world how or what we felt when shoeless, hatless, many almost naked from the force of the water, some bruised and broken, we stood there and looked upon that scene of death and desolation, it's near impossible to describe the true horrors of it."

Reverend Beale continued by using examples of those who had lived through, and perished in, the waters. He spoke of Noah and how God had used his family to start humanity again and, even then, sin had infiltrated their lives. "We must live these days with caution. Our behavior, our character, and even our faith have all been tested and *will* be tested in the days to come."

Drunkenness, thievery, greed, lust of all kinds—Monty had seen it all over the past ten days. General Hastings' men had seized liquor arriving on the trains and sent a good portion of it back to its origin to keep it from exacerbating the riotous brawls. He kept small amounts at his headquarters for medicinal purposes and its disinfecting properties.

Prostitutes were another problem permeating the valley. So were thieves, who made great promises to those who had money or possessions left to bargain with and left them more destitute. The Hungarians and Swedes, called "Hunkies," accused in the papers of mutilating the dead for their possessions, lived in fear of mobs hungry for justice. A few of those accounts had been true but embellished, and many of the accounts printed had been lies. General Hastings demanded the reporters print the truth and stop inflating tales to sell papers.

Monty had heard that a group of vigilantes had traveled up the mountain to South Fork and onto the fishing and hunting club property in search of club members. But the summer season at the club didn't begin until mid-June, and none of them would come now with no lake to sail on or fish in. Any club members present when the dam collapsed had already fled.

" 'Wherefore,' " the reverend said, pointing to a passage in his Bible, " 'have I seen them dismayed and turned away back? And their mighty ones are beaten down, and are fled apace, and look not back: for fear was round about, saith the Lord. Let not the swift flee away, nor the mighty man escape; they shall stumble, and fall toward the north by the river Euphrates.' "

"Or Lake Conemaugh," someone from the group yelled.

Agreeing voices took over. Reverend Beale silenced the crowd with a raised palm then finished reading. " 'Who is this that cometh up as a flood, whose waters are moved as the rivers?' Let us not forget folks, 'The Lord sitteth upon the flood; yea, the Lord sitteth King for ever.' "

Both men and women shouted. Hands waved in the air.

John Fulton of the Cambria Iron Works joined Reverend Beale on his dais. His hair had grayed considerably since Monty had seen the man last. "Rest assured, each and every Cambria shop will rebuild."

"Amen!" someone shouted.

"Johnstown is going to be rebuilt." Fulton's almond-shaped eyes pierced the crowd with conviction.

A woman standing beside Monty, wearing a dress that would be better off used as rags, wiped a tear and said, "Thank God!"

"What about Gautier?" a man shouted.

Fulton's broad shoulders left little room for the reverend. "I cannot speak for the Gautier works. However, I am certain they too will rebuild, and bigger than ever. The Cambria men will be taken care of, and if you still have your family left, then God bless your soul, man, you're rich."

A renewed energy seemed to take over their little corner. More spectators joined Monty, filling in as far back as the next street. Reverend Beale stepped off the platform, either allowing Fulton to give his own sermon or feeling he had no choice.

"Get to work," Fulton continued. "Clean up your department. Set your lathes going again. The furnaces are all right. The steel works are all right. Get to work, I say. That's the way to look at this sort of thing. . . . Think how much worse this could have been."

Fulton's voice and intensity rose with every sentence. "Give thanks for that great stone bridge that saved hundreds of lives. Yes, it took lives too, but had it not existed or the bridge collapsed, the whole town would have washed down the valley. Give thanks that the flood did not come in the night. *Trust in God.*

"Johnstown had its day of woe and ruin. It will have its day of renewed prosperity. Labor, energy, capital—by God's grace—shall make this city more thriving than ever in the past."

"Amen!" Fists punched the air.

Reverend Beale clapped along with others in the crowd. Unfortunately, Johnstown put more faith in the Cambria Company than in God. Monty had learned that on his first day and had worked to flip their mindset the same as Reverend Beale, mostly to no avail. Sure, faith abounded, but it fluctuated based on the success of the mills.

Monty gazed across the landscape, still in ruin. Fulton was right though. This was their home, and they must fight for it. The question was, how long would it take to get the town functioning once more?

"Now. . ." Fulton held up a paper crinkled in his hand. "I hold in my possession today—and I thank God that I do—my own report, made years ago, in which I told these people who, for purposes I will not mention, desired to seclude themselves in the mountains, that their dam was dangerous."

Strained silence settled over the crowd. Bodies crowded closer to hear.

Fulton lowered his thick, dark eyebrows into a *V*. "I told them that the dam would break sometime and cause just such a disaster as this."

With that, the thoughts that had been circulating in town for days were declared aloud. And by one of the most respected men in Johnstown. Fulton was the general manager and mining engineer for the Cambria Iron Works. In the interest of his company, his family, and the people of Johnstown, he'd inspected the South Fork dam and had written a report declaring its flaws.

He'd been ridiculed by many club members, including Monty's Uncle Henry, who'd casually joked at dinner about someone needing to "silence the man." Monty had been fifteen and believed it an unthreatening statement. In the years that followed, his Uncle Henry would squash any lingering naivete that he was bluffing when spouting threats, and the cold hard truth of his uncle's darkness would cause Monty to flee Clayton.

Fulton went on to reveal that years earlier Daniel J. Morrell, the former manager of the Cambria Iron Works, offered to invest money to stabilize the dam if the club would allow Cambria use of the water during times of drought. Benjamin Ruff, the man who originally purchased the property from the Pennsylvania Railroad and later sold shares to create the club, promptly refused Morrell's offer. Morrell purchased a share in the club so he could monitor the dam and other events within the organization. Both men had passed away a few years ago, and Morrell's club membership transferred to Cyrus Elder.

Despite how Elder viewed the situation, the paper clutched in Fulton's hand may very well be the link to holding the club accountable.

———————•◦•———————

"Watch yo'self, Miss Worthington."

Annamae gripped the bundle of mail tighter and shuffled out of the path of men carrying crates of disinfectant to the wagon. The gentleman who had issued the warning was as thick and strong as an oak tree. Cedric, as he'd introduced himself, had eyes and skin the same dark color and a laugh that coaxed one from those around him. Although she was intimidated by his size upon first glance, his gentle, boyish grin and kind nature quickly set her at ease.

The crate landed in the wagon with a *thud*. The horses startled, but a passerby grabbed the reins and calmed the beasts.

"Thank you, Mr. Cedric." The bustling South Fork depot, though tiny in comparison, rivaled the operation of Washington's Union Station platform with crates, barrels, and trunks delivered and loaded, some stacked two or three high. Relief for the people of Johnstown was coming faster than folks could transport it down the mountain. Passengers filled the waiting rooms for either a way into the town or for a way out.

Until the viaduct between Mineral Point and South Fork was restored, there was no way to get supplies into the heart of Johnstown by train. The Pennsylvania Railroad crew worked around the clock to build a temporary bridge and restore the lines until they could repair the original viaduct. They were close to finishing, according to the papers. In the meantime, the South Fork and Sang Hollow depots were as close as anyone could get.

General Hastings filled the doorway of the station, scowled at the surrounding view, and then stalked toward a team of horses tied to a hitching post. Annamae intercepted the grumpy general. Upon seeing her, his face softened, and he tipped his hat.

"Good evening, General."

His white mustache twitched. "It would be if I didn't have to police all of Pennsylvania and could concentrate on the safety of Johnstown."

She raised a brow in question.

"I must spare two of my men and leave them here to turn away anyone who doesn't have a legitimate reason to be in Johnstown. Folks are coming from all over the country just to say they saw the disaster for themselves. Despicable souls."

"Oh, my." General Hastings, although the kindest of men, was not one to make an enemy of.

He unwound his horse's reins. "And how is the Red Cross faring?" His tone was considerably less aggressive.

"Doctor Hamilton, the surgeon general, has arrived with disinfectants. I'm to help with distribution and training on how to use the chemicals. With time, it should help eliminate typhoid cases."

"Yes, I've heard it's spreading rapidly. Hopefully, these disinfectants will help freshen the air as well."

Now that the torrents of rain seemed to have passed and the early summer temperature was rising, the putrid smell of filth and decomposing corpses had gotten worse.

General Hastings placed his foot in the stirrup, swung his leg over the horse, and dropped onto his saddle. "Good day to you, Miss Worthington. I must go before it gets dark. Please send my regards to Miss Barton."

"I will do that, sir." Annamae smiled.

Clara and the general had formed quite the unique friendship since their arrival. In fact, if Annamae had to guess, she'd say the general was impressed with the little warrior. No doubt, her dedication and determination rivaled any he'd seen from his men.

Doctor Hamilton exited the depot and held up his hand when he spotted her by the post. She followed him to the wagon. He took the bundle of mail from her and assisted her up. She maneuvered her large skirt to make room for them both and Mr. Cedric.

"Miss Worthington." The doctor squeezed in beside her, handing her the mail. "Are the stories of looting and lynching I've read in the papers true?"

"Most were sensationalized to sell papers. Captain Hart, General Hastings, and the military are doing their utmost to keep order and assure safety to the Johnstown residents and volunteers."

Doctor Hamilton seemed satisfied with her answer.

"What of Washington?" she asked. "Is it true investigations have commenced regarding the dam and its property owners?"

The doctor glanced around to see if they had an audience. He kept his voice low. "It's true. The property used to be part of the Pennsylvania Canal but was sold to the man who started the South Fork Fishing and Hunting Club in '79. There's speculation that the club members were warned several times over the last decade that the dam's structure was no longer safe and would someday collapse."

Her mouth fell open. "You mean this could have been prevented?"

Doctor Hamilton shrugged. "I suppose that will be for the courts to decide."

Mr. Cedric slapped the reins on the horses' backs and set them into motion. The path was rough and would take them much longer than the traditional way, but with all the debris and the railroad men laying new tracks, they were forced to travel the east side of the terrain to Johnstown that was comprised of flatter ground to withstand their heavy load.

Annamae clasped her hands in her lap, unable to keep from rocking into the men boxing her in. "Surely any wise and honorable judge will make certain the club members are held accountable if they are guilty of negligence."

A wry smile curled one side of the doctor's mouth. "One can hope. Unfortunately, it seems as if the club roster is a secret. The identities are held with lock and key by the most powerful men in the country."

"How does keeping the identities of the club secret benefit the powerful men?"

"Because they're the members."

"If membership is secret, how do you know that?"

His expression was that of an adult speaking to a naive child. "Simple deduction, Miss Worthington. The average working man can't afford luxury or time away from work, and men of high ranking in the government or military rarely get time for sporting. Only the kings of industry have the time and wealth for such devices."

The hairs on Annamae's arms rose. The most powerful men in the country were men like Andrew Carnegie, Henry Clay Frick, John D. Rockefeller, the Vanderbilts, J.P. Morgan, and John Jacob Astor. Men who relied on others to build their fortunes.

Men who could afford to pay a judge to rule in their favor.

The wagon hit a rut, jarring her teeth. She clutched her small bundle to keep from losing it. The horses shifted to brace the heavy load down the incline. Anguish welled inside her as they passed the former towns of Mineral Point and Woodvale. Areas just as devastated as Johnstown, but on a smaller scale.

Suddenly, she missed her father. Missed the comfort of her small apartment in Washington. She even missed the mundane routine she got lost in when loneliness crept its fingers around her heart. She thought of Monty and the sweet friendship she'd found in him but pushed the thoughts aside when she recalled Clara's warning. Her mentor was right. She must guard her heart. There was no sense in forming an attachment when she'd go back to Washington once the Red Cross finished their work here.

It was almost dark when Mr. Cedric pulled the wagon to a stop at the warehouse. She delivered the bundle of mail to headquarters and helped Doctor Hamilton and Clara catalog the various disinfectants in their logbook. At a quarter to nine, Clara informed her that Pastor Childs had stopped by to offer his services as chaplain, and then dismissed Annamae to her tent. Though Annamae had tried to elicit an indifferent attitude, Clara no doubt noticed the slight uptick at the corners of her mouth.

She'd never mastered the art of keeping her feelings off her face.

Annamae gazed at the full moon as she walked to her quarters. "Good night, Papa," she whispered.

Holding back a yawn, Annamae undressed and slipped beneath the blanket. Tomorrow, the real work began.

Chapter Fifteen

"Then after burying, mourning the dead, (Faithful to them, found or unfound, forgetting not, bearing the past, here now musing,) A day—a passing moment or an hour—we bow ourselves— America itself bends low, Silent, resign'd submissive."

~Leaf two of "A Voice from Death" written by Walt Whitman, published in the *New York World* a week after the disaster

SATURDAY, JUNE 15

On a garbled sigh, Mrs. Clavin, who'd run the schoolhouse for almost twenty years before marrying, left this world for the next. Mr. Clavin had perished in the flood when a pipe spinning in the churning waters harpooned him through the chest. Husband and wife were together again.

"We commend thy soul to Jesus." Monty slid the sheet over her face.

He searched the tent for Annamae, but she still had not arrived. Something kept her this morning, and he missed her company. They'd seen each other every day since he'd agreed to act as chaplain, even if their exchanges only comprised a greeting in passing. When time had allowed, they'd discussed things that better acquainted them with one another. Likes and dislikes, present and past experiences. Nothing of true significance, but enough to endear her to him even more.

She was a flicker of hope in these dark days. A place where he could glean encouragement. Someone with whom he could feel something besides grief and loss. He'd told her once she was a godsend, and he meant it.

The nurses on duty cared for other typhoid patients clinging to life. The tent reeked and, as bad as some areas of Johnstown still smelled, the fresher air outside of the oiled canvas was welcome. He entered headquarters and informed Hetty of Mrs. Clavin's passing and requested her body be prepared for burial. "I'll return in a few hours. If you need my services, I'll be at the church."

"Thank you, Mr. Childs." She put her pen down and flexed her fingers then shook her wrist.

He couldn't imagine spending hours a day hunched over a desk, copying information from one source to another. Monty moved to leave but hesitated, wanting to inquire about Annamae, yet deeming it unwise.

"Is there something else?" Hetty asked, stretching her neck from side to side.

"No, miss." Monty left before he opened his mouth and revealed his thoughts.

He had too much work to do, rebuilding his church and home and serving his congregation, to allow a pretty nurse who would leave Johnstown to distract him. Even if she had pulled him out of his darkness and brought him back to the land of the living.

Construction noise yanked him from his reverie. Supplies to meet almost every need poured in from around the country, including lumber, nails, plaster, and other building materials, but Monty didn't feel right using any for himself. He could put the inheritance he'd received from his parents to good use and purchase the materials on his own. Then his past circle of wealth and privilege would serve a purpose on the current path God had called him to travel. He would send a wire to his bank in Pittsburgh for the amount he needed to be sent to the Babcock Lumber Company.

All around him, the groaning of construction and cleanup pulsed in the background to dynamite blasts and the B&O Railroad whistle blasts.

The new depot in Mineral Point was finished, and the lines from there to Johnstown were set. The obliteration of the roundhouse made travel tricky, so a small loading dock had been raised a few days ago where supplies and passengers could disembark before the train moved along to Sang Hollow.

The First National Bank once stood near the roundhouse, but it too was gone. Thankfully, a crew had found the two bank vaults encased in mud and the contents inside were unharmed. Rumors spread through town that anyone with an existing mortgage was covered by the monetary donations pouring in, settling their debt with the banks. Any mortgages not covered would be seized by the bank without default for them to resell the plot to the many businessmen seeking to erect institutions on the foundation of the new Johnstown.

Monty waited for a horse and buggy to pass before crossing Main to Washington Street. Not that they resembled the once parallel routes anymore. But the Johnstown Savings Bank, where Monty held an account for wire transfers, miraculously stood on the corner with minimal damage and access to the lone telegraph line sending messages in and out of the valley.

In the shadow of the savings and loan building stood Cyrus Elder, talking to a reporter. Monty couldn't believe it. After ten days of attempting to find the man, here he was, as if he'd known Monty had planned to visit.

Soldiers milled about on foot and horseback, making it feel less like home and more like a military camp or a mining town. Their tents split Johnstown in half, a wall of oiled canvas peaks running right through the middle of the ruins.

Monty started forward, but a soldier leaning against a post blocked his path. "What's your business here, sir?"

His attention flitted between Elder and the soldier. "Pardon?"

"Your business in Johnstown. What is it?"

Annoyance sluiced through Monty and brought an un-pastorly response to his tongue that he chose to not utter. He scratched the skin of his cheek, appalled by the beard that sprouted there. "I'm a resident of Johnstown and pastor of what *was* the Valley Baptist Church. I'm here to speak to the bank manager as well as Cyrus Elder. Excuse me."

Elder must have overheard his name, because they held eye contact an instant later. Monty brushed past the young, arrogant soldier who needed someone to knock some manners into him. Elder's posture straightened to full height as Monty approached.

"That's all I have to say on the matter," Elder told the reporter, who stuck his pencil behind his ear and dashed off, presumably to write his article in enough time to make the evening paper.

Elder smiled. "Monty Childs. Glad to see you alive and well."

A dynamite blast sounded on the other end of town, sending a plume into the air.

"You as well. I heard about your wife and daughter. I'm deeply sorry for your loss."

Elder's head dropped, and his chin bobbed against his collar in a nod. "I'd just returned from Chicago. Found my street covered by four feet of water. I could see my house. Water almost covered the porch steps where my girls waved their handkerchiefs at me, greeting my arrival."

He shook his head. "I didn't want to get my shoes and trousers wet, so I secured a raft some kid had made of rough boards and attempted to paddle the rest of the way home. It overturned in front of my brother's house, so I went in for dry clothing. The flood came while I was dressing. Washed my girls right off the porch."

If every member of Johnstown, no matter their station, lined up and told their stories, the horrific tales would last for months. One thing the newspaper headlines had correct: the disaster was something "no pen could describe."

Monty bowed his head and prayed for God to give Cyrus strength, as well as himself for what he was about to say. "So much loss and pain. Almost more than we can bear." He cleared his throat. "Cyrus, there's talk all this suffering could've been prevented."

Elder snapped out of his grief and returned to the hard businessman at his core, searing Monty with a glare. "I know everyone blames the fishing and hunting club, but it isn't so, as I told that reporter." He pointed in the direction where the reporter had gone. "I will stick to my position. I've inspected that dam myself and never had cause to believe the structure was faulty. No dam could withstand the rain and flooding that poured in from upstream. If anyone is to blame, I suppose we ourselves are among them, for we have indeed been very careless in this most important matter, and most of us have paid the penalty of our neglect. Including me."

The young soldier walked toward them, right hand resting on the pistol at his hip. "Is there a problem here, Mr. Elder?"

Monty refrained from rolling his eyes and telling the squirt this town had bigger problems to monitor than two men in a heated discussion. "No, young man. There isn't."

"It's corporal." The kid stepped forward to project intimidation that was lost on Monty.

Monty noted the smooth, pale flesh on the corporal's face. Had his cheeks ever seen a razor? He barely looked old enough to be out of primary school.

Elder glanced at Monty. "Everything is fine here, Corporal."

"Best we keep it that way." With a nod at Elder and a scowl at Monty, the soldier returned to his lazy stance against the post, watching them like an eagle watched its prey.

Monty reconsidered his approach. Elder had just as much reason to be angry at the club as anyone, and yet he stood his ground. As for Elder's personal inspection of the dam, he wasn't a qualified engineer; therefore, his report meant nothing.

Monty slipped his hands into his pockets. "My quarrel isn't with you personally, Cyrus, but this disaster is of a caliber this country has never seen. If man was the cause, there needs to be consequences. What does the club plan to do about this?"

Elder ran a hand through his hair. "I repeat, it's *we* who have been careless."

The residents of Johnstown? "Careless how?"

"We've ignored the growing intensity of the spring floods each year." Elder scrubbed his hand down his face. "The town was booming. All this building, this progress. It takes lumber. We took the lumber from the hills around us. That left fewer trees with roots to absorb the water and slow the downhill flow of rain, creating higher flooding in the valley."

Monty rocked from heels to toes, considering Elder's point. "I won't deny that. It doesn't explain the crumbling structure of the dam, however. There are witnesses who say streams of water were shooting out twenty feet above the bottom of the dam days before the collapse. Why wasn't warning given then?"

Elder chuckled sarcastically. "Witnesses who didn't have authority to be on that property to begin with? Yeah, I'd take their words as gospel." He rubbed his temple, revealing the dirty cuffs on his shirt. "Benjamin Ruff put on record after he purchased the property that those shoots were natural springs."

A lie, but even if it were true, what imbecile would have an earthen dam surrounded by natural springs that would saturate and weaken the structure? That alone would be grounds for restructuring the dam.

Elder sighed. "Rumor of the dam breaking was a boy-who-cried-wolf tale repeated for decades. Robert Pitcairn of the Pennsylvania Railroad sent numerous warnings the morning of the flood, giving everyone plenty of time to flee to the hills. Few took it seriously until it was too late."

He choked on the last word.

The man made valid points, but he still hadn't addressed the club's negligence. "Fulton is saying—"

"I know what Fulton is saying." Elder shuffled his feet. "We've always stood strong together. But not on this."

Elder turned to go inside the bank.

"Cyrus—"

"Look." Elder swiveled and poked a finger at Monty's chest. "The club didn't build the dam. The Pennsylvania Railroad did. From there, it changed hands before Benjamin Ruff sold shares to the club. The collapse could be the fault of many poor decisions made over time or an act of God. Sometimes we don't get answers to our questions. Sometimes God takes good things from us. Allows things to happen. This event certainly didn't take Him by surprise. You, of all people, should know that."

Elder went into the bank, and Monty let him go. Elder was right. God knew this disaster would happen before He created the earth. It was a difficult and sobering thought. However, it didn't negate the consequences if human action was at fault.

Monty stalked away. He'd come back and wire for his money another day.

Elder was a good man who'd done many great things for this town over the last generation. Shame washed over Monty for attacking him in that manner. Perhaps he'd let his passion for helping others see what was right overtake his sensibility and compassion.

Surely none of the club members had intended for the dam to break. But they'd also failed to improve its structure. Earthen dams were centuries old and should work fine for holding back water. If the dam had collapsed, it was due to water seeping internally and weakening its structure. The amount of rain shouldn't have affected its strength if the spillway and sluice pipes worked properly. Monty knew that Ruff had removed the sluice pipes upon purchase and sold them for scrap and that the control tower the Pennsylvania Canal built for raising and lowering water had burned years earlier as well. Even so, the spillway, if working properly, should have been enough to keep the lake from cresting over the dam. So what had happened that day?

The answers were out there, and someone needed to find them.

***

Annamae sipped tepid coffee from the tin cup and relished the warm sun blanketing her shoulders. The activities at the commissary buzzed all around her. There were two things that kept a steady delivery to Johnstown for which she was grateful—coffee and newspapers. One kept her connected to her faculties while the other kept her connected to the world outside the valley. Currently, she was reading about the new cable car service in Los Angeles, California, and a new structure called the Eiffel Tower in Paris, France. She was ignoring the telegram from Matthew burning a hole in her pocket.

PAPERS PRINTING THE WORST *STOP* PLEASE SEND WORD OF YOUR SAFETY *STOP* DOCTOR MARTIN *STOP*

Matthew's concern was sweet. After all, she didn't have family left to care about her safety. Though she had friends, none of them were close enough to worry about her. She should quit procrastinating and reply instead of occupying her mind with the news, which wasn't working as much of a distraction anyway.

Various good feelings bubbled inside her when she was around Matthew—respect, awe for his ability not only to diagnose a patient correctly but to know how best to treat them even if the method wasn't conventional, and laughter. He had a wonderful sense of humor. But were any of those things strong enough to build a marriage with? She doubted it.

Annamae was certain Matthew would soon declare his desire for a courtship, which made a marriage proposal nearly guaranteed. Her coffee turned acidic in her stomach.

A heavy weight lowered onto the bench beside her. She looked up in surprise.

Monty. With a day's growth of beard.

Her skin flushed beneath her uniform, making the combination of her reaction and the sun beating down on her entirely too hot. She resisted the urge to fan herself with the newspaper. This man certainly ignited more ardent feelings inside her than Matthew did.

"Hello, Miss Annamae." The blue of his eyes competed with the cloudless sky.

She smiled. Something she didn't do often, as Matthew had pointed out on more than one occasion, accusing her of taking life too seriously.

The action of her mouth made his gaze lower there, which made her skin blaze. "Do I have coffee on my face?"

She touched her lips and found them dry. His eyes traced her every movement. "I haven't seen you smile before. Not fully. It's lovely. You should do it more often."

His appreciation had a touch of confident arrogance to it, as if he was skilled in the art of flirtation. Which was ridiculous, him being a pastor and all.

One of his thick brows quirked, and his lips pursed in amusement. In that moment, he reminded her of Austen's Mr. Darcy: aristocratic, noble, and impish in a subtle way that captured one's fancy before they could stop it. Aware of this, she should practice caution. Yet, she didn't.

He breathed a chuckle and leaned in as if she was going to tell him a secret. That was when she realized her head had dipped closer to him first, and she drew back with a start.

Air. She needed cool and stirring air.

"Thank you," she squeaked.

His lips twitched beneath his mustache that hadn't grown as thick as the hair along his jaws. "How is your work with the Red Cross?"

She cleared the desire from her throat. "Miss Barton moved me from the typhoid tents to help Doctor Hamilton with training the committees on how to properly use the disinfectants that arrived. I just finished instructing the commissary on cleaning all eating utensils and vessels. You?"

"I salvaged what I could of my belongings, and we brought my house down. We've been burning small piles at a time to keep the fire under control. Once finished, we'll begin reconstruction on the church."

"I'm sorry. It must be difficult to watch your home fade to ashes."

"It's not any harder than watching a wave sweep it off its foundation. Or being trapped inside when it does."

Oh, this poor man.

She resisted the urge to reach out to him. "Where are you storing your belongings? In the church?"

"All of my worldly possessions fit into a knapsack."

"I'm sorry again."

He bumped her elbow with his. "Material possessions are replaceable. Besides, I have a grander home and possessions waiting for me in eternity."

She tilted her head. "You seem in much better spirits today."

Monty leaned his forearms on the table and clasped his hands. "I just had a conversation with a friend who reminded me that my losses don't compare to many of those around me."

Such things certainly brought one into perspective.

"How is Joanna?"

He looked away. "She still hasn't spoken much to anyone since Ben died. A few families have come from outlying areas to adopt the orphaned children, but she's so quiet they pass her over. She's being cared for by the Stineys right now, but Reverend Beale plans to hold a special meeting soon, inviting anyone wishing to adopt to Johnstown. They've had several inquiries and expect folks to come from as far as Indiana. Pray for her. The children who don't find homes will be sent to orphanages in Philadelphia and beyond."

Remorse leaked through every word.

"Of course." She reached to touch his arm then snatched her hand back when she realized what she was doing. She *must* heed Clara's warning, no matter how strong her attraction to Monty. "Maybe I could try coaxing something out of her. I would be closer to her mama's age than Mrs. Stiney. Perhaps we could find some common ground."

His forehead creased in thought. "I'll consider that."

"Did you hear about Jake Kilrain?" She pointed at the newspaper, changing the subject to ease the lines on his face. "He held an exhibition fight with Charley Mitchell in Madison Square Garden specifically to raise money to send to Johnstown."

"I hadn't heard that." Monty sat taller and took the paper, his eyes communicating that he appreciated her attempt to lift his mood.

"And at the Metropolitan Opera House, Edwin Booth played the third act of *Othello*, raising twenty-five hundred dollars for the victims."

"He plays a better Hamlet."

She gaped at him. "You've seen Edwin Booth perform?"

"Uh, once." Monty squirmed.

"Then how do you know he plays a mediocre Othello?"

"Okay, twice." He pointed at the paper. "What else have you discovered?"

Narrowing one eye at him, she continued, though she was determined to pry the details from him another time. "To help raise money for Johnstown, John Philip Sousa gave a band concert."

She pointed to the article and ran her finger along the print. "Buffalo Bill, who's in Paris, put on a special production to help victims—and the Prince of Wales attended! And there's some monstrosity of iron there now called the Eiffel Tower."

He angled his body toward her to see the image of the structure. "That's amazing." He propped his upper body against the table as if she'd caused all his cares to evaporate on the wind. "Go on."

She chuckled. "You actually enjoy my chatter?"

His voice dipped an octave. "I very much enjoy your chatter."

Delightful chills started at her center and radiated outward. There was much more to this man than what bubbled on the surface, and she wanted to learn every facet.

"Tiffany & Co., R.H. Macy, the Astors, the sultan of Turkey, and even President Harrison have contributed funds."

"That's quite a list of influential people. Does it say anything about the Carnegies, Fricks, Mellons, or James Reed contributing?"

The first two names always sent her spirit tumbling. "It doesn't."

Though it didn't surprise her. She knew well the heartlessness of Henry Clay Frick and Andrew Carnegie. Men like that were rich because they refused to part with their money.

Monty's jaw hardened. "Didn't figure it would."

Annamae assessed the surrounding crowd. She'd debated within herself whether to share what she'd overheard yesterday and decided if she could confide in anyone, it would be Monty.

"Can we take a walk? There's something I'd like to tell you. In confidence."

He nodded but took his time leaving the table. His sudden reluctance to converse with her was confusing. Clara's warning flitted through her memory. Was he afraid that walking with her unaccompanied might jeopardize his position within the church?

If that was the case, though, why did he sit down with her in the first place?

She allowed him to set the pace, which he set at slow. He buried his hands in his pockets. She recognized the gesture as something he did both when he was at ease and when he faced a difficult situation. Which mood was he in now?

The toe of his shoe sent a pebble skipping a few feet ahead of them. "Does what you want to tell me have anything to do with my seeing Edwin Booth perform?"

"What?" She chuckled. "No. Though I would like to hear more about that if you're ever willing to share."

Why he wanted to keep such a silly thing secret seemed odd to her.

WHEN THE WATERS CAME

Perhaps it had something to do with his confession under the moonlight regarding Shakespeare.

His mood brightened. "What did you want to ask me then?"

The sudden change in aura nearly gave her whiplash.

"Well…" She looked around them. Any chance of an audience grew thinner the farther they walked from the commissary. Normally, she wouldn't worry about being overheard, but she'd learned yesterday what all a person could glean if they kept their mouth quiet and listened.

She steered them even farther away. "Last evening, Clara asked me to instruct the nurses on duty how to clean the ticks using chloride of lime. While I was in the typhoid tent, someone brought in an Italian man raging with fever. He kept mumbling that he can prove the South Fork Fishing and Hunting Club is responsible for the dam's break."

Monty leaned away in surprise. "How?"

She shrugged. "He's been in and out of consciousness since. I've also heard this club referred to as 'The Bosses Club' because it consists of powerful men from Pittsburgh who own factories and started the club to escape the smoggy air their industries create. Do you know if that's true?"

"Did you read that in a newspaper?"

"No. I heard it from a colleague in Washington. He said several investigations into the club have opened about the matter. Though the names of these club members haven't been released."

Monty worked his jaw.

"If you hear anything else about this, will you please tell me?"

He rounded to face her, brows knit. "Why?"

She linked her pointer fingers together to keep her hands busy. Perhaps confiding in him wasn't wise after all.

"What I told you the other night about my father? I've not told another soul since it happened. I trust you, Monty. Please. If you hear anything else regarding the club or the investigations, will you tell me?"

"You still haven't answered my question."

She sighed. "I have my suspicions about who these powerful men are. They've destroyed enough lives, including mine. I don't want to see them get away with it again."

"And what do you expect to do about it?"

His displeasure hurt. "I don't know. I only know I must do something."

"If you're correct in your suspicion, those aren't the kind of men to trifle with, Annamae."

"You think I don't know that?" She inhaled and exhaled slowly to simmer her ire at his scolding. "I just want to be kept aware of the investigation. Victims everywhere are telling their stories, and if any of those details could aid in a conviction—"

Monty tugged her sleeve and pulled them even farther away from listening ears. "Why do you think it's your responsibility to see them convicted?"

The agony of missing her father and the rage that followed when she recalled the circumstances that stole him away twisted within her. "Murder requires justice."

He studied her for a long moment as if examining every layer to understand the true motive that lay beneath. His scrutiny invited vulnerability, her least favorite emotion. Guilt poked at her, but she pushed it away. Wanting justice was never something to feel guilty over.

He scratched his cheek. "I'll keep you informed of what I hear if you promise to do the same."

"Thank you."

"But *only* if you promise to let the authorities handle anything we discover."

"What if—"

He held up his hand and lowered his voice to a whisper. "If you're correct and they were ruthless enough to murder one of their employees for cooperating with the union, they won't think twice about silencing a young, pretty nurse with no family connections."

She blinked.

"I'm not trying to be cruel. I'm trying to get you to see how they'll view your involvement."

Her pulse raced, both from their interaction and his comment. "You think I'm pretty?"

"What?" Realizing his confession, he grinned and shook his head sheepishly. "Is that all you got from my impassioned speech?"

"Was that part of the speech impassioned?" She held her breath.

The tension drained from his shoulders, and he relaxed his stance. "Well." He smoothed the bristly hairs at his chin. "I believe in always telling the truth."

Pleasure burst inside her and grew like a wilted flower stretching to the sun.

"Promise me, Annamae."

"I promise."

Chapter Sixteen

"The ghosts of Johnstown are the ghosts of American labor that is dead."

~Chicago Herald

TUESDAY, JUNE 18

"My boys died so those men could fish?" Robert Townsend growled and threw the folded newspaper. It sailed through the air before landing at Monty's feet in the cracked, dry dirt. They'd just carried all the church pews outside and were determining which ones to salvage and which to burn when Jim arrived with the morning paper.

The atmosphere of the town had shifted from despair to enmity. Now that reporters had declared the disaster as manmade, folks wanted answers. Everyone wanted justice, including Monty. And reporters manipulated information and fed on the emotions of the flood victims and the periodical's subscribers, which made an already precarious situation volatile.

Like Jacob with the angel, Monty had wrestled with himself every night since his meeting with Cyrus Elder, trying to figure out where he fit into all this. Monty knew the identities of the club members. Most of them, anyway. He'd also known the sagging condition of the dam when he'd joined Uncle Henry at the clubhouse two summers ago for both business and leisure. He knew that any paperwork involving a club member or any permits to build on the property were purposely filed at the Allegheny Courthouse in Pittsburgh and not—as state guidelines required—at the Cambria County Courthouse, making the details of the club's conception secretive.

Was Monty wrong to withhold the information?

What good would come from revealing it? The damage was done.

The condition of the dam was no secret. Over the past several years, many concerned citizens from Johnstown had either snuck onto the property to examine the dam themselves or filed a complaint with the county inspector. The court system would discover and investigate the club members. Revealing the list unethically would most definitely cause a mob riot on the members' homes, and Monty didn't want to be responsible for any deaths. He hadn't seen his family in over two years, so he had no knowledge or proof of any doings at the club recently that would aid in the investigations.

Revealing his knowledge would also reveal his family connections. Not only would he lose his congregation, but it would invite an angry mob to his own door. If he had one. He knew well the sin of omission. If anyone asked him a question that would elicit the need to tell them who he really was, he would. But choosing not to declare every detail of his life wasn't lying.

Monty bent and picked up the newspaper, the summer heat and weight of the situation bearing down on him. He glanced around. Jim Parkes sat in the dirt and rested his head against the side of the church, eyes falling closed. Ernie approached from the back of the church where he'd slept on a pallet last night. The man shook with the need for a drink.

A small breeze stirred a corner of the front page. He dropped onto a stump and stretched his legs in front of him, crossing them at the ankles.

Many thousand human lives—Butchered husbands, slaughtered wives, Mangled daughters, bleeding sons, Hosts of martyred little ones, (Worse than Herod's awful crime) Sent to heaven before their time; Lovers burnt and sweethearts drowned, Darlings lost but never found! All the horrors that hell could wish, Such was the price that was paid for—fish!

A man named Isaac Reed had written the poem, and the caption stated the poem's popularity in several prominent papers. It was accompanied by an article quoting James McGregor, a South Fork Fishing and Hunting Club member, who wasn't afraid to divulge his identity. The daft man claimed the flood was caused by a different dam breaking and that the club had been putting fifteen to twenty thousand a year into the property for upkeep and improvements. *"I am going up there to fish the latter part of this month. I am a club member, and I believe the dam is standing there the same as it ever was."*

The gall.

Monty dropped the paper on his legs and rubbed the hair on his upper lip. How dare anyone claim this calamity as a farce? If only he had the power to force those men to come here to see the valley of death for themselves.

"Can you believe that fool?" Robert curled his fists then flopped onto a pew facing Macedonia Street.

"They'd think differently if it were their wives and children," Monty said. He handed the paper to Ernie, only to remember too late the man couldn't read.

Robert stood again and paced like a caged lion. "Ruff put screens over the spillway so the club wouldn't lose their precious fish."

Shame plowed into Monty. He remembered Uncle Henry bragging about the fish they'd stocked in the lake for "only a thousand dollars." Delivered by train from all over the country, only one had arrived dead. Ruff added screens over the spillway so the fish wouldn't wash downstream when the water level rose. Prized fish that Monty had caught himself when visiting the clubhouse.

"Ruff was only ever in it for himself," Jim mumbled.

Benjamin Ruff had sold three shares of the fishing and hunting club he'd founded to Uncle Henry. Monty had only heard Ruff's name, but many native residents in Johnstown remembered the man well.

"Fulton's saying Ruff removed the sluice pipes for scrap and never replaced them." The anger radiating from Robert was close to bursting through his skin. "There was no way to release excess water in the reservoir without sluice pipes. The spillway wasn't big enough to handle all the water. He's also saying Ruff removed the culvert and packed it with all kinds of junk that made it sag in the middle. It's no wonder the water breached the top."

"If you ask me," Jim said, "that right there is what did us in. The only place for all that rain to go was up and over. With an earthen dam, once the water goes over, that's the end. They're right when they say no dam could withstand that much water, but that dam wasn't in proper working order to begin with."

Tears traveled down Robert's cheeks the way they often did these days. "One paper said the creeks that feed into Lake Conemaugh dumped all kinds of small trees and debris into the lake the day before. Said it clogged up the screens so no water could get through the spillway."

Monty stood and laid a firm grip on Robert's shoulder. He'd been doing a lot of that lately as words were hollow and reciting scripture only took him so far. The Lord's words were powerful, His promises true, but one had to open their soul and allow it to soak in, to nourish, to heal. Circumstances such as these made trusting anything difficult.

Even for a pastor.

Truth was, even if the screens weren't covering the spillway, the small trees would have traveled with the flow of water and jammed the spillway anyway. Not that he was defending the club.

The jangle of a horse and cart came from down the rough street. Monty lifted his hand to shield his eyes from the sunlight. With nearly all the livestock drowned, the sight of a man and a woman riding on the narrow bench looked out of place among the chaos. Something commonplace they'd taken for granted in their previous lives. Sadly, that was how they'd view their lives from now on—before the flood and after.

Monty lowered his arm to go back to work when his brain registered the woman's nursing uniform. Annamae was riding in the cart. Sitting next to a man she bumped into with every uneven spot in the road. A possessive heat churned in Monty's gut. He wasn't sure why. He only knew he didn't like the visual of her in close proximity to another man.

Land sakes, he had more obstacles to work through than he'd thought.

As the man with a dark and neatly trimmed Vandyke beard pulled the horse to a stop, Annamae glanced at Monty and smiled. His pulse galloped. Hopefully, she didn't smile like that for this other fellow.

Before anyone else had time to react, Monty jogged to Annamae's side of the cart and assisted her to the ground. Her grin widened, exposing straight teeth above a plump bottom lip.

He looked away.

She curled her fingers around his arm. "Are you all right? You're not feeling ill, are you?"

Yes he was, but not in the way she meant.

"No, I'm fine. What brings you by?"

"Oh." As if she'd forgotten about the gentleman who'd driven her there, she lifted a small basket from the wagon and pivoted toward the man who stood on the other side of the carriage. "This is—"

"Doctor John B. Hamilton, United States Surgeon General." The thin man tugged on the points of his vest.

The doctor said it with such authority, Monty wasn't sure whether to shake his hand or salute. "Pastor Monty Childs."

"Miss Worthington and I are traveling to every district with disinfectants to train folks in how to use them. We need a few leading men in each locale who can train others within their district. Your area starts at Clinton Street and covers all parallel streets southwest to the hillside. Miss Worthington suggested you'd be a good man for the job. Can you do this for us?"

Monty wanted to remind the doctor the town was no longer divided into streets and that deciphering where the old ones lay wasn't easy, but he kept it to himself. If Annamae thought him capable for the job, he'd do it.

"Yes, Doctor," Monty replied.

Doctor Hamilton instructed the men to help him unload the contents of the cart. Ernie took one look at Annamae and slunk away in embarrassment. Annamae stepped aside not seeming to notice.

The barrels were marked QUICKLIME and CHLORIDE OF LIME. Monty reached for a smaller keg, but the doc stopped him with a hand splayed across the top. "Not this one. It's nitric acid. It goes to the commissary for disinfecting the communal plates, cups, and utensils."

The man spoke as if he were reciting a passage from a medical book. He wore a thin gold band on his left fourth finger. Monty reached for one of the other barrels and carried it beside the church, relieved at that revelation. Annamae showed him where to stack the barrels while the doctor carried a sack across his shoulders. Metal clanked from inside with each step.

"Aside from rebuilding, this will be the most important thing you'll do in this town." The sack dropped at the doctor's feet.

The orange tabby Monty had yet to name jumped from his lazy curl in the windowsill and bolted away in the direction Ernie had gone.

"Please heed Miss Worthington's instructions while I deliver the remaining barrels to the commissary. Miss Worthington, I'll be back shortly."

"Yes, Doctor Hamilton."

Annamae rested her basket on the ground and asked Robert to fetch a pail of water from the pump routed directly to the nearest stream. Robert obliged but with lackluster movements.

The clop of horse's hooves joined the other sounds before the cart disappeared altogether. Annamae removed a small pry bar from the sack and loosened the lid on the nearest barrel. Monty helped her remove it the rest of the way.

"This, gentlemen, is chloride of lime. It is a highly potent disinfectant. You must use it cautiously." Robert returned with the pail, and she thanked him. "This works well to clean and disinfect hard surfaces and wood containing any mold or other harmful substances. It's vital that you dilute it properly. It will turn dyed cloth white, and it can cause chemical burn on the skin if the solution is too strong."

Using a piece of chalk she removed from her pocket, she wrote measurements on the barrel lid for dilution instructions. Then she demonstrated how to mix the solution. A pungent odor filled the air around them. It smelled clean, but the sharpness of it also tickled Monty's nose and stung his eyes. After she finished mixing, she dipped a rag into the pail, squeezed out the excess liquid, and walked inside the church. The men followed.

Ernie peered around the back of the building, and Monty motioned for him to join them.

Craning her slender neck, Annamae gaped at the hole in the church where his house had crashed. Part of the home's foundation remained on the lot next door, but any evidence beyond that was now ashes.

Annamae looked around at what remained until she found something that suited her. She inspected an upturned pew they'd decided earlier needed to be burned. White and black mold, along with dirt, clung to the legs. She scrubbed the rag over the mold, and, little by little, the offense disappeared.

"Would'ya look at that," Jim said.

Monty covered his nose and sneezed.

She grinned at him. "It can do that too."

When she finished cleaning the entire leg, wet, shiny wood was the result. A few hairline cracks appeared, but they wouldn't affect the pew's stability. Perhaps they could salvage more pews than they'd originally thought. She held the filthy rag away from her apron. "Chloride of lime is great to use on anything that's still functional but needs to be cleaned."

Annamae returned to the outdoors, and the men followed. Ernie joined them as she replaced the lid on the chloride of lime barrel. Then she went through instructions with the barrel marked QUICKLIME.

"This powder is wonderful for sprinkling in yards or lots. It disinfects the ground without harming livestock or wildlife."

Ernie concentrated on the earth beneath his shoes. "Excuse me, ma'am, but is it necessary to clean the dirt?"

She assessed Ernie in two blinks of an eye, the way Monty had witnessed her do many times at the Red Cross tents. While judgment usually followed Ernie's attempts to converse, compassion filled her answer. "Absolutely. God only knows the things mixed in that water when it swept through town. This dirt is more contaminated than you can imagine. If it isn't disinfected and folks build on top of it, it could make them very sick.

You'll be doing a very noble thing by helping to disinfect it."

Ernie's posture improved, and he nodded as if she'd bestowed a great honor on him.

She pulled a scoop from the bag, filled an empty pail with quicklime, and then used the scoop to spread an even amount of powder on the ground. "Do this three times a week or more often as you see the powder fade away. By mid-July, you can limit application to once a week."

She handed Ernie the scoop then guided it with her own hand, demonstrating the sprinkle. "If you get any on you, wash the area with soap and water right away. Though it's safe for animals, it can cause skin allergies in humans."

"Yes, ma'am." Ernie worked hard to control his shaking when Annamae left him on his own, Monty could tell. The old man lit up in a way Monty had never observed from him before.

She had a way of doing that to a man.

As she helped them prepare more chloride of lime, she answered questions, promised Monty she and Doctor Hamilton would deliver more barrels, and explained once again which areas would fall under his district.

"Thank you for doing this. Within a few weeks, the typhoid cases should drop significantly."

"I'm willing to help in any way I can."

She tipped her head to the side, surveying him for something he hoped he could give. "You could help with one more thing."

He nodded for her to continue.

She made sure the others were far enough away not to overhear. "The Italian man I told you about. The typhoid has weakened him, but he's still alive. He told me he was one of the workers installing new plumbing in the South Fork clubhouse the day the dam burst." She whispered the last sentence. "A man on the property named Colonel Unger knew the dam would break if they didn't do something quickly. He commanded the crew of plumbers to dig trenches to release excess water before the entire dam gave way. Unger was told if they cut off the screens covering the spillway, it would help lower the water level. He refused."

Monty inhaled deeply.

"The man claims this Colonel Unger was afraid of what the club's shareholders would do when they discovered they had no prized fish. When their efforts to dig trenches failed, he allowed permission to remove the screens. But it was too late."

Monty's stomach roiled. "What is it you think I can do?"

"I want to report this, but I don't know whom to trust."

"Let the Italian tell his story."

"He's too weak to appear before the courts, and he may not make it through the night. This might very well be the information the judges need to hold the club accountable."

"I told you the other day, these are not the kind of men to trifle with."

"And that's what makes them untouchable." She pinched her lips to control her irritation. "If we don't stand up and fight for ourselves, who will?"

No one. But fighting men like Uncle Henry was also a guaranteed defeat. After all, the upper-crust lawyers who defended such cases were also members of the club.

In order to keep Annamae safe and her information out of the wrong hands, he must convince her to let him lead. "Don't say anything to anyone yet. I know a couple of men I can talk to. I'll see what I can do."

She touched his sleeve. "Thank you, Monty. One more thing?"

He was beginning to dread that phrase. "What am I, a genie?"

"This isn't a request. It's a gift."

She reached inside her basket and pulled out a paper-wrapped square. He knew what it was without even removing the paper. The weight of it in his hand, the familiar thickness. A Bible.

"You mentioned yours got ruined in the flood, and your first service since the flood is nearing, so I'm loaning you mine until you find another. Keep it as long as you need."

The paper slid off easily to reveal a cover worn in all the right spots. Monty opened to the first page, where she'd written her name in looping cursive. He ran his fingertips over the scrawl.

Horse hooves clomped, and he spotted Doctor Hamilton returning for her. "This is very thoughtful."

She smiled. "Friends think about each other."

The wagon jerked to a stop beside them. She allowed the doctor to help her up, settled in, and waved as they drove away.

He'd spend the rest of his day thinking about more than friendship.

Chapter Seventeen

⁓○

"There are those who tell us they want only the religion of sunshine, art, blue sky, and beautiful grass. The book of nature must be their book. Let me ask such persons what they make out of the floods in Pennsylvania."

~Reverend T. DeWitt Talmage, a quote spoken to his congregation in New York

SUNDAY, JUNE 23

Annamae stood at the back of the large crowd, listening in awe to Monty's sermon. It was his first since the flood, and he'd mentioned to her yesterday that he was anxious. She'd woken extra early to help finish stocking the newly built hotel provided by the Red Cross to house misplaced victims of the flood so she could attend services. It was important to her to support her friend but also to meet Joanna and offer some token of kindness she hoped would comfort the girl.

It was a lovely day for an outdoor service. The temperature was comfortable, and the birds trilled. A magnificent change from all the banging and blasting that normally filled their days. Even if not everyone in the town attended a service, at least they honored the Sabbath by resting from labor.

The church grounds were clear of debris. The iron fencing surrounding the small cemetery stood once again, but several headstones lay broken. Ernie had assured her he'd thoroughly disinfected the areas on both sides of the church. Since the side of the building still held a gaping hole, congregants spread blankets on the dry earth or stood on the fringes to worship.

The angle where she stood offered the perfect glimpse of Monty's strong, shaven jaw. Someone had trimmed his hair and, in this light, she caught faint strands of red and blond near his forehead as he bent his head to read from her Bible cradled in his palm.

The timbre of his voice rippled over the crowd. " 'The floods have lifted up, O Lord, the floods have lifted up their voice; the floods lift up their waves.' "

Monty stared into their faces. "The newspapers are reporting many preachers across the nation using this very text to convict their congregations, saying our wicked town was under the judgment of God or that we've become the greatest example of needing to be prepared to meet our Maker. But the passage in Psalm 93 doesn't end there."

He paused. As if they were all tethered to the same string, they leaned closer for his next words.

" 'The Lord on high is mightier than the noise of many waters—' "

Amens exploded into the air.

" 'Yea, than the mighty waves of the sea.' "

The man standing next to Annamae wiped the deluge of tears from his cheeks with the cap he'd strangled in his fist.

"None of us is fit to claim the Lord's reason for allowing this flood to take place. Only He knows that answer. But I know one thing. He's caring for our loved ones in heaven better than we ever could. Those of us left behind must continue carrying out His purpose. For He is mightier than the noise of many waters."

Monty swallowed, and when he spoke again, his voice wobbled with emotion. "Those of us who heard the intensity of those mighty waters know how powerful a promise that is."

Annamae's skin pebbled from head to foot. She couldn't imagine the horrors the people standing around her had endured. It was a reminder to always be kind, because one never knew the pain that lurked inside another's heart.

Monty went on assuring the people of God's provision and how He was meeting their needs through charitable donations of food, supplies, money, and the many doctors and nurses who'd traveled from their homes to donate their time and skills to keep folks healthy. His gaze found hers and locked there. The serious angles of his face softened, and the message of appreciation and attraction meant for only her crackled in the air between them.

Her body grew languid with a serenity she'd never experienced. The connection between them felt wholesome and true and right. She didn't care that in a few short weeks or months her work here would end and the Red Cross would return home. All she wanted was to learn everything about this man who watched over and fed people's souls.

But romantic feelings would only complicate the comfortable structure of her life. She wasn't one for fanciful daydreams and impractical flirtations. As Matthew had pointed out many times, she watched life move around her through somber glasses, rarely taking part. Monty poured energy into her dormant heart, awakening a longing she couldn't ignore.

After the closing prayer, the congregation, mostly composed of men, shook Monty's hand before going about their day. Annamae stood beside Ernie, slipping her hands into the folds of her skirt. She waited and watched Monty focus on each person, asking how they fared and if they needed anything.

This side of him was new to her. She'd first been introduced to the man, but seeing him slip into the role of pastor left her awestruck. It also challenged her to be someone worthy of standing by his side.

She'd worn her plain blue calico today as a reprieve from her uniform, her hair secured into a loose knot at her crown. A few of the men gathered by the road instead of leaving. They conversed with one another while sneaking glances her way.

Monty had mentioned how many marriage ceremonies he'd performed since the flood as most men had lost their wives. Marriages of convenience, not of love. She avoided direct contact with their prowling gazes, not wanting to encourage any attention.

An orange cat sauntered out the church door with its tail in the air. Annamae smiled. The feline had put on some weight since its invasion of Monty's bed at the Red Cross tent. Its coat was no longer mangled but was smooth and shiny. The lids around its missing eye had crusted over with a scar, but overall, the cat seemed to do well as Monty's companion.

She knelt and coaxed the cat to her. It sniffed the tips of her fingers before rubbing against her skirt. She scratched its head, giggled when it purred, and then scooped it up and nestled it in her arms.

"May I escort you anywhere, Miss Worthington?" Ernie's voice rattled.

"It's very kind of you to offer, but I'm waiting for Pastor Childs."

Thin skin sunk on Ernie's cheeks. His bloodshot eyes moved from her to Monty then back again. He winked. "He needs himself a fine woman. You enjoy your afternoon."

The poor man smelled as if he hadn't seen a bar of soap since the flood. "Thank you, Mr. Ernie. If you need anything at all, ask for me at the Red Cross."

"Will do, ma'am." His movements were less shaky today than yesterday, and alcohol clung to his breath, indicating he'd given in to his craving sometime last night.

During one of her visits to deliver more disinfectants, she'd found Ernie passed out behind the church. Fearing him dead, she'd discovered a pulse and slapped his cheek to rouse him. He'd awoken, words slurring. She'd recognized the symptoms. Ernie had shared the story of losing his wife and daughter to cholera fifteen years ago and how he'd crawled inside of a bottle and never climbed out.

The men gathered at the road shifted away as Ernie walked past. Hypocrites. She wanted to race to them and issue a good tongue lashing. Instead, she held the cat tighter. It purred deeper and kneaded its paws on her sleeve.

Monty headed her way, his casual stride and confident grin snuffing out her anger. He stopped in front of her. Lazily, his eyes traveled over her as if she were a rare flower he wanted to take time observing. Heat stole into her cheeks.

"Thank you for attending the service today." He tucked her Bible against his side.

"You spoke powerful words of honesty and encouragement. Your congregation is blessed to have you."

Monty glanced to the side and swiped his thumb at the end of his nose. She'd embarrassed him with her praises. How adorable.

"I was hoping to meet Joanna."

"They couldn't get her to come. I think she's afraid if she does, she'll be taken to a new family."

"Oh, poor girl."

"Will you join me for lunch?" He scratched the cat's head, making its ear twitch. "Afterward, maybe we can see if she's up for company."

"I'd love to."

"I wish I could treat you to a meal at one of our cafés, but since they're no longer open and I have no money, how about the commissary?"

"Best place in town." She set the cat on its feet and stood, reaching her hand out to curl around his arm but stopped short. Though the gesture was common practice for a gentleman escorting a lady, perhaps it wasn't common practice for a clergyman.

"What's wrong?" He frowned at his outstretched elbow.

"Are you allowed to escort me this way? I don't want to tarnish your reputation."

Monty laughed. "Annamae, you worry too much. And you're certainly not the type of woman who'd tarnish my reputation." He offered his arm again. "I'm a pastor, but I'm also a man, and I'd like to escort the prettiest woman in town to lunch."

"Well, when you say it that way." Her fingertips brushed the fabric of his faded suit coat. The muscle that lay beneath hardened as they walked.

She should wipe off the silly grin she knew stuck to her face. "The first of the Red Cross hotels is finished. I helped make the beds and stock supplies this morning. I secured a place on the list for you. There are many beds in one room and only a small crate beside each one for belongings, but it'll keep you from sleeping on a hard pew."

"I appreciate that, but I'm sure there are others in more need than I."

"All the widows and children already have beds in Holt House and Alma Hall. This hotel is for the men. A second hotel will be completed any day. There'll be six in all. The Red Cross will ensure everyone a place to stay."

"Thank you." His arm pressed her wrist tight against him. "Your friendship has become one of the most important in my life."

"Handsome *and* a suave elocutionist. That's a dangerous combination."

"Only for women."

She laughed. The airy cheerfulness of it struck her like an arrow. When was the last time she'd truly laughed without the slightest weight holding it down? Before her father died? She tried but couldn't recall a time with Matthew when she'd lived wholly in the moment and laughed joyously.

They took short, slow steps, neither seeming to be in a hurry to reach the commissary.

"May I ask a bold question?" She tilted her head to look up at him.

He scratched his forehead, smiling. "Your inquisitive nature concerns me."

She chuckled. "Papa always used to accuse me of asking too many questions."

The familiar tide of emotions that came with her father's memory threatened to steal the sunshine from her day. She pushed it away, wanting to enjoy the afternoon.

"What is it you want to know?"

"Why isn't there a Mrs. Monty Childs?"

"Ah, that." His eyes narrowed in contemplation. "I've been waiting for the person my soul connects with. For the woman who brings out the best in me, and I in her. I want a marriage like my parents had—humble, loving, persevering when life gets tough."

A suave elocutionist indeed.

"You said had. Did something happen to them?"

"Mmm, that is a question for another day."

"Fair enough." Grass grew in the patch of earth where they crossed a road declared as Market Street on a crude, handwritten board stuck in the ground. The green was a stark contrast to the dry dirt throughout the town.

"My turn. Why isn't there a mister in your life?"

She started to tell him about Matthew but thought better of it. Matthew hadn't asked for her future. In fact, he hadn't officially asked to court her either, but his attentions left no doubt he wanted to. Her feelings for him didn't extend beyond friendship, so, really, there was nothing to tell.

"For the same reason as yours. I've kept mostly to myself since Papa's death. No time for courtship. I don't remember what my parents' marriage was like, but the love that leaked from Papa's voice when he talked about my mother made it clear he never stopped loving her. Perhaps a love like that is as rare as a glimpse of Halley's Comet."

His steps slowed even more. His gaze roamed her face. The motion of the town faded to her periphery as her focus stuck solely on him. "It may not be as rare as you think."

Annamae swallowed, wanting to savor this moment for as long as possible. She didn't know what it was about him that kept drawing her to his presence, but it was raw and powerful.

A delightful scent carried on the breeze, coaxing their noses into the air.

Monty smiled. "Is that fried chicken?"

She sniffed. "I believe it is."

He sighed in contentment. "Thank the good Lord. Come on, let's eat."

Chapter Eighteen

~

*"To maintain a dam to form a lake for pleasure
purposes is an enterprise no less legitimate than
to build a dam for running a mill wheel."*

~*Forest and Stream* magazine 1889, in defense of the club,
stating sportsmen who appreciate nature are essentially good
men and can't be held responsible for the dam's breaking

WEDNESDAY, JUNE 26

Monty was furious. He stepped around Richard Hearst without his usual greeting. The man blocked half the doorway of the Red Cross hotel, chatting with Jim Parkes, who whittled a wooden block in his aged hands. Monty was in no mood to act friendly, though he should make himself. Uncle Henry had declared war after two years of silence, and Monty's blood boiled hot enough to scald anyone in his path.

His room was mostly empty, the other tenants either taking supper or utilizing one of the bathhouses at this time of the evening. He removed his boots and eased onto his bed. His weary bones sighed, grateful he no longer had to sleep on a hard pew. Though this hotel was nothing like the luxurious Greenbrier or the Grand Hotel or even his personal quarters at Clayton, it was warm, functional, stocked with supplies, and protected him from the outside elements.

That made it the best public lodging he'd ever experienced.

Besides, he didn't fit into the world of servants and ballrooms and debutantes anymore—as Uncle Henry had reminded him. This was Monty's world now, and these were his people. He wanted it no other way.

Pain shot through his back, and he winced. His whole body hurt. The moldy plaster inside the church wasn't salvageable, so they'd spent hours ripping it out. Ernie wasn't much help with physical labor, so they'd sent him to Red Cross headquarters for more disinfectant. He returned with Annamae and a wagon full of cleaner.

At first, Monty's dirty, sweaty appearance embarrassed him. Then the heat of attraction had softened Annamae's hazel eyes, and he set all reservations aside. A working man was likely the only kind she'd ever known. He needn't bring aspects of his old life to impress her. Annamae wore her heart out in the open, without false simpering flirtation or guile. She didn't claim her role as a respectable lady while acting otherwise behind closed doors.

The pretense of society had always made his stomach sour. At least here folks didn't hide their secrets behind expensive cigars and glittering jewels.

That was what he liked about Annamae—plus her grit, her intellect, her caring and serving heart. For years, Aunt Adelaide had scolded him for being too picky when he had scores of young women from the cream of society offering their attention. He hadn't wanted any of those women. Sure, they were beautiful on the outside, but then what? Time passed, and beauty faded. He wanted a woman who challenged him, inspired him, and wanted to work beside him.

Annamae was that woman.

Walking to the commissary after Sunday service with her on his arm had felt as natural as breathing. He'd rarely been that comfortable with anyone, and he sensed he could tell her anything.

Except that he was Henry Clay Frick's nephew.

How would she feel about him, knowing he came from the very family she held responsible for killing her father? She would see him differently.

Might even hold him as responsible as Uncle Henry simply for sharing the same blood.

Which made his need to keep her from getting involved in any investigation critical. Monty had been dismissed from his uncle's home and his uncle's life the day he packed his luggage for seminary and denounced the offered position at Frick & Company. Since he and his uncle no longer shared ties, there was no reason for Annamae to know of his heritage. The time would come for that later. Right now, she was asking too many questions. His uncle was a dangerous man when threatened, and Monty wanted to keep her out of it.

The battle was between him and his uncle, and it was about to get ugly.

The audacity of Uncle Henry to freeze his accounts in Pittsburgh, claiming they awaited proof that Monty had survived, was hogwash. Pretending he cared and wanted to make certain no fraudulent schemes would infiltrate Monty's inheritance. As if any of them were concerned whether he'd lived or died. Uncle Henry was Monty's closest relative, and Monty's inheritance, pennies compared to his uncle's fortune, would fall to Uncle Henry upon Monty's passing. Unless he married, of course. Uncle Henry was freezing Monty's accounts to make a statement as to the power he wielded over his nephew.

Monty swung his legs up onto the bed, leaned back against the wall, and placed a book on his bent knees. He reached for his writing materials on the small crate beside the bed. He pressed the pointed lead to paper and let the slanted dips and swirls speak his frustration.

He opened his letter demanding that Uncle Henry unfreeze his accounts. He also informed his uncle that he had issued sufficient proof to the bank of his existence. Satisfied, Monty added, *You know as well as I, the flood that destroyed Johnstown was caused by the club's oversight to properly repair the dam. Members were aware of its deteriorating condition. At your very table, I heard you shirk responsibility for the faulty structure and insist the carriage road be lowered and widened for the convenience of two carriages to pass simultaneously. You have a responsibility to the people of Johnstown. If you do not fulfill it, I will release your name and every detail regarding your dealings at the club to every reporter here.*

Uncle Henry had always appreciated forthrightness, so Monty closed there and signed his name.

He folded the letter, slipped it into an envelope, and wrote the address on the outside. First thing tomorrow, he'd take the letter to the temporary post office set up on Walnut Street and pay its postage. Then he'd wait to see how long it took for money from Frick & Company to roll into town.

———————

I'M WELL. *Stop*. BUSY. *Stop*. RETURN UNCERTAIN. *Stop*.

Annamae knew she should say more to Matthew but didn't wish to pay extra to include details she could relay the next time they saw each other. She also didn't want to give him false hope. He didn't stir her blood the way Monty did with a single look. He didn't provoke her to confront the hard things in life the way Monty did. While Matthew wanted to shield her from work, Monty seemed to enjoy her working beside him.

There was no question who held her true affection. And though Monty was here now, he wouldn't be in Washington when it was time for her to return home. The idea of going back to her sparse apartment, where she would spend every evening alone, made her stomach hollow.

What if Monty didn't ask her to stay?

If he did, would she?

"Is this all, miss?" The lanky man behind the counter raised one eyebrow over the gold spectacles perched on the end of his nose. His fingers drummed on the surface between them.

"Yes, thank you." She handed him the paper and the appropriate coins then watched him tap the message.

The room was full of people on both sides of the counter. Judging by the yawns and purple shading beneath their eyes, the telegraph operators worked around the clock to send and receive messages for the residents, military, volunteers, and reporters. Everyone was working themselves to the bone to serve one another and rebuild, while the club members remained silent.

An article in the morning edition of the *Tribune* had made her breath quicken with fury. Though the membership list was still a mystery, an investigation into the club's financial status revealed that the club itself was invested at thirty-five thousand dollars and that twenty thousand was owed in mortgage, leaving a mere fifteen thousand to be distributed among victims should the club be declared guilty by a court of law. Since lawsuits would be filed against the club and not wealthy individual members, there wasn't enough capital for survivors to collect in restitution.

Not that any amount, no matter how large, would right the wrong.

Yet, the knowledge that those men would once again get away with murder feasted on Annamae. She couldn't sit idle and allow it to happen. Someone needed to stop them, and if she had to be the sacrifice, so be it.

The telegraph operator returned. "Message sent, miss."

She thanked him and wove through the press of men to the exit.

The street was full of workers restoring the city's street lamps and cable car tracks. The air smelled of dirt and sweat, and the reek of decay lingered. A man holding a shovelful of dirt spun and almost collided with her. A dark clump rolled off the pile and onto her skirt. "Sorry, miss. Take care to watch where you're going."

She should take care?

Ignoring his rudeness, she yanked at her skirt to dislodge the clod and moved around him. Good thing the fabric was similar in color to the stain. She hoped to see Monty later today and wished to be presentable.

A shingle constructed from a crude plank of wood hung from the building across the street. Newspaper Offices. Like a beacon, she went toward it, unsure why. For news of the investigation, she supposed. A desire to see justice burned like fire in her heart. The restless agitation, the sour taste of bitterness, stayed with her like a festering wound.

She'd give anything to feel her father's arms around her once more. To lie on a blanket and tell stories under the stars. Monty had told her not to repeat what she'd heard regarding Colonel Unger's refusal to cut the screens on the spillway, wanting her to let him handle the matter. Every time they were together, however, he would deflect the conversation. She suspected his course of action was putting it off long enough for the prosecutors to handle the evidence.

But what if the prosecutors didn't know about the spillway? What if the information they had wasn't enough evidence to convict? Annamae would go crazy knowing corruption had won.

She peeked through the cracked glass on the shack's door. She didn't know how some of the sturdiest buildings in town had collapsed and this one had survived. Through the grime, shadows rushed about, preparing for the evening editions she presumed.

"You going in, ma'am?"

Annamae pivoted toward the boyish voice beside her.

"If not, I need 'round ya, please."

"Are you an aspiring reporter?" Annamae smiled.

"No, ma'am. They're paying me a dollar a day to run their messages to the telegraph office and to other folks 'round town if they need. You see now, that's why I need 'round ya if you're not going in."

She stepped out of the way. "My apologies, good sir."

The boy, who couldn't be older than nine, burst through the door, leaving it wide open. Men in shirts with their sleeves rolled to their elbows sat behind typewriters, clicking keys and puffing on cigars. Others scribbled on paper or passed notes to the tiny couriers who nearly knocked her out of the way to do their bidding. A few men napped in chairs, their boots resting on their desk.

A handsome gentleman with a stylish mustache sat at the front desk. He glanced up from his mug of coffee then quickly set it down. "How can I help you, miss?"

He stood.

She wasn't sure. When had she walked inside?

"Um. . .I was looking for something."

One side of his mouth curled in a roguish grin, and he circled the desk. "My name's Colt. I'd like to say you found it, but you'll have to give me more details than that."

He was flirting. Brazenly, she might add. "Forgive me, but I was searching for information regarding a person."

His face grew sober. "Have you checked the casualty list compiled by the Ladies Committee of Johnstown? They update the list daily at the

Second Presbyterian Church on Vine Street."

"Oh no, I'm not missing anyone. I'm here working as a volunteer. I'm searching for information on a Colonel Elias J. Unger."

Surprise lifted his features. "Colonel Unger." He crossed his arms and ankles and leaned against the wall. "What information were you hoping to find?"

His brown eyes were eagle sharp, and she squirmed, feeling as if he could see into her mind and read her thoughts.

"Are these past editions?" She pointed to a window seat piled two feet high with newspapers.

"Every single one since we arrived in Johnstown. If you'll tell me what you're hoping to know about the colonel, I can assist you in finding which paper it would be in."

Monty's warning blared through her brain. *Those men aren't the kind to trifle with, Annamae.*

She smiled coyly and fluttered her lashes the way she'd done as a child when wanting to appear innocent. "I don't know what I'm looking for, as I've never met the colonel. I simply wished to know more about his dealings in Johnstown before the flood so I might better assist with my work here."

The work she put in against the club members, of course, not her nursing. Sunlight poured in through the window. Small strips of wood divided the large rectangle into sections, but the glass was absent. Dust motes danced in the beam that yellowed the pages.

"Where are you volunteering?" The thin vertical stripes on Colt's shirt matched the hue of his brown suspenders.

She shuffled through papers. "I aid in helping others feel their best."

"Then you work for the Red Cross?"

Shocked, she turned to him. Her twirling skirt almost knocked the papers onto the floor.

He chuckled. "Your brassard gave you away."

She frowned at her arm where his finger pointed. Embarrassment flamed her face. She had worn the white strip of fabric with the red cross around her arm so often, she forgot it was there most times.

Grinning, Colt leaned down until he was eye level with her. "Why does a pretty lady like you think information on Colonel Unger would help to better serve patients?"

Annamae huffed at his probing. "My reasons are my own. Do you have any information regarding Colonel Unger and the ongoing South Fork Dam investigations or not?"

He blinked at her change of tone and stood to full height. "To my knowledge, no reporter has printed anything specific regarding Colonel Unger and any potential role in the dam's collapse, if that's what you're asking. However, I'd like to take a stroll with you if you have any theories or information regarding such. The *Pittsburgh Post* is loyal to their readers in relaying the truth and would be glad to be the first to print such news should it prove valid."

Should she tell him? He was young and handsome and charming but also had an air of coarseness about him that made her apprehensive. Monty had asked her to trust him, and she'd promised him she would.

"I've nothing to share. I heard a story about him that made me curious to learn about his time during the war and his role in Johnstown."

His shoulders shook as his lips ticked up. How dare he laugh at her?

She moved to leave, but he stayed her by the arm.

"Look, miss," he whispered, leaning close. The noise of the typewriters and chatter around them made it hard for her to hear his low tone. "I'm not sure what you're up to, but you should know that Colonel Unger never served in the war. It's simply an honorary title given him years ago for the way he conducted business as a hotel manager."

Colt dug through the papers. She wanted to flee but had a feeling she should hear what else this man had to say. He lifted an issue, threw it back, then pulled out another. He passed it to her. "After watching the dam burst before his eyes, helpless to aid anyone in its path, he collapsed. When an angry mob arrived days later, he'd already fled to Pittsburgh."

She scanned the front-page headlines until her gaze rested on an article about the mob. His attention focused more sharply on her.

"If there's something regarding Colonel Unger we've left out, please confide in me. The residents of Johnstown, of America, deserve to know what really happened. You can trust me."

She stared into his coffee-brown eyes. Could she?

Annamae tapped the paper against her open palm. "If someone did know something, how would telling a reporter help the investigation?"

He tilted his head back. His sharp gaze softened in a knowing gleam. "It isn't just the folks of Johnstown that are livid about the dam's collapse. The entire country is. All of us want closure. If it's an act of God, fine. But new details are emerging every day that verify the club members are responsible for this disaster, and we all deserve the truth."

Truth. Yes.

She wanted so badly to spill what she knew, but she'd promised Monty that she'd trust him to relay the information in his own way. Revealing what she knew to this reporter would make *her* truth a lie.

"I pray the courts will discover all truth and that justice will be served hard and swiftly." She passed the paper back to Colt. "Thank you. I'll keep my ears open for anything of interest."

Chapter Nineteen

"We think we know what struck us, and it was not the hand of Providence. Our misery is the work of man. A rat caught in a trap and placed in a bucket would not be more helpless than we were."

~George Swank, Johnstown resident, to the *Tribune*

SUNDAY, JUNE 30

Annamae's laughter lifted into the trees above them like tinkling glass. Even the hemlock enjoyed it, wagging its branches in the breeze, making the sunlight flicker about. It was strange, sitting on a blanket on the forest floor, enjoying the company of a beautiful woman near the very spot he'd wrapped himself inside a petticoat for warmth. Had it really been only a month ago?

Aside from the flashes of memory reminding him of that awful day, Monty was content. He was alone with Annamae, except for God's creation, the noises and smells of town in the distance.

She tilted her head back as her laughter built, and his fingers itched to know if the skin at her throat was as soft as it looked. The sound of her mirth helped chase away the screaming voices that often surfaced when he found himself in a familiar place that involved the tragedy. He'd hesitated to come here, but this place was the best to steal away together without the prying eyes and ears of others to witness their exchange. They needed to discuss his uncle, and they needed privacy.

Her laughter eased to chuckles, and she attempted to catch her breath. She placed a hand on her stomach. "That's the funniest story I've heard in ages. So funny it hurts. Though, I imagine your poor mother must've been livid."

He grinned. "She was. Not only did I receive a good spanking but so did the neighbor boy."

Annamae dabbed at the tears spilling over the corners of her eyes. What would it be like to make her laugh every day for the rest of their lives? The thought was premature in light of the short time they'd known one another. Life was a vapor, and Annamae was a remarkable woman.

She leaned back on her palms and closed her eyes, mouth upturned. Her breath left on a sigh.

Was she as content as he?

One eye peeked open to catch him staring at her. "The moral of that tale goes along with your sermon this morning. You should have shared it with the congregation."

He barked a laugh. "I will never share that with the congregation."

She twisted to face him, mischief radiating from her face. "Why not? Are you afraid they'll find out you're human?"

Monty opened his mouth to speak, but nothing escaped. Something thrummed inside his chest, like a plucked harp string. He knew the members of his congregation well—their backgrounds, likes and dislikes, weaknesses and strengths. But other than his character and comings and goings in Johnstown, they didn't know him at all. In fact, he couldn't recall a single time he'd shared a personal story or memory with them.

Always scripture, always something that pointed them to the Almighty. That was what his calling was about, not about bringing attention to himself. He'd also kept his personal life and background concealed because if they knew he was raised in a mansion with every possession and opportunity at his whim while they worked sixteen-hour days in deplorable conditions for wages that barely fed their families, they'd send him out of town on the next train. They'd never see past his gilded surface to hear the messages God laid on his heart.

"Did I say something wrong?" The joy fell from Annamae's features, and she stared at him with those big innocent eyes.

"No. You said something right."

A small mound formed between her brows as she waited for him to continue.

He stared into the tree line. "I don't share things about my life with the congregation."

"Why? Is your past scandalous?" she teased.

"Far from it." By the grace of God, he'd seen what his future would have been like with Frick Coke and had fled from Clayton.

"Share things with me, then. Were you a naughty but good-hearted boy like Huckleberry Finn? Or were you hard and mysterious and always seeking adventure like Captain Nemo?"

"Neither."

She sat erect, hands plopped into her lap, ready to listen with rapt attention. "Then what were you like?"

Melancholy.

Monty plucked a blade of grass and twisted it in his fingers. "I lost my parents and younger sisters when I was fourteen. They'd gone to England on business. I'd whined about staying home with my cousins, and my aunt agreed to let me stay with them for the summer. On their return trip to the States, they sailed right into a hurricane. No survivors."

"Oh, Monty," she whispered. "I'm so sorry."

Tiny branches on the hemlock trees danced in the warm breeze.

After a respectable amount of silence, she asked, "Who took care of you?"

They'd circled around to things he didn't share with other people. He didn't want to hold back from Annamae. He wanted to know everything about her, which would require divulging everything about himself in return.

"My aunt and uncle were gracious enough to take me in." He smoothed the bent blade.

"You were blessed to have family and avoid an orphanage."

Her words hit him square in the mouth. She'd had no one to take her in when her father died. She'd survived and succeeded on her own.

Monty's admiration for her grew.

"The tension in your face makes me think your memories aren't fond ones. Were they not good to you?" She scooted closer on the blanket, giving him her full attention the way she did with her patients.

"They gave me refuge in Pittsburgh, but they tolerated my presence more than wanted it. My aunt's intention was to be helpful, but she was constantly trying to make me into a man I was not. My uncle, well, he raised me with the objective that I would show my appreciation one day by joining the family business. When I bucked at the idea of being his puppet, he became downright vicious."

Her hand covered the top of his, numbing the stab of memories. She was a nurturer to her very center. And she was good at healing his broken places. "What was the family business?"

"Depends on which one you're referring to. My ancestors succeeded in almost every endeavor: flour merchants, distilling whiskey—"

"Ah, that makes sense. Liquor contradicts your calling." She tapped her finger on the Bible resting beside them.

She'd agreed to accompany him on a picnic after the service. They'd gone straight to the commissary to retrieve their lunches, and he'd skipped the extra time it would take to drop the Bible off at his room in the Red Cross hotel.

"I'm glad you chose the church over alcohol. I've seen it destroy too many lives."

He started to correct her misconception of the business his uncle wanted him running but decided it was best to let it go for now. Revealing too much too soon might cause him to lose her before he proved his worth with a courtship. There would be time later to tell her when she believed without a doubt that the complication with his family wouldn't affect their future.

Monty tossed the blade of grass aside. "You're great with Ernie, and I appreciate that. Most folks, even ones in the congregation, ignore and ridicule him for being weaker than the bottle."

She uncurled her legs hidden beneath her skirt and stretched them out in front of her, pointing and flexing her toes. "He told me about his wife and daughter. I would think the others would show more compassion for him as many understand the loss of a spouse and children now."

"To my knowledge, you're the only other person he's shared his story with besides me."

She asked him about Joanna's progress and the adoption service scheduled in a few days. Nothing had changed, and he dreaded telling her goodbye. The girl would leave Johnstown the afternoon of the service, whether it was with another family or on a train to the nearest orphanage.

Annamae leaned back, supporting herself with her arms. "I'm sorry if my questions put a damper on this otherwise wonderful day. My inquisitiveness is a character flaw that needs improvement."

"Don't. I like you just the way you are." He slid his hand over hers, gliding his fingertips up to her wrist. Scars marred the back of his hands and looked incongruous beside her perfect flesh.

Her lashes blinked away her surprise then fluttered languidly over her cheeks that had heightened in color. When she didn't pull away, his thumb grazed her knuckles. She stared at their hands, her chest rising and falling in quick succession. Her pulse raced beneath his fingertips. His pumped hard too.

It was foolish to court a woman who would leave when she finished her volunteer work, but the pull between them was strong. It could take months to rebuild Johnstown. Maybe it would allow enough time for her to fall in love with him, and she'd stay when he asked.

As if she'd tugged an invisible string around his neck, he moved closer. His gaze flicked to her lips, and her mouth parted slightly. *Just another inch.*

She spun away. "I went to the newspaper office on Friday."

Her blurted confession doused his yearning. Was this her way of rejecting him? Surely he hadn't misread the desire in her eyes.

Monty leaned away and rubbed his hands along his pant legs, clearing his throat. "Why?"

She worried her lip. "I was curious how the investigations were going. I wanted to find out if they knew about Colonel Unger and the spillway and if they'd discovered the identities of the secretive club members."

He rubbed his eyes with a thumb and forefinger. "You didn't tell them anything, did you?"

"No. But I came close."

"You promised to let me handle it."

"And have you?" Her accusatory tone sparked his ire.

Monty tugged at his collar, his neck growing hot. How had they gone from almost kissing to an argument? "I've written to someone who has sway in the matter."

"And?"

"I haven't gotten a response." Her shoulders drooped. "Yet. There hasn't been enough time."

Annamae stood and walked twenty feet to the nearest spruce. The circumference of its trunk easily made four of her. She leaned against it, facing the town lying in the valley below.

Monty joined her. "Are you angry with me?"

He shoved his hands into his pockets.

"Of course not." She turned and placed her hand on his chest, and her eyes immediately widened in shock at her action. Before she could pull away in embarrassment, he caught her hand and held it against his heart. He wanted her to feel this comfortable with him.

She sighed. "My behavior is despicable."

"Because you rejected my kiss?" He shook his head. "You didn't do anything wrong. I apologize for making you uncomfortable."

"What? No. The last thing you make me feel is uncomfortable. I'm despicable for taking my frustration out on you."

He shrugged. "Aggravation is a part of life. At times, part of a relationship."

"Clara says I have an unhealthy balance between crusader and nurturer. I let one overshadow the other." She inhaled a deep breath. "To be clear, I wasn't rejecting your affection. I wanted you to know what I'd done so there'd be no secrets between us."

Guilt slithered across Monty's shoulders like a predatory snake. "Then I have some confessing to do as well."

He lowered their hands to rest beside them. "I know who the club members are. Not all of them, but some."

"What?"

He silenced her outraged shock by pressing a finger gently to her lips. "My background afforded me entrance into the most prominent circles of society. I know those men, Annamae, and what they're capable of. I know you want to seek justice for what they've caused here. For your father. But I don't want you involved."

Releasing her hand, he brushed his knuckles against her cheek. "I'm trying to keep you safe."

"When you asked me that day at the commissary if Carnegie, Frick, Reed, and Mellon had contributed to the survivors, it's because they're members, aren't they?"

He sighed. "Among others. The anonymity of their club was so important to them, they convinced a judge to let them file their charter at the Court of Common Pleas in Allegheny County instead of at the Cambria County courthouse as Pennsylvania law demands. They'll go to great lengths to keep their names cleared."

"We need to tell someone, Monty. If the judges don't know who they are, how can they convict them?"

He returned their joined hands to his chest. "The lawsuits filed are against the *club*, not the individual members. If the courts find the club guilty, a judge will subpoena the membership list. That will force them to reveal themselves. And keep you safe."

She dropped her hand in frustration. "But if the public knew the names of the club members, they could file lawsuits against them individually instead of the club itself and see justice served."

"It doesn't work that way. Lawsuits can't be filed on specific members since the fault lies with negligence by the entire club, not just certain members."

"Yes, but this Colonel Unger, he—"

"Owns a farm beside the club and helps to oversee the club's property as the club's president. From what I hear, he collapsed after watching the dam crumble and had to be carried back to his house. His health has failed since. The structure of the dam wasn't in his jurisdiction. The fault doesn't lie with him."

Tears welled in her eyes, and she turned away.

"Listen." Monty lowered his voice, sidling up behind her. He put his hands on her shoulders, relishing the feel of her. "I read in the paper this morning that another investigation has been opened into why the club applied for a mortgage for *improvements* days before the dam collapsed. The theory is they knew the dam was dangerous and finally planned to repair it. The country is outraged. There will be lawsuits filed for months if not years. Their actions will catch up with them. We need to be patient."

She swiped at her cheek. "If I can't help ensure these men go down for their crimes, then my work here has been for nought."

His spirit deflated. Her hunger for justice went much deeper than the folks of Johnstown. She wanted revenge for her father.

"Look at me." He spun her around and lifted her chin with his finger. "You came here with the Red Cross to help and to heal, and you're doing a wonderful job. Without you, I'd probably still be wandering around in a shocked stupor. Your work here has been vital. For others, but especially to me."

She tucked her head against his shoulder. He pressed her against him and held tight, rubbing circles on her back. "We mustn't forget that the Lord died for the rich and the privileged too." She stiffened beneath his palm. "Promise me you'll keep what I shared with you today in confidence. Let me protect you," he whispered.

She lifted her head until their lips were inches apart. Her cheek was like velvet. His touch made her eyelids flutter closed. Oh, how he wanted to lean in and attempt that kiss again, but he would wait. Her emotions were vulnerable in this moment, and when he kissed her, he wanted her mind and heart clear.

He settled for her cheek instead, just above the corner of her mouth. "Come on. Let's enjoy the rest of the day."

They explored the forest, strolling along the patches of violets and ferns blossoming between the trees. The air smelled of honeysuckle with a faint trace of smoke. He asked her about working with Clara Barton, her life in Washington, what her apartment was like, and what she enjoyed doing with friends when she wasn't working.

After a while, they went back to the blanket and snacked on the berries and cheese they'd brought along. He described the layout of Johnstown the way it had been on the day of the parade, pointing to various parts of town. "Why are the tree trunks black where the edges of town meet the tree line?" she asked.

"The mills. Their smoke chokes the air, robbing the trees of the oxygen they need. I'm surprised any of them survived. The flood mowed many of them down because their roots are so weak."

She tilted her head. "If the smoky air does that to the trees, think of what it's doing to people."

"Without the mills, there's no work. Without work, there's no people, and Johnstown becomes a ghost town."

Hours passed like minutes as they took their time learning about each other through questions and stories. When evening waned, they walked back to town, her hand nestled in the crook of his arm. As they neared the Red Cross tents, the first of the streetlights flickered on. How he'd missed something as simple as gaslight. That small flame lit the road to recovery, which ignited a little more hope.

At her tent, he handed her the blanket she'd borrowed from the warehouse. "Thank you for spending the day with me, Annamae."

She yawned, then giggled. "Sorry. I'm just so relaxed."

"I'm glad."

"Next Sunday, then?" Expectation sparkled in her eyes.

"I'll be counting the days."

She smiled and squeezed his hand then entered the tent, giving him one last lingering look before disappearing completely. My, she was beautiful. Though he hated the circumstances in which they'd met, he'd never regret their meeting.

Refraining from the upbeat tune his lips wanted to whistle, he strolled in the direction of the church. Folks milled about, many heading to the two Red Cross hotels. A third was in progress, predicted to be completed within a fortnight. He turned the corner, and a face in the crowd made him stumble. He hoped his vision was playing some kind of cruel trick.

A hulking man with a black mustache and thick eyebrows glared at him from the back side of the old depot.

Knuckles.

Alarm zinged up Monty's spine. He didn't know what the man's real name was, but he'd recognize his uncle's henchman anywhere. Uncle Henry had a few thugs he rotated depending on the situation, and Knuckles was the most ruthless.

Monty turned and raced through the alleyway, weaving between shacks and debris piles, bonfires and drunkards. He had to be the reason the man was here. He dashed into the church and pressed against the wall, letting the darkness swallow his shadow. Through the window, he saw Knuckles crest the knoll in front of the building, look both ways, and then head in the opposite direction.

Monty released a breath.

Uncle Henry had finally responded to his letter, and this was his answer. This was why Monty didn't want Annamae involved. A slight thing like Annamae would vanish, and no one would ever know what became of her. His uncle always silenced those who spoke too loudly.

And Monty had yelled.

He slid against the wall until his backside was flush with the dirt floor. The long week caught up with him, and eventually he dozed, chin against his chest, until the sound of breaking glass jarred him awake. Raucous laughter followed. Someone bellowed a warning to stay off their property. Lizzie Thompson's place. The one business that hadn't slowed since the disaster.

Cracking his neck, Monty stood, trying to decide whether to wait the night here or sneak back to the hotel. There he'd have safety in numbers.

An instant later, a hard fist connected with his jaw. He didn't need to decide anything. His uncle's henchman had decided for him.

Chapter Twenty

~~~

"What is done in love is done well."

~Vincent van Gogh

MONDAY, JULY 1

Annamae finished wrapping Katie Lynn's arm and tucked the end of the bandage into the taut coil. During a three-legged race at the schoolhouse, organized for the orphans before the adoption meeting on Wednesday, Katie Lynn had tripped over a pipe sticking out of the ground. She was lucky to get away with only a sprain. The girl had smiled at Annamae through her tears, exposing a mouthful of crooked teeth, and said, "We won!"

While Katie Lynn's spirit was to be admired, her injury would be uncomfortable for the active child for the next few weeks, at least. "Promise me you'll take it easy on that arm. No activity for a week."

"Yes'm," the girl said around a peppermint stick Annamae had given her to distract from the pain. She turned to the caregiver and handed her a small bottle. "If the pain is too great over the next few days, administer half a teaspoon of laudanum morning and night."

"Thank you." The woman tucked the bottle into her pocket. She helped Katie Lynn to the ground, and the little girl waved to Annamae as they left the tent.

Annamae chuckled and rolled the leftover bandage for future use. Mary grunted as she passed by the tent, balancing a load of clean blankets stacked as high as her head. Annamae rushed to help the nurse she'd befriended from the Philadelphia Red Cross even though Clara had banished the society to another area for not heeding her instructions.

The little warrior hadn't done it out of arrogance. Clara simply hadn't tolerance for anyone—especially a man—who acted as if they could run the organization better.

"Here, Mary, let me help." Annamae snatched blankets off the top of the stack and draped them over her arm.

Mary sagged with relief. "Oh, thank you."

"Warehouse?"

"Commissary."

An energizing walk and another cup of coffee were welcome. She'd stayed up too late last night helping Clara transfer information to the record books, since Hetty had been absent for a few days with a severe headache. Fighting a yawn, she walked beside Mary through the bustle of laborers and down the street to the commissary.

As they neared the plot filled with tables, chairs, and the scent of cooking meat, she spotted two men carrying someone on a makeshift stretcher. Another construction accident? They'd doctored many injuries of that nature. Some fatal.

Closer now, she grimaced at the poor man's swollen and purple face. His busted lip oozed blood, and a nasty gash split his forehead. She'd guess the injuries stemmed from a beating more than a fall. Another saloon fight?

Her focus narrowed on the men carrying the stretcher. Was that Mr. Townsend and Mr. Parkes? She'd only worked around them a few times when training and delivering disinfectants to Monty's district, and this man bore the same telltale defect across his left eyebrow as Mr. Parkes. The men headed toward the Red Cross hospital.

Hefting her load of blankets higher, Annamae stared at the men as they passed. She noticed the old scars on the injured man's hands and spun with a gasp. "Monty?"

Mr. Parkes craned his head and fastened his gaze on her. "Miss Worthington, thank God."

The men stopped walking. "What happened to him?" she asked.

Her heart pounded in her throat.

"We're not sure." Sweat poured down Mr. Parke's face. He hefted Monty's weight higher. "I found him lying on the church floor like this. Looks to me like someone beat him half to death."

Who? Why? Monty was the sweetest man she'd ever met.

"Sorry, Mary, but I've got to go." Annamae returned her stack on top of Mary's and rushed away, not bothering to make sure Mary had the bundle secure.

She spoke to Mr. Parkes. "I'll go ahead of you and prepare a bed."

With each step, the grotesque deformity of Monty's handsome face swelled in her mind and fear pulsed at the severity of his injuries. Why would someone beat him and leave him inside the church? She recalled the newspaper articles about the Hungarians cutting the fingers and ears from corpses for jewelry and anything else of value. Had someone thought Monty possessed something expensive or that he had money hidden inside the church?

A horse and wagon trotted toward her from the east. She lifted her skirt and raced ahead, not wishing to delay a second of Monty's care. The driver jerked the reins, and horse hooves skittered on the dirt. A deep voice bellowed his displeasure, but she kept running. She had to. Preparing a bed and alerting a doctor was the only way she could help the man she loved.

She almost tripped at the revelation. Did she love him?

Yes, she did. He was wholesome and wonderful and had transformed her dull existence to vibrant living. She thought of their almost kiss the day before and how desperately she'd wanted his lips on hers.

Yes, she loved him. And she would stay by his side and do everything she could to help him heal.

Sprinting from tent to tent, she searched for Doctor Rose. Her lungs burned from exertion, and her chest rose and fell to keep up with her racing heartbeat.

"Annamae, what's wrong? Why do you look so—"

She grabbed Clara's arm. "Have you seen Doctor Rose?"

Clara's features went on alert. "To the commissary to get lunch, I believe. What's happened?"

Annamae turned to see Mr. Parkes and Mr. Townsend carrying Monty toward them. "Someone beat a man and left him to die. His injuries are likely extensive."

Clara snapped into action. "I'll fetch the doctor. Prepare a bed and do what you can until we get back."

The woman set off in the opposite direction. Annamae waved her arm high and wide to signal to the men where to bring Monty. Inside the nearest tent, she found an empty bed, added two blankets to add more cushioning, and started gathering items she knew the doctor would need.

The men entered, and she helped them transfer Monty to the bed. Mr. Parkes wiped sweat off his forehead with his sleeve, panting from carrying Monty's weight so great a distance. She looked Monty over and flinched. He had to be okay. He had to survive.

Gazing down into his bloated face, love for him welled inside her chest.

"Is he alive?" Mr. Townsend asked.

Annamae probed for a pulse. There. It fluttered against her fingertips, unsteady. She released a breath. "He is, but as bad as he looks on the outside, he could be worse on the inside."

Mr. Parkes nodded. "That's what I'm afraid of."

"Me too," she whispered, raking her gaze across Monty again. "Thank you for bringing him in. The doctor is on his way."

"I'll stop by and check on him later." Mr. Parkes wiped another round of sweat. "We'll continue our work on the church while we pray."

That was all any of them could do at this point. Even the most precise doctoring and a skilled pair of hands couldn't change what God willed. Monty's healing was completely out of her control, and she wanted to scream. She hated not having control.

Annamae gripped Mr. Parkes's forearm. "Bless you."

He patted her hand, and the men left.

She began removing Monty's boots. He didn't stir. The more comfortable they could make him, the better.

Odor assaulted her as she dropped one boot onto the ground then the other. Flesh peeked out from a hole in his sock, and his heels were visible on both where the knitting had worn thin. Pressing gently, she felt up and down his legs and around his kneecaps. Nothing seemed broken, but the doctor's examination would provide more accurate results.

She dipped a rag in water and cleaned dried blood from the hands she loved to caress her. Then she worked on his neck. Next, his beloved face. By the time she finished cleaning the skin around the wounds, the water in the basin was as red as if she'd bled him.

"Who did this to you?" she whispered.

His eyelids twitched, but otherwise, he gave no sign he'd heard.

Her heart ached, unable to fathom why anyone would want to hurt this man. Surely he had no enemies. His kind heart stretched as far as the day was long, so it was doubtful he'd made anyone angry or—

She stepped away. The basin pressed against her sloshed bloody water onto her apron. The information regarding the South Fork Fishing and Hunting Club. He told her he'd passed the information to a reliable source. Could it be that the source wasn't reliable? Had this person leaked Monty's name to the club members?

"These are not the kind of men to trifle with." Monty's voice rang through her mind like a gong.

Thoughts of her father and the brutal way he'd died raced through her mind. She'd pushed Monty to share the information. If what she feared was true—if Monty died—it would be all her fault.

————◆◆◆————

Night crickets serenaded the dark hillsides. Annamae loved that sound, but tonight it only served as the accompanying tune to her anguish. Doctor Rose had thoroughly examined Monty, and the prognosis wasn't good. A broken nose, a subconjunctival hemorrhage in his left eye, cracked ribs, and several lacerations deep enough to cause infection. His abdomen was too swollen to ascertain damage, and the possibility remained that his organs held damage as well.

If only doctors could somehow see inside the body.

She leaned forward in her chair by his bedside and rubbed her weary eyes. He hadn't stirred during the examination and likely wouldn't for several hours yet from the laudanum Doctor Rose had administered to help with pain and allow him to rest. Clara had tried to convince Annamae to sleep in her tent, but Annamae refused—much to the dismay of her mentor, who thought a nurse shouldn't give her heart away.

Well, Annamae had.

Besides, she wasn't like Clara. While she loved using her skills to help others, she didn't want to give up life and love for it. She used to look up at the night sky with her father and wish on a falling star for a husband and children someday. Silly tradition, yes, but children often exchanged nonsensical thoughts for things too difficult for their minds to grasp. She'd chosen her profession after her father died because she had no choice but to support herself. How glorious it would be to share her life with a good man who would walk beside her in every circumstance.

She thought she'd found such a man in Monty, despite their short time together. One thing was certain. In the scant number of days they'd known each other, the aching tenderness with which he'd held Joanna and the gentle care he'd shown for Ben spoke of his character. The character she wanted in a husband.

A fly buzzed around Monty's face. She stood to shoo it away and noticed the sweat beading on his forehead. She retrieved a clean basin of cool water, wet a cloth, and wiped his brow. "I'm sorry, Monty. Please don't give up. Fight to get well. . .for me."

Nothing.

She sighed deeply and dipped the rag into the bowl again. The other nurse on duty gathered some soiled sheets and left the tent. Annamae took advantage of the time alone and whispered a kiss against his lips. "Get well. For me."

His mouth twitched in the barest of smiles.

She stood erect, studying his mouth in case she'd imagined it.

"You kissed me." His voice sounded like a croaking frog.

She barked a laugh. Tears sprang to her eyes. "I did."

He grimaced then moaned. "I'm. . .telling Miss Barton."

His muscles went limp.

Annamae sniffed, her heart lighter.

While it would take several days to determine if Monty would survive, a sense of humor was a good sign.

She believed he would get through this. Prayed he would. The alternative was too horrible a thought to bear.

Chapter Twenty-One

*"The need of charity is always the result of
the evils produced by man's greed."*

~Tom L. Johnson, partner in the Johnson Steel Rail Company

TUESDAY, JULY 2

Pain ricocheted through Monty, squeezing the very air from his lungs. Darkness engulfed him. Had a horse and carriage trampled him? A stampede of buffalo? That didn't seem right. He searched through the fog of his memory for any clue. Rushing water started faintly, then grew in intensity. The flood. The wall of water rushing down the mountain. It had burst through his front door and overtaken him. Like a cyclone, he'd spun through the raging swirl that snatched debris and dead bodies along the way.

Fire.

Screaming.

Lightning struck his skull. He moaned.

Rain, cold and unrelenting, pelted his body. He was standing on his rooftop with a little girl in his arms. Why was he holding a child?

He clawed through the fog. That was right. He'd survived the flood somehow. That event was in the past, and his mind was merely spewing memories. Then what was wrong with him? Why was he trapped in the dark, every nerve in his body crying out in excruciating misery?

A cool sensation brushed his head. He moaned again. Or tried. Was he floating outside his body? He didn't think such a thing was possible, but his conscience drifted on the strangest sensation.

A soft, feminine voice wrapped around his ear. "Get well. For me."

Was he sick? Dying?

Parts of his body he didn't know he had throbbed with pain, yet he felt dead.

"I love you. Please, fight."

The vision of a beautiful woman in a nurse's uniform, dark hair spilling out of her cap, large brown eyes and full pink lips promising him a lifetime of love and passion filled his memory. Annamae. He didn't know what he was supposed to fight against, but for her, he would fight against anything.

Another flash of lightning ripped through his brain.

A man's scarred face snarled at him before a huge fist slammed into his nose. *Knuckles.* One fist multiplied to two and pummeled every square inch of Monty's flesh. *"That was from your uncle. For being stupid enough to threaten him."*

The hard toe of Knuckles' boot slammed into Monty's ribs.

"That was from me."

Somehow the stench of liquor and rotten teeth broke through the barricade of blood pouring from Monty's nose. *"Any more lessons you need teachin', I'll be teachin' on that pretty little nurse of yours."*

Knuckles relayed his plans for Annamae using vulgar words and anatomical terms. Bile rose in Monty's throat. He had to warn her away. Had to keep Annamae safe.

His tongue was thick and heavy as a tree trunk. His eyelids refused to open.

"Shh. You're okay, Monty. I'm here. I won't leave your side."

She had to leave his side. She had to get far away from here.

He wriggled and groaned, forcing his tongue to work. Garbled babble sounded in his ears.

Cool liquid trickled into his mouth, cutting him off. He swallowed, relishing the trail it worked down his parched throat.

A soft, velvety surface rubbed the water that had spilled out the sides of his mouth. "Everything's going to be all right. I'm here. I won't leave you."

Run, Annamae, run.

It was his last thought before he slipped into oblivion.

WEDNESDAY, JULY 3

Annamae's head dipped forward, jerking her awake. She blinked to clear her blurry vision. Her neck ached from sleeping upright, and she'd give almost anything to curl up somewhere and sleep to her heart's content. She forced her eyelids to stay open. The orange tabby slept, curled against Monty's side. His arm had slipped off the table, and his hand dangled toward the ground. The lack of circulation had caused his fingers to turn blue.

The unnatural hue was enough to pull her awake. She stood, scooped the cat into her arms, placed it in the chair she'd vacated, and tucked Monty's arm against his side. Holding his hand with hers, she squeezed a healthy color into it then checked his pulse. Thready but present. She pushed her hand into the small of her back and stretched.

"How's our patient this morning?" Doctor Rose asked from behind her.

She startled and yanked her fingers away from Monty's. "His sleep was fitful most of the night. He finally fell into a peaceful rest in the wee hours."

Annamae searched Doctor Rose's face for signs of displeasure. If the doctor had noticed her indiscretion, he hid it well.

He shooed the cat from the tent then examined Monty for several minutes, making notations on a paper they'd started last night to keep track of the ailments his body suffered. "Spoon as much broth into him as he'll allow. Keep the wounds dressed, and watch for any sign of infection. Continue administering laudanum every six hours for the next couple of days.

"I'll be back to check on him this evening. I volunteered to examine the orphans this morning before the adoption meeting at the Methodist church. Doctor Hubbell will be around if you need anything."

She'd forgotten the adoption meeting was today.

Joanna.

Her gaze trailed over Monty. He wouldn't be there to offer words of comfort to Joanna. To ask all the right questions to the couple who showed an interest in welcoming her into their family. To pray over her.

It didn't matter that exhaustion pressed on Annamae like a boulder tumbling downhill. Monty would want someone to go in his stead if he could not go himself. Annamae would go for him. That way, when he awakened, she could ease his worry by filling in the details he'd missed.

She'd been that orphaned girl once. No one should have to walk that path alone.

The Methodist church shadowing Annamae at the corner of Locust and Franklin Streets was a miracle in itself. The wave that tumbled from South Fork into Johnstown had split at the chapel, half spilling down Market and Vine Streets toward the cemetery and the other half destroying Kernville. Reverend Beale claimed it was like the parting of the Red Sea and the church was the dry ground on which survivors could walk.

At first, the sanctuary had been a place of refuge for the homeless. Then, a temporary morgue. Committee meetings were held inside its doors, volunteer groups founded, worship services held, and now it was a haven for orphaned children to connect with families.

Annamae didn't know what to say to Joanna to ease her fear, especially since they'd never met. She only knew she had to be Monty's eyes and ears and hands.

Men and women filled the pews with hopeful expressions and nervous energy. Spectators filled the side aisles against the walls. The room was stifling and held a strange mix of unwashed bodies and perfume. Annamae occupied a space near the back and searched the faces of the children lined at the front.

Toddlers to teenagers stood awkwardly before their audience, most looking everywhere but at the crowd. Siblings clung to one another, terrified of being ripped apart. Some would probably never see each other again.

Reverend Beale quieted the murmuring voices and introduced the children down the line, telling each one's background, age, likes, and interests. Doctor Rose sat on the front pew, answering any medical questions asked.

An hour later, the couples were encouraged to approach the children they were interested in. Any who felt a specific child or set of siblings met their needs could make arrangements with Reverend Beale to sign the papers and take them home.

Farmers chose the teenage boys first. Promised room and board and three square meals a day for their help in the fields. The older girls went next, likely so they could help care for younger children already in the home. The youngest children went last.

They separated two sets of siblings. Their cries echoed off the walls and crashed into Annamae with enough force to produce tears. At the last, one boy and two girls stood alone and without new homes. One of those girls was Joanna, who'd curled in on herself and wouldn't speak to anyone.

Annamae approached the girl. At eleven, Joanna looked much younger, with a braid trailing over each shoulder and her arms wrapped around herself. Annamae knelt in front of her.

"Hello, Joanna. My name is Annamae Worthington. I'm a friend of Pastor Monty Childs."

The girl's head snapped up, and she stared at Annamae.

"Pastor Childs wanted to be here with you today, but he suffered an injury and is recouping in the Red Cross hospital. I came in his place."

Joanna's eyes rounded, and tears rushed to the edges. Annamae quickly realized what had caused the alarm and worked to rectify her mistake. "He'll be fine. He's a strong man. I've been taking excellent care of him. He's resting right now."

Beside them, a man from the Blessed Hope Orphanage in Philadelphia made arrangements with the reverend to take the unwanted children with him.

Unwanted.

No child should be unwanted.

Annamae swallowed. If only she had a husband and the means to adopt them all herself.

Something pressed against her arm. Joanna had raised a finger and was tracing the Red Cross symbol on her brassard. Fat tears dripped down her freckled cheeks. "My momma. . ."

The words scraped against Joanna's throat.

"What about your momma, sweetheart?"

Joanna sniffed. "She was good at taking care of people. She told me she dreamed of being a Red Cross nurse."

Annamae closed her eyes and let her own tears fall. She wrapped the girl in a hug. Joanna's braid tickled the side of Annamae's face. "You're going to be okay. Be strong. As soon as Pastor Childs is well enough, he'll write you a letter."

Joanna sobbed on her shoulder until the man from the orphanage commanded the children to accompany him to the train station. Before Joanna walked away, Annamae ripped off the brassard and thrust it into her small hands. "Never take your eyes off the cross. No matter what happens in your life, you'll always find healing at the cross."

The girl clutched it in her fingers, confusion pulling at her features as she went out the door.

Annamae's heart had been ripped from her chest, beaten, and stuffed back in. As soon as Monty was well, they'd both write to the sweet girl. In the meantime, Annamae would work on living the truth of what she'd told Joanna.

SATURDAY, JULY 6

Riddled with fever, Monty had drifted in and out of consciousness for the last four days. When he did awaken, he mumbled words about the dam and money and her life being in danger. His frantic pleas cracked Annamae's heart wide open. From the pieces she could fit together, whoever had done this to him had done it because of the information he shared regarding the dam's spillway. The information she'd pressed him to relay.

She never should have involved Monty. That was clear now. They'd become such fast friends, and after all the broken lives she'd witnessed and all the injuries she'd bound, this town's fight had become hers too. She knew what it was like to suffer from the selfish natures of the Pittsburgh elite. It didn't matter that they'd already amassed fortunes to rival the kings of the ancient world. They'd lie, cheat, and steal from a poor man for a few more pennies. It didn't matter that they owned homes as large as a city block. They must take over another man's land as well, even if their comfort meant putting lives at stake.

And they would get away with it all because there was no one to stop them.

What the folks in this town had suffered went beyond the worst of her grieving. Death and destruction on this massive a scale demanded accountability. If God withheld His swift hand of judgment, then the judgment of the courts must prevail.

She lifted a rag from the basin of water, letting the cool drips saturate Monty's scalp the way his words from their picnic tried to saturate her heart. *"We mustn't forget that the Lord died for the rich and the privileged too."*

That might be, but it didn't mean they should escape the consequences of their actions. Whoever did this to Monty would answer to her.

She pressed the rag against his cheek. He needed a good scrubbing, and the July heat made that fact more apparent. His skin beaded with sweat, and the nightshirt the doctor and two male nurses wrestled him into days ago was damp and stained. She was vigilant to spoon broth and cool water into his mouth hourly, but he never allowed her to administer as much as she'd like.

She'd prayed, she'd nursed, and she'd spoken soft words of encouragement, but still he lay there, battling God only knew what injuries on the inside. All because of her.

He had to get better. Had to. She couldn't lose another man that meant so much to her.

"Fight, Monty. Fight." She clasped his hand.

He didn't stir.

If it wasn't for his pulse twitching against her thumb, she'd think him dead. The thought of never again seeing his haughty smirk when he teased her or how his blue eyes darkened at her nearness, never having the privilege of running her fingers through his thick dark hair in times of health, made tears blur her vision.

She hadn't allowed herself to get close to anyone since her father died. Life was short, and the sorrow that swallowed those left behind was almost too much to bear. But from nearly the first moment she'd spotted Monty meandering through the tents, she'd felt a connection that made her lay her fears aside and open her heart to him. He'd taught her things about servanthood and love she'd thought she'd already mastered.

Now, she would put those lessons into practice. The Bible said, "Greater love hath no man than this, that a man lay down his life for his friends." Well, Monty meant more to her than a mere friend, and she was certain he reciprocated those feelings.

She would be the sacrifice and ensure whoever was responsible for this paid. For Monty, for the people of Johnstown, and for her father. And she knew just where to go to make sure the information landed in the right place.

The men of the South Fork Fishing and Hunting Club might evade a judge and jury or two, but they could not evade the citizens of the United States of America.

Annamae finished tracing the wet rag over Monty's neck and clavicles then dropped the rag into the basin. She dried her hands on her apron as she stalked through the tent with the fiery purpose of a lioness.

Like Clara Barton of old, Annamae was ready for war.

Footfalls pounded the dirt behind her, growing louder at their approach. "Annamae."

Someone touched her arm, and she turned. Her fire sizzled out. "Matthew."

His smile was tender, his gaze heated like that of a man reuniting with his lover. "You used my given name."

Her stomach soured.

She stood dumbfounded, unable to form words after her charge to meet the foe.

Matthew's gaze traced every nuance of her face. "My, you're a sight for sore eyes." He moved closer and whispered, "I've missed you."

She stared up at him, mouth gaping, unable to return the sentiment.

Chapter Twenty-Two

⁓

"If they should be held liable in civil suits for damages it is probable
that many, if not all of them, will be financially ruined."
~New York Sun, referring to the South Fork
Fishing and Hunting Club members

SUNDAY, JULY 7

Every inch of Monty's body hurt. His face felt lumpy and distorted, like
creek bubbles building against a rock. He could eat a bear but suspected
food wouldn't stay in his stomach. He peeled one eye open, the one that
wasn't swollen shut, and took in his surroundings.

Beds were lined up in rows, some occupied, some empty. Nurses flitted about the space. He was in a Red Cross tent. Where was Annamae?

The sun beat down on the canopy, making the air thick with heat.
Sweat and grime coated his skin, and his clothes stuck to him. What he
wouldn't give for a swim in a cool stream. What had happened to him?

His attempt to sit up sent pain slicing through his ribs, stealing the
air from his lungs. He hadn't hurt this badly since the time a horse threw
his cocky hide during equestrian lessons. Had he learned this instruction

the hard way too?

Staring at the peak of the tent, he searched the memory in his pounding head for the cause of his predicament. He remembered spending a glorious day with Annamae and walking her back to her tent. The sun was setting. He looked forward to retiring to his room. Then—

His uncle's henchman.

Panic seized Monty. He thought he'd covered his trail to the church, but. . .

Every punch, every swift kick to his vital organs had caused suffering, but when Knuckles had threatened to lay his hands on Annamae, Monty's heart had torn in half, and he'd pushed through the pain to fight back even harder. He would not allow the tentacles of his uncle's evil to harm her. No matter what he had to do to prevent it.

Monty needed to tell her who he was. Even if it meant losing her.

He'd come to Johnstown with little money and plain clothes to blend in with the very congregation he'd hoped to build. So he could assimilate with the people most like the man at his core. To prove he wasn't that arrogant apprentice to Henry Clay Frick anymore.

If he was honest with himself, he didn't quite fit in either world.

"You're awake." Annamae's smiling face hovered over him. Her fingers entwined with his for a moment before she released them.

A twinge of misery shot through his hip, and he flinched. "I think I'd rather be asleep."

At least then the pain was tolerable.

She placed her hand on his forehead. Relief lifted her lips. "Your fever has finally broken. You've been asleep for four days."

Her fingers brushed back the hair sticking to his forehead in the gentle, loving way of a mother to a child. Or a wife to her husband. Her eyes glittered with too many emotions to decipher. Not that he had the energy to do so anyway. One thing he was sure of. He'd like for her to go on touching him like this for the rest of his life.

He wanted to pull Annamae into his arms and keep her there until the threat passed. "There's something I need to tell you."

Her face grew somber. "If you're going to confess how you ended up here, I already know."

"Have you run into any trouble?" He tried to sit again.

Gentle pressure pushed him down, inciting more pain. "No. You woke just enough during the worst fits of your fever to mumble about the spillway and dangerous men come to harm me. And you kept talking about your knuckles."

He'd laugh at the last sentence if the agony of the action wouldn't kill him.

"I'm sorry I involved you in my crusade," she said. "For pushing you to be as passionate about it as I. Your condition is my fault, and I'm very sorry."

He frowned, which made his eye hurt. Despite the consequences, he needed to tell her the full truth. "It wasn't your fault. It was mine. I haven't told you that—"

"The patient's awake." A man Monty didn't recognize approached the bed. Professionalism held the man stiff. The doctor, Monty presumed. He would not have this conversation with anyone but Annamae. It would have to wait.

"How do you feel?" the doctor asked.

"I survived." Monty took a careful breath. "What's the damage?"

The doctor's close-clipped mustache, a blend of red and brown, twitched as he looked at Annamae. Had his hand settled on Annamae's back, or was Monty hallucinating?

Her lips flattened, and she slid sideways. He wasn't hallucinating.

If Monty could move without help, he'd pummel the man for his bold gesture and for making her uncomfortable. Her gaze softened on Monty. "You have three cracked ribs, a burst blood vessel in your eye, a broken nose, and numerous cuts and bruises," she said. "We feared the worst regarding internal injuries, but now that your fever has passed and there's no sign of complications, we believe you'll make a full—though painful—recovery."

The doctor clung to her every word, looking as proud as a mother hen with her chicks. Who was this guy? In all the time Monty had spent at the Red Cross tents and around town helping train folks to use the disinfectants, he didn't recall seeing this doctor before.

"How long do I have to stay in this bed?" Monty asked Annamae, since the doctor seemed to prefer that she speak for him.

"It would be best to get you up and moving as soon as possible. Though you'll want to ease into your routine. Start with sitting up today. Eat and drink what you can manage. Each day you can add a little more activity and food if you promise to rest plenty in between. Rest and hydration is the fastest course to healing."

"Will you help me sit up?"

Annamae placed one hand beneath his sweaty back and one beneath his armpit. The doctor did the same on his other side, and they pulled him to a sitting position. Teeth clenched, Monty fought a groan.

They let him catch his breath before releasing him. His surroundings spun like a top.

"If the pain gets too bad, I can administer laudanum." Annamae lifted his eyelids to check his pupils. "Though I'd prefer to wait until it's absolutely necessary. You've had a fair amount the last few days."

Monty nodded. It was about the only thing he could do on his own.

"Do you have any recollection of what happened?" the doctor asked.

Annamae answered for Monty. "Still not clear."

Strange. Her statement wasn't fully true, and it seemed as if she didn't want him and the doctor speaking to each other.

She turned to the man. "How about we get some broth inside him before he falls asleep again? Would you mind getting some?"

"Uh, sure." The man searched her face a little too long before stalking away.

Annamae sagged with relief.

"Who's he?" Monty cleared his throat. His head pounded like a war drum.

"Doctor Martin." She dipped a rag into a basin of cool water, squeezed it out, and bathed his face and neck.

"Doctor Martin is smitten with you. Is he with the Philadelphia Red Cross? I haven't seen him here before."

She made dipping the rag in the basin and wringing it out an art, as if every movement would make a difference in his healing. "Mr. Parkes and Mr. Townsend have checked on you daily. Ernie stopped by once. Poor thing shook like a sapling in a windstorm. You were sleeping, but he told me to tell you he was staying strong for you, so you needed to stay strong for him."

Something stirred in Monty's chest. He hoped Ernie meant he was staying away from the bottle.

Annamae ran the cool rag over his dirty arms. He closed his eyes, a thousand thoughts racing through his mind. "Thank you for taking care of me," he whispered.

"I wouldn't be anywhere else for all the money in the world," she whispered back.

He cracked his eyelids open. The worry lines on her face eased, and she gave him a coy smile. This bond they had created, this attraction—was it as strong for her as it was for him? Maybe almost losing him had forced her to examine her feelings.

"I return bearing gifts." Doctor Martin broke the spell. He held a cup of broth. Jim and Robert followed on his heels.

"How are you, Pastor?" Jim planted his hands on his waist the way he always did when wanting to get a rise out of Monty. "You're certainly looking better than you were yesterday."

"Can't keep a good man down," Robert said.

A little girl's voice from outside the tent brought Joanna to the forefront of Monty's memory. "Oh, no."

He tried to wiggle off the table, but his injuries wouldn't allow it.

"Where do you think you're going?" Annamae scolded.

A draft rushed up Monty's leg, and he realized he wore a nightshirt. What in the world? He yanked it over his knee, but the wadded fabric underneath him wouldn't allow it to fully cover his calf. "Joanna. The adoption."

Annamae's hand lowered to his shoulder. "The meeting was four days ago. I went for you." Intense eyes explored his. "Joanna didn't find a home. She's at the Blessed Hope Orphanage in Philadelphia. I spoke to her before she left."

"What did she say?"

"She told me about her mother. How she'd dreamed of being a Red

Cross nurse. I sent her away with my brassard in memory of her mother and gave her the same advice I thought you might give."

Monty reached his arm across his chest to grip her hand on his shoulder. "Thank you, Annamae."

Doctor Martin raised an eyebrow. "It's nice to see that Annamae is as keen with her skills here as she is in Washington."

He handed Monty the cup of broth. Annamae released Monty and put space between them.

Monty sipped the warm beef broth. It tasted better than any meal he'd ever had.

"I shouldn't be surprised though. She's quite a woman." Doctor Martin inched closer to Annamae.

Monty didn't like it.

"You're from D.C. too? I'm surprised the city is giving up all their medical staff for the Red Cross." Monty swallowed another sip.

"Oh, I'm not with the Red Cross," Doctor Martin said. "We work together at the Jericho Square Hospital. I came to make sure Annamae was safe and settled. She had me worried when she didn't respond to my telegrams."

The broth churned in Monty's gut. Why would her superior at the hospital send her telegrams and travel all the way here to inquire about her safety unless. . .

Annamae clenched her lip between her teeth and stared at the ground, her arms crossed over her middle.

Ah.

His heart hurt worse than the rest of him. Here he'd thought. . . It didn't matter what he'd thought. Neither of them had declared any intentions. It made sense that she had a life before arriving in Johnstown with the Red Cross. That she'd made an attachment back home. She was beautiful in every way, and any man who didn't see that was an idiot.

Monty couldn't fault this man for appreciating her the same way he did. He swirled the cup of broth, his appetite gone. "How goes it at the church?"

Jim and Robert glanced at each other. "What is it?" Monty asked.

"A miracle." Robert smiled. "Someone has anonymously donated money and supplies specifically to rebuild our church and your home."

"Both?" Monty's head spun.

"And grander than anything you can imagine," Jim said. "Fifteen thousand dollars total."

Annamae gasped.

Good thing Monty wasn't drinking broth at the moment, or he might have choked. "Did I hear you right?"

"The men of the church decided after all you'd been through with saving little Gertrude Quinn's life and helping us like you have, caring for Ben and Joanna, and now suffering physically, it was time we give to you. After we put you in Miss Worthington's care, we rounded up a large crew and got started on your new house."

No one owed him a thing. He'd served them gratefully.

Tears stung his eyes. That was the beauty of God's grace, wasn't it? Gifts given in undeserving circumstances.

Monty swallowed, and he turned his attention to drinking the rest of the broth. He was going to need his strength to work beside these fine men. To repair the broken church, the broken congregation that had become more family than the one he'd been born into. To repair the broken places inside his heart where he'd dared to imagine a future with Annamae.

Clenching his back molars, he forced his body to move and rose from the edge of the bed onto shaky legs. "If one of you gentlemen will fetch my boots, I'd like to seek solace in our church. If my calculations are correct, today is the Sabbath."

Doctor Martin accepted the cup Monty held out to him. "That's not wise this soon."

Annamae touched his arm then recoiled in embarrassment. "Yes, Monty, I think you should stay under my care for a few more days."

Monty didn't miss Doctor Martin's questioning look. There was something going on between Annamae and this man, and Monty wasn't going to step in the middle.

"Thank you for all you've done, Miss Worthington. You've been a true friend in my time of need." Monty lifted one leg to put on his boot, and torment radiated through his entire lower abdomen. Jim and Robert steadied him while he slipped his foot inside the shoe. He repeated the action on the other side. When he finished, sweat covered his entire body, and he was ready to go back to bed and sleep another four days.

Monty took a tentative step and knew it was going to be a long, excruciating walk to the church. In a nightshirt at that. At least now it fell past the top of his boots.

"Monty, please," Annamae said.

Turning his head but not daring to turn his torso for fear that his broken ribs would puncture his lungs, he gave her a resolute glance. "It's time for me to go."

Her throat worked, and she seemed to shrink beside him. Doctor Martin's gaze bounced from Monty to Annamae before his hand, once again, cradled the small of her back.

Monty looked at the long distance ahead of him to the church. Yes, it was time to go.

Chapter Twenty-Three

"If they were unable or failed to cope with forces of nature which they called into action, the responsibility is theirs, and as they have sown so must they reap, even if the harvest is the whirlwind."

~*Boston Post*, regarding the club members' responsibility for the flood

TUESDAY, JULY 9

The orange glow of morning filtered through the stained-glass windows of the church, bringing the peace of God's presence over the sanctuary and to Monty's soul. Alone, except for Ernie sleeping on a pew across the room, Monty closed his eyes and let his prayer flow through his throbbing mortal body and upward to the Throne. This was what he needed more than a home, more than Annamae, more than justice for what this town had suffered.

Amid the disaster and horrible aftermath, he'd lost sight of his purpose. Of his responsibility to his fellow man. Sure, he'd helped save Gertrude Quinn, tried his best to save Ben, and helped in the typhoid tents, among other things. But he'd also allowed his faith to falter, allowed a pretty face and a desperate need for companionship to distract him from truly meeting with God. He'd even allowed his complicated feelings for his uncle to couple with Annamae's need for revenge and feed his old cocky attitude.

Thankfully, the Lord listened to the pleas of His children, especially their pleas for forgiveness.

Ernie stirred awake, and Monty opened his eyes. The thin blanket draped over the emaciated man slipped to the floor. Ernie sat up and rubbed his eyes. "Pastor? What ya doin' here? You should be restin'."

"I am." Monty tapped his heart.

Pale eyes surrounded by drooping skin filled with understanding. Ernie had asked permission yesterday to sleep inside the building. He was attempting to sober up and remain that way, and he felt that the solace of the church would make it harder for him to wander out and fulfill his lust for liquor. A few men in the congregation working to rebuild the church weren't keen on the idea, but Monty wasn't about to refuse the request. Sometimes rules and formalities were just the excuse someone needed to continue their stray, and Ernie had strayed long enough.

Bracing his withered hand on the back of the pew, Ernie stood on unsteady legs, stepped over the blanket heaped on the ground, and walked to Monty's pew. "The pull is strong this morning."

Monty patted the spot beside him. Ernie dropped next to him, the stench of unwashed clothing and rancid body odor hitting Monty hard. Thankfully, Robert and Jim had offered to help Monty into the men's bathing house before bed last night, setting a chair inside the small private area beside the barrel of fresh water and the cake of soap. It had taken Monty three times longer to wash than usual, but despite the pain and the cold water, he'd felt like a new man.

"Stay strong, Ernie. Satan wants nothing more than to see you give in to that pull. Don't give him the satisfaction. He's all that's waiting for you at the bottom of that bottle."

"I—" Ernie clamped his hands together to keep them from quavering. "I suppose coffee will do fine this morning."

Monty patted the man's shoulder, wincing at the pain that shot through his ribs.

Ernie stood and shuffled toward the doors.

"Bring me some back?"

Monty knew Ernie was trembling so much that there wouldn't be a lot of coffee left in the mug when he returned, but the task would keep him accountable to return shortly and not stray into one of the taverns reopening for business.

Ernie nodded. Seconds passed, but he didn't loosen his grip on the door handle. "I'm afraid, Pastor."

Monty tilted his head, letting the sunlight from the window bathe his bruised face. "So am I. But we must remember that 'God hath not given us the spirit of fear; but of power, and of love, and of a sound mind.'"

The door opened, and Ernie blinked into the sunlight. "I'll be right back."

In the quiet moments that followed, Monty dozed, but woke when the crew arrived to work in the church. Everett McDonough, whom Monty hadn't seen since the day of the parade, stumbled to a halt. "Well, look who's ready to supervise our sorry hides."

Monty chuckled. "Someone must. How are you faring, Everett?"

"Faring okay. I took Sally and Edward to stay with my folks in Ohio for a spell. I came back to see what more damage I could do."

"Thank you for helping."

Soon, James Quinn entered the building and thanked Monty for the thousandth time for helping Max save Gertrude.

"It was my pleasure." The same response Monty always gave. "How is the family?"

Mr. Quinn scratched his cheek. "Doing well. Still in Kansas with Rosina's sister. Gertrude's ready to come back and giving the Mrs. fits."

Monty smiled. "Praise God, she's still around to cause mischief."

"Amen to that."

The church came alive with the sound of hammers and the slap of boards coming together. Some worked on the new floor, while others spread plaster on the walls that held fresh lumber. A few of the men sanded the new pulpit and pews on the front lawn. Monty watched each group for a few minutes simply to feel as if he was doing something productive.

A good half-hour passed before Ernie returned with a mug partially full of coffee. Brown drips coated one side and wet Monty's fingers as he gripped the cup. The liquid was tepid and the flavor bitter, but Monty thanked Ernie and sipped it as if it were the best he'd ever tasted.

An ache started at the base of his neck and gradually made its way to his crown. He motioned Jim over. "I'm running out of steam. Let the guys know I'm gonna head to my room, but I'll be back after a nap."

"Can I help you get there?" Jim asked.

"It's not far. I'll be fine."

The fierce July heat made Monty wish for rain.

Crazy.

As he started off the church property, a feminine voice called his name. *Annamae.*

Tempted to keep walking as if he hadn't heard, he instead stopped and smiled cordially. "Good morning, Miss Worthington."

She finished her jog toward him, winded. "I went by the hotel to check on you, but they said you were here. You should be in bed, resting."

"I was off to do just that." He took two normal strides forward and regretted it as pain pulsed through his abdomen and ribcage.

"Please, wait." Desperation leeched from her voice.

Monty hung his head and inhaled a breath for patience. "What is it, Miss Worthington?"

"Would you stop calling me that?" She sidled close to his side. "I should've told you about Matthew—Doctor Martin. I apologize, I—"

"You don't owe me an explanation." Monty noticed Robert glimpsing them from the corner of the church, trying to act as if he wasn't being nosy but failing.

"Oh. I see." She looked down at her hands and blinked.

He hadn't meant to wound her, but she'd done her share of the injuring. "He seems like a good man, Annamae. And fully in love with you."

That lit a spark in her soulful eyes. "What I'm trying to tell you is that Matthew and I don't have an understanding. We never have. We work together at the hospital. He's a wonderful friend and benefactor, and I know he wants more, but I don't, which is why I didn't respond right away to his telegrams."

The events of the past week, the state of his beaten body, and the heat of the day made this conversation too much at the moment. "I need to sleep."

Obviously, his words elicited a different reaction than what she'd hoped for, and she backed away. "Of—of course. I just wanted to make sure you understood. Do you need help getting to the hotel?"

"I'll be fine." He needed her to leave in case he collapsed. If there was one thing he didn't want to be at this moment, it was weak.

With one last disappointed look of longing, she started toward the Red Cross tents. She didn't love Doctor Martin. That buoyed his heart. Was she telling Monty because she wanted more with him?

His head pounded, and his thoughts were unclear. He needed rest.

Monty concentrated on taking one uncomfortable step at a time, the orange tabby keeping stride beside him. He'd named the cat Job for his unwavering patience. Job came and went as he pleased, yet he always made his way back.

Robert strode beside him as Monty crossed the street.

After Robert's third sidelong glance, Monty said, "I think that hurt worse than my injuries."

"Women are skilled like that." Robert pulled a set of keys from his pocket. A small, intricate pendant dangled from the ring. A small pearl nestled in the middle.

"Rosie's?" Monty pressed his palm against his ribs. The pressure hurt, but his jarring steps made it hurt worse.

"Yep. We almost didn't get married."

Monty raised a brow.

"I've never told you that story? Well, our papas didn't like each other. Some old feud about a fence line and a poker game. But Rosie and I didn't care about all that. Or at least, I thought. One day while we lazed by the river, I spouted some insult about her daddy, and she nearly took my head off. I finally won her over again, but it wasn't easy. When our parents found out we planned to wed, her daddy spouted an insult at me, and she nearly took his head off."

Robert laughed. "Guess the insults were okay, as long as she was the one giving 'em."

Monty stopped for a breath. Job rushed ahead, batting at a bug taking flight. "Then you moved here and lived happily ever after."

As soon as the phrase left Monty's mouth, he wanted to black his other eye. "I'm sorry, I didn't mean…"

"It's alright. I know what you meant." They continued to the hotel. "Though our time together didn't even reach ten years, it was the sweetest of my life. Not always happy, mind you, but sweet."

Robert went quiet.

"I sense you wanting to say more." Monty told himself it was only twenty additional feet to the hotel entrance and he could do this.

"You're always the one giving advice. It might not be fitting for me to advise you."

He added more pressure to his ribs. "With age comes wisdom. I'm not too proud to listen to my elders."

Robert huffed. "Thirty hardly makes me your elder."

Monty winked. "Say your piece. I'll chew on it during my nap."

"Don't let a misunderstanding keep you from pursuing Miss Worthington, if she's who you want."

Oh, he wanted her all right.

"I'm just saying, until she's married to another man, there's still hope. Don't let the sun go down upon your wrath, and all that."

Annamae had made it clear she didn't love Doctor Martin.

"Are you advising me to pursue Annamae?" Monty stopped when he reached the hotel door, relieved his bed was feet away.

"I guess I am. Life is fleeting, as we've all learned. We mustn't live the days granted to us with regrets."

Robert took a step then swiveled back around. "Miss Worthington has us all convinced she's your match. Has cared for each of us the way a pastor's wife would. She's stolen a little piece of all our hearts."

Monty had noticed the respect and appreciation his congregation had for her nurturing.

"What do you suggest I do?" Monty asked.

"Tell her how you feel. That may be all she's waiting for to send this doctor on the next train east."

Annamae had let him know she and the doctor had no formal understanding. Was that her way of telling Monty she was free for him to declare his intentions? How different the nature of courtship was here compared to the society balls and marriages arranged for financial benefit he'd grown up witnessing.

"Thank you, Robert."

"Promise me that after you chew, you'll swallow."

Monty smiled, called for Job, and walked the short distance to his room. The beds were mostly empty, as the majority of the town was working. He pressed his toes into the heels of his boots to remove them without bending. Then he settled on top of his made bed, sleep claiming him before his head hit the pillow.

Chapter Twenty-Four

"It was through their indifference that this great disaster was precipitated upon the residents of the peaceful valley. Remorse, if nothing else, should lead them to alleviate to the fullest extent of their wealth the suffering they have caused."

~New York Daily Graphic

THURSDAY, JULY 11

Two days had passed with no word from Monty. Annamae wanted to go to him, to see how his injuries were healing and talk candidly about anything and everything the way they'd always done. She wanted to be near him. To bask in his wisdom and learn all the things that made him the man he was. She'd thought they'd crossed the threshold from friendship to something more the day he'd taken her on that picnic outside Kernville, on the forested hillside.

Apparently, she'd been wrong.

Or the danger she'd gotten him into had changed his mind about getting involved with her. She couldn't blame him. She'd been battling the Carnegie corporation on her own for years now. Why would anyone else want to join her crusade? The survivors of Johnstown certainly had good reason to, but that didn't mean her fight was theirs.

Monty was the first person since her father died she felt she could trust with every part of herself. That trust had encouraged her to open her heart and her life. He'd seemed intent on protecting her, and it was nice to have someone looking after her well-being for once. Matthew's efforts left her suffocating, while Monty's made her feel cherished.

But fighting for justice was her cross to bear.

Alone.

She hated the men at the Edgar Thomson Steel Works for taking her father from her. She was furious that they put the lives of their workers in jeopardy every day so each spare coin made in profit could further fatten their coffers. Livid at their negligence to repair the dam because the time they spent in leisure meant more to them than the thousands of people who lived below. Enraged that they valued their empires so much they would send a thug to beat the life out of a humble pastor.

The culprits needed to pay for all they'd done, and she was going to see that they did.

She removed her nurse's apron and folded it into a neat square on her bed. She used the small mirror on the only bureau in the tent to smooth the stray hairs in the braided coil at the back of her head. The gray shirtwaist, though worn, was presentable, and she figured Mr. Colt from the newspaper office wouldn't care what she wore as long as she shared her gossip.

After checking to be sure none of the other nurses were dressing, she pushed the tent flap to the side and stepped into the afternoon sun. She hadn't made it twenty feet when Matthew stopped her. "There you are. Are you hungry? I thought we could eat lunch at the commissary and then tour the new opera house. They've yet to place all the seats and curtains, but they've finished the basic construction. It boasts to be nicer than the original."

Shame puddled at her feet. Matthew was trying hard to court her, and her apprehension before she left Washington had kept him tethered by a string of hope. Now that she was certain they could never have a future together, she needed to cut the string.

Matthew had known the companionship and intimacy of marriage, and he wanted that again. He wanted—no, deserved—a woman who was certain of her affection for him and who would enter a marriage with joy.

No matter how Monty felt about her, or she him, Annamae knew without a doubt that she wasn't the woman for Matthew. "Let's start with lunch."

After she told him the truth, touring the opera house would most definitely be cut from his plans.

Her palms beaded with sweat as they walked along, their steps unequal. They didn't sync in any way. Surely he saw it too.

"I can tell you have something on your mind, and it's far from lunch." He gave her a sad smile. "You're going to tell me we have no future together and send me home, aren't you?"

Annamae's mouth dropped open, and she faced him, shadowing her eyes from the sun with her hand.

Matthew gazed at the distant mountains. "Or have I misread you? If I have, I'll be relieved."

How she hated to be the killer of the hope lighting his eyes. "You're not mistaken."

Her words were barely above a whisper.

He let out a breath. "I thought so. I've suspected it for a while now but thought for sure I could win you over. After seeing the mournful longing in your face the day that pastor walked out of the infirmary, I knew."

"Knew what?" She swallowed.

"That he had completely captured your heart."

Emotions swirled inside her, making her eyes water. Her feelings for Monty weren't just something she'd secreted in her heart. They were real and strong enough that others saw them too.

"I'm sorry, Matthew." She gripped the folds of her skirt like a vise.

He nodded, looking at the ground. "Me too."

As if seeing the world differently now, he lifted his head and gazed at his surroundings. "Sometimes it takes tragedy to open our eyes to what the Almighty has for us. Getting through the tragedy and onto the other side is the hard part."

"Matthew, I—"

"Don't." He slipped his hands into his pockets, watching her. "Truth is, I can't fault you, Annamae. From the first moment I met you, I saw the screen of aloofness you live behind. Never letting anyone get too close. Never letting others know the Annamae that lives beneath the surface. I'd hoped that one day I would get the privilege of tearing that screen away, of knowing what had caused that solitary part of you to dominate.

"The way you looked at the pastor that day, the tender way you touched him and spoke to him. . . It was the first time in all the years I've known you that the screen was gone." He sighed. "It was beautiful."

A tear snaked down her cheek. Her rejection cut him deeply, and she hated herself for it.

"If you'd still like to join me for lunch, I'd be honored to eat with my friend," he said. "Though I admit my appetite has waned considerably."

"I'm not much hungry anymore either." Her voice wavered.

Matthew brushed her damp cheek with his thumb. "We'll both be all right. I'll go back to the hospital, and you'll finish your work here with the Red Cross. Then we'll see what life brings us next."

"You're a good man. I'm not sure I deserved you anyway."

"Let's hope this pastor fellow endeavors to deserve *you*."

Matthew dropped his hand, gave her one last curl of his mouth, and walked away. She watched as he grew smaller in the distance then blended into the crowd altogether.

Annamae inhaled, her breath catching a time or two as she worked to steady her emotions. She certainly hadn't expected this confrontation when she'd awakened this morning. As heavy as her rejection made her steps, peace enveloped her heart. Whether or not Monty spoke to her again, she knew she'd done the right thing in letting Matthew go. There was a better-suited woman out there for him, and now he was free to pursue her.

Scrubbing the last salty tears from her cheeks, she gathered her wits and strode around town until she was in control again.

Workers were finishing up the last of the streetcar line repairs. Almost all the telegraph lines once again towered over the city. Businesses, old and new, lined the streets. Though many weren't open yet, inventory beckoned from their windows. The papers reported that several companies destroyed by the flood had decided not to rebuild, and entrepreneurs from other towns had purchased the properties, seizing the opportunity for success once the town flourished again.

And Johnstown would. It was evident in the way folks had banded together to clean debris, share shelter with one another, disperse supplies, and work to repair the damage. The assistance of the Red Cross wouldn't be needed much longer. Maybe another month or two at most. Soon, she would return to Washington, and Monty would continue his life here. In the meantime, she would ensure that the folks in this town, and folks in any other, wouldn't have to live in fear of the Pittsburgh elite anymore.

With renewed determination, she strode to the end of town where the newspaper offices clustered together in small shacks. She searched for the crude shingle that read PITTSBURGH POST. She stepped inside, and it took a few moments for her eyes to adjust to the dim lighting. The scene was like the last time she'd visited: reporters typing furiously, cigars dangling from their lips, young couriers running in and out, and men napping with their feet propped on their workspace.

"May I help you, ma'am?" A rotund fellow with a clean-shaven face standing two inches shorter than she rounded a desk, wearing a smile.

Annamae shifted awkwardly, guilt clawing at her conscience. Revealing the list of club members would break the confidence Monty had entrusted to her. Was she doing the right thing?

Fear pushed her one step closer to the exit.

"Miss?" The reporter frowned.

She spied Mr. Colt at the back of the room, speaking with another gentleman over a newspaper, arms extended, pointing to various sections of the print.

The moment of truth. Leave or stay?

A young boy ran inside the building, brushed against her skirt, and nearly knocked her over. The rounded reporter hollered at the lad, gaining the attention of most everyone in the room. Mr. Colt's eyebrows rose when he spotted Annamae. He set the paper down.

Panic seized her with every step he took forward. Was Monty right about letting the courts decide where the guilt lay? About allowing God's vengeance to repay and not her own?

Mr. Colt's pleasant face warmed with a smile. A smile on a young, robust body while Monty's sported bruises and scabs. The members of the South Fork Fishing and Hunting Club deserved the vengeance of the entire world. If Monty wouldn't fight for himself and these people, she would.

"What can I do for you, Miss Worthington?" Mr. Colt offered a small bow.

She glowered at the rotund reporter next to them, salivating for gossip, and addressed Mr. Colt. "May we talk somewhere, in private? Perhaps we could chat outdoors on this lovely day. The sky is clouding over, and the temperature is more tolerable than it has been of late."

Mr. Colt immediately reached for a notebook and pencil on the desk behind him, slipped them into his shirt pocket, and gestured for her to lead the way.

She had no idea where the best place was to speak privately, so she walked while he made companionable chatter, all the while searching for the right spot. On the edge of town, where the stone bridge was being repaired, lay a small hill that the water had created with its forceful swirl. The dirt was dry now, and sprigs of grass popped through small cracks of earth. Work was still ongoing as they repaired the stones, but she and Colt stood far enough away no one should overhear.

Annamae shaded her eyes and pretended interest in the bridge's progress.

"What is it I can do for you, Miss Worthington?" Mr. Colt stood casually beside her, wearing no overcoat. Only his suspenders hugged his muscular frame. He'd rolled his sleeves to his elbows, and ink smudges soiled his fingers and forearms.

Guilt speared her again. A flash of Monty lying half dead in the infirmary lit her memory, and she pushed the guilt aside, pressing on before she lost her nerve. "I have a list of members of the South Fork Fishing and Hunting Club. Well, a partial list anyway."

Mr. Colt didn't try to hide his surprise. "Why are you choosing to share this list with me?"

She took a deep breath. "Because this isn't the first time those men have hurt the ones I love. I want justice, and I want to see this never happens again."

He searched her face, as if scouring for any untruth. Then he removed his notebook and pencil. "I'm listening."

Nausea swirled in her belly with each name she spoke aloud. Five in all. She was betraying Monty. A man she was falling in love with. But she was doing it for his benefit. She couldn't be wrong. Could she?

Mr. Colt closed his notebook and slipped the pencil behind his ear. "How do I know this is an accurate list? These are some of the most powerful men in the country. I can't just go printing their names without proof to back it up."

The group at the bridge stopped their digging along the bank and lifted a small body. Annamae flinched and looked away. "Corporate charter for the club wasn't registered in Cambria County per the laws of Pennsylvania. It's filed in the Court of Common Pleas in Allegheny County. You may check there to verify my information."

Mr. Colt shook his head. "How do you know all this?"

She placed a palm flat against her middle to quell her nerves. "Someone I know and trust has ties to those men and has insight into their transactions."

"Who is this trusted source?" Mr. Colt removed the pencil in preparation for writing.

"That is a tidbit I won't be sharing with you, Mr. Colt."

He smiled his understanding and returned the pencil to his ear. "Anything else?"

"This information is going to sell a lot of papers for your company. It may even boost your reputation as a reporter. In return, I ask that you leave my name and occupation out of your articles, present and future."

"Done."

Mr. Colt stuck out his hand. She eyed it warily then accepted.

They parted ways, and the entire walk back to the Red Cross, she couldn't shake the feeling that she'd just made a deal with the devil.

Chapter Twenty-Five

"Modern industries are handling the forces of nature on a stupendous scale. Woe to the people who trust these powers to the hands of fools."
~Major John Wesley Powell, director of the U.S. Geological Survey, *North American Review*, August 1889

MONDAY, JULY 15

The whistle of the Cambria Iron Works shrieked through the hills, announcing its first operating day since the flood. The men working in the church glanced at one another and cheered. Everything inside the mill had been cleaned, repaired, and replaced, and all shifts were running. Business meant work, and work meant money. An honest day's wage made a man able to rest his head peacefully on his pillow at night.

"Boy howdy, that's a good sound." Irving Thibault, a middle-aged chap whose accent bordered on Irish and southern twang, clapped his hands in two staccato beats.

The man's place in Woodvale had been destroyed, and the water had thrown him several feet into the air before tossing him on top of a root cellar built into the hillside. Tree trunks and debris had piled up around him, making a cave of safety from the worst of it. He'd been trapped for four days, drinking rainwater from his cupped hands from where it dripped between the trees. At last, someone heard him yelling, and a crew had worked to free him.

"How close is the woolen mill to opening?" Monty asked, running his hands over the smooth, sturdy pulpit Robert had fashioned. His friend had a fine talent for wooden craftsmanship but had returned to his position at the Cambria mill.

"'Nother month yet, I'd say." Irving lifted a wooden cross and held it steady while Monty directed to assure centeredness. Once set, Jim nailed it to the wall behind the pulpit.

A thing of beauty.

A shuffling sound behind him caught Monty's attention, and he turned cautiously as to not disturb the muscles around his ribcage. Ernie walked in, appearing more human than the day before.

"Join us, friend." Monty gestured him over. "Isn't it perfect?"

Ernie's nod was exaggerated by his trembling. If the man remained sober for a year, Monty doubted the tremors would stop.

Removing his cap, Ernie wiped sweat from his temple, wafting the smell of his unwashed body. "I was on my way to the commissary for coffee and walked past the train station. I saw that doctor fellow of Miss Annamae's boarding with bags in hand. Thought I'd better tell you straight away."

Ernie had such a tender heart for others. If only the man would stop destroying himself.

"Thank you." Monty patted the man's shoulder, knowing how much Ernie needed to nurse a mug of coffee right now instead of matchmaking.

Jim laid the hammer on a board they used as a makeshift table. "You're going to go talk to her, aren't you?"

Monty wasn't sure why his congregation was invested in his romantic attachment. He supposed it was because Annamae had captured pieces of their hearts too, as Robert had said. Robert had also confessed to Monty that after all they'd gone through, if he found a good woman and blazed a new trail, it would give the rest of them hope they could too.

Stalling, Monty rolled his sleeves to his elbows. "I may see her around sometime soon."

Jim rolled his eyes. "Go now. It's not like you can do anything to help here anyway."

"Sure I can," Monty said. "I can supervise and make sure you hang the cross up straight."

Besides, he didn't want to make a declaration of love sporting a black eye. Well, more greenish yellow now, but still.

"We just hung it," Jim huffed. "For a man wise on righteous living, you're still a boy in knee pants when it comes to women. Haven't you ever read the Song of Solomon?"

Monty headed for the exit.

"I'll be back," he called over his shoulder.

He didn't know what he'd say to Annamae, but he knew he was not discussing the Song of Solomon inside the church.

Summer was upon them now, bringing oppressive heat that would mix with the thick smoke produced by the iron works. He understood the South Fork club's intentions. The air on the mountain was as pure as the landscape. Much different from Johnstown and Pittsburgh and Philadelphia where the factories produced round the clock. Enjoying the nature God had created and balancing work and pleasure wasn't a sin in and of itself. But when nature became one's God, that was a different story. The club members valued recreation and luxury above human life. They had sinned against mankind, but more so against God.

Monty trusted the Lord would fight for the people of the valleys.

Activity in town hustled as usual. Now that the railroad had replaced most of the lines, transporting cargo to and from the town kept the railroad workers busy. Construction on the new roundhouse was progressing, but the temporary turn track worked fine.

It took longer to reach the Red Cross tents than Monty bargained for. He walked at a snail's pace as to not jar his abdomen and ribs. Last night when he'd awoken to sneeze, he'd thought a steel beam had plowed into his face. Stars had filled his vision, and the pain in his broken nose and ribcage had stolen his breath. Moments later, blood had oozed from his nose, and he'd soaked two handkerchiefs trying to get it under control.

It was probably a good idea to have a doctor look him over to make sure his nose was healing properly and that the break wouldn't disfigure his face.

"Can I help you?" A grandmotherly nurse approached him, carrying a clipboard.

Monty tucked his hands into his pockets. "I was treated last week for a broken nose and other injuries. I was told to come back for an examination."

"Follow me, please."

He obeyed, and she took him two tents over where only one other person sat waiting for a nurse. With the rise in disinfectant use, patients at the Red Cross tents had thinned considerably over the last few weeks. Monty recognized the man as Phillip Lowman, one of the streetcar conductors. The man raised a hand in greeting, as did Monty. The grand-motherly nurse assured him she'd fetch the doctor.

As Monty waited, he thought about what he wanted to say to Annamae, but nothing sounded right. Then, as if he'd conjured her before him, she sidled past the tent, forehead scrunched in thought, carrying a small crate with bottles poking out of the top. "Miss Worthington."

She jerked to a stop. Then her shoulders lowered. "You scared me."

The conductor chuckled, and Monty smiled an apology. Had her wandering thoughts involved him?

Appearing less amused than the men, she ducked beneath the angled tent flap and relinquished the crate to a nearby bed. Hands on hips, she assessed Monty. "You're looking better. Are you here for an examination or to strike fear into the staff?"

While he preferred her unruffled, that spark that lit her up when riled made his blood pump harder. "I came to ask if I could court you properly."

Her pretty lips parted and almost curled into a smile before they closed again, and she shrugged. "You and every other unwed man who sweeps through here. Except Mr. Lowman." She hitched her thumb at the conductor. "He's about the only gentleman in this town with his wits about him."

Lowman cackled.

A warm sensation trickled down Monty's upper lip. Annamae rushed to a bureau, pulled out a rag, and told him to hold it against his nostrils without adding pressure. The doctor walked in and informed Mr. Lowman the nurse was fetching the salve he needed and that once she returned, he'd be free to leave.

The tall doctor focused his attention on Monty. "Ah, I remember you. Mr. Childs, is it?"

Monty offered his free hand, and Doctor Rose shook it with a firm grip. Monty tried not to wince from the jolt that shot through his ribcage.

"Mr. Childs came in to have his head examined," Annamae said.

This earned yet another chuckle from Mr. Lowman and a questioning look from the doctor. "His broken nose and other injuries," she clarified.

Her narrowed gaze and incensed attitude told him she wasn't going to make this easy. She was angry with him for being flippant about her explanation of Matthew's arrival. As well she should be, he guessed. He could have acted more graciously.

Annamae left to continue her duties while the doctor poked and prodded until Monty wanted to punch the guy. About the time he felt like he couldn't take another second of the examination, the doctor straightened up.

"You're healing as well as you can be at this point. I'm confident the threat of any serious internal injury is over. Nasal bleeding is common after a break. Unfortunately, you will sneeze as you continue to heal. It's your body's natural way of cleaning and clearing the nasal passages. I understand it hurts. It will get better, I promise."

All Monty could do was grunt.

"Keeping your ribs bound tight will not only help with pain but also healing. Let me collect a roll of bandages large enough to do the job. I'll be back."

While Monty waited, a nurse brought Mr. Lowman his salve. She steadied the older man as he maneuvered from the bed to the ground. Once he stood fine on his own, she left the tent.

Mr. Lowman shuffled past Monty. "Good luck, son."

His cackle followed him outside.

Now if he could keep Annamae from laughing him away as well.

———————◆◦◆———————

Annamae's head spun with Monty's declaration. He wanted to court her? Surely he was jesting. No, that wasn't Monty's way. He was all truth and gravity with the perfect amount of humor, but never at another's expense.

Guilt slithered around her throat and squeezed.

She had betrayed his confidence.

Alone in the warehouse, she reached inside a crate stacked with clean, folded blankets and clenched the cotton with all her strength. Why did this war continue blasting inside her? She'd done what she had for the right cause. Mr. Colt had assured her he would check her list against the records in Allegheny County and would see to it the breaking story would end up in the correct hands once the information was verified. The rulers of industry would be exposed, justice served, and she could finally have peace.

Tears filled her vision. All she wanted was peace.

She also wanted a future with Monty. Was it possible to have both?

"Miss Worthington, do you know where the rolls of bandages are?"

The voice startled her. She didn't see anyone else but recognized Doctor Rose's voice.

Embarrassed to be seen in such a state of agitation, she shook herself into action. "They're here, sir."

She fumbled on a top shelf and gripped the roll.

Doctor Rose rounded the corner. "Wonderful. Will you assist me in binding Mr. Childs' ribs, please? Mrs. Heimlich has admitted another patient. Infection in the leg that will need drained."

"I'll be right there, Doctor."

He left with the bandages.

Taking a few cleansing breaths, she stepped into the sunlight and prepared herself for whatever Monty had to say. She would not feel guilty about what she had done. She was a juror in the court of human life, and she was seeing to it that the club members paid for their crimes.

The air seemed thicker than it had been before. Her nerves stood on edge as she ducked beneath the tent flap. Mrs. Heimlich was speaking with the other patient, and Doctor Rose was assisting Monty in removing his shirt. Annamae halted abruptly. Monty's gaze met hers over the doctor's shoulder.

Her mouth went dry.

Blood, vomit, death—she took it all like a good soldier. Monty's naked chest made her want to run the other way. Actually, it made her want to stay and appreciate his male form, which is why she should run the other way.

"Miss Worthington," Doctor Rose called, sensing her presence. "Can you stand behind him and hold the end of the bandage below his armpit while I wrap? Be mindful of his bruise."

She did as the doctor asked, careful of the angry knot on his side, and nearly jumped to the ceiling when her fingers touched his bare skin. Goose bumps fanned across the cord of muscles on his back. The sight would be perfection if it weren't for the blotches of purple and yellow covering his flesh.

Wounds she was responsible for.

What if releasing the club membership to Mr. Colt put Monty in danger again? This time, they might aim to kill. Oh, why hadn't she thought of that sooner?

Doctor Rose wound the bandage across Monty's front then handed it to Annamae for her to continue the circle around his back. They exchanged the ball of rags four times before they ran out of fabric. Mrs. Heimlich called the doctor over to her patient while Annamae crossed to the front of Monty, holding the end of the bandage tight. She tried to avoid his gaze, but cat-like curiosity had always been one of her weaknesses. She raised her eyelashes to look at him.

Monty watched her, a smile touching his lips. He knew this affected her, and it amused him.

Clamping her teeth over her lower lip, she concentrated on tucking the end of the bandage inside the coil around his ribs.

"You seem flustered," Monty whispered.

"I'm a professional," she whispered back. "I don't get flustered."

Affection and desire flared in his eyes. Annamae glanced at the others in the corner to see if they were paying attention.

"Your face has turned a lovely shade of pink." He brushed his fingers over hers.

She stiffened. "Then explain the redness in your cheeks as well. And don't give me the excuse of being in pain or I'll pull this bandage even tighter."

He laughed softly. "I'm not sure whether to be embarrassed or flattered."

She handed him his shirt. "Be both and get dressed."

Busying her tingling fingers with whatever she could find to distract them, she waited—back turned—for Monty to cover himself.

"Thank you, Doctor." Monty brushed past her.

"Return in two days, and we'll give you a fresh bandage." Doctor Rose raised his hand in farewell then returned to the patient with the leg infection.

Monty strutted from the tent.

Annamae trailed after him. "Where do you think you're going?"

"To the church."

"I thought you had something to ask me."

He feigned ignorance.

She slapped his arm.

"Ouch." Monty snickered. "I guess I came for a purpose, didn't I?"

She waited while he stared at her. "Well?"

"Come with me. There's something I'd like to show you."

He'd likely want to show her the first train back to Washington if he knew she'd spoken with Mr. Colt. The story hadn't gone to print yet, and even when it did, Mr. Colt had assured her she would remain anonymous. Therefore, people would think that anyone could have provided him the information. Or that a reporter investigated deeply enough to discover it. So why let it spoil the moment?

If Monty ever asked her, she'd tell him the truth. Otherwise, they could move on in their relationship.

"Let me change out of this apron and tell the administering nurse I'm leaving. I'll meet you outside the new general store in fifteen minutes."

Monty agreed, and she rushed into her tent to freshen up. Small ringlets of damp hair burst from beneath her cap but would dry soon without it on. She wiped her face, neck, and chest with a wet cloth, then applied a splash of rosewater. How she wished she had one of her nicer dresses for the occasion. But she had left anything impractical back at her apartment in Washington.

As promised, she met Monty outside the general store. Insecurity filled the space between them as she walked beside him toward the church. Finally, he spoke. "I heard Doctor Martin left. Did you give him a reason to go home, or had his time away from Washington expired?"

She cut him a sidelong glance. "If you're asking if I rejected his offer of courtship, the answer is yes. I told you weeks ago that I wasn't married because I hadn't yet met a man I could tolerate spending the rest of my life with. That comment included Doctor Martin."

Monty's hands fell into his pockets. "Do you still feel you haven't met a man you could tolerate spending the rest of your life with?"

Her irritation grew by the second. His confidence had filled the infirmary, and he had blurted his intentions in front of Mr. Lowman. Why was he being coy now?

"Yes," she answered.

His steps halted, and his brows creased.

"I mean, yes, you can court me."

He blinked. "You made that easier than I thought you would."

She wrapped her hand around his arm, careful not to hurt him. "There's no point in dragging this out. It won't be long before the Red Cross will pack up and return to whence they came."

"What about your life in Washington?"

She thought for a moment as they walked along. "I've grown fond of my life there, but after coming here, after meeting you, I've come to realize I'm not exactly happy living an independent life of solitude."

"Neither am I."

They neared the church, and amazement filled her at how much progress they'd made since her last visit.

"This disaster has reminded me how short and precious life is," Monty said. "I want the days I have remaining to be spent with a good and honest woman by my side. Someone who loves the members of my congregation as much as I do. As much as God does."

He stopped in front of the open doors of the church, wrapped an arm around her shoulders, and pulled her close without touching his bruised side. Job trotted toward them and greeted Annamae, rubbing against her skirt. Monty bent, and he whispered in her ear, sending shivers down her spine. "You're the woman I need, Annamae."

Remorse attacked her conscience like a hungry lion. Would he still feel that way about her when he discovered what she'd done?

Chapter Twenty-Six

~~~~~~~~~

"The lesson of the Conemaugh Valley flood is that the catastrophes of Nature have to be regarded in the structures of man as well as its ordinary laws."

~New England newspaper, as quoted in *The Johnstown Flood* by David G. McCullough

SATURDAY, JULY 20

Annamae had betrayed his trust.

Monty slammed the newspaper on the commissary table, fuming. The reporter had described that an anonymous source revealed the names of the most prominent club members, as well as the location of the charter filed at the Court of Common Pleas in Allegheny County. Judge Edwin H. Stowe approved and signed the charter. Several days of investigation proved the source was true.

From there, it listed the names of the four most prominent members—Andrew Carnegie of Carnegie Steel; Henry Clay Frick, the "King of Coke"; Philander C. Knox, assistant district attorney for the western district of Pennsylvania; and Robert Pitcairn, superintendent of the Pittsburgh Railways.

That anonymous source exposed details too specific for anyone outside of the club to know. Details like the ones he'd shared with Annamae.

He'd confided in her. Trusted her.

Trusted that she would trust him.

When had she done it? Why?

He already knew the answer to his last question. She'd done it to avenge her father's death.

Monty got up from the table and dumped the rest of his coffee on the ground. He stalked to the washtub and tossed the tin mug in with the other utensils. Soapy water splashed against the side of the building. Pain zinged across his middle. Though he was healing well, when he pushed himself too hard, his body reminded him he had yet to make a full recovery.

Right now, his adrenaline ran high enough to power the B&O all the way to Pittsburgh.

He could no longer protect her. Uncle Henry would not only finish him. As promised, he'd go after Annamae too. The stench of Knuckles' whiskey-coated breath filled his memory, along with his deep-throated threat. *"Any more lessons you need teachin', I'll be teachin' on that pretty little nurse of yours."*

Heaven help him. If Knuckles or any other man laid a violent hand on her, Monty would kill him. And that would go against everything he stood for.

He needed to compose himself before confronting her. Their past week of courtship had been wonderful. Picnics around Kernville, savoring baked goods from the Ladies Aid Society, walks along Millcreek and the Stony Creek River, both nearly dry from little rain and the summer heat. He'd even rented a horse and buggy so they could check the progress of the nearby towns of Sheridan and Sang Hollow.

She'd told him what it was like growing up in the tenement houses, about her Scottish neighbor who'd taught her how to make haggis, and when she'd first discovered her talent for nursing. He'd shared about life with his parents, about the difficult transition after their deaths, and his experience getting to hear the great D.L. Moody preach in London when he'd accompanied his aunt and uncle to Europe at sixteen. How that sermon had opened his heart to Jesus, latched on to him for the next six years, and drove him to discover God's calling.

All the while, they'd been building certainty in one another. A confidence that, in their honest and open exchanges, their lives were being knit together.

And then this.

His gut churned with disappointment and frustration the entire way to the church. They were setting the new pews today, and Mrs. Rollins and Mrs. Bixby had volunteered to "clean God's house to a shine." Monty had planned to show Annamae the progress he and the crew had made to his home this evening.

Now he wasn't sure what to do.

The hot day passed like molasses through a funnel. The tension in his neck and shoulders wound tighter with each passing hour. In late afternoon, clouds overcast the sky and the dark gray hue on the horizon promised rain. One thing was certain. No matter how much it poured, they wouldn't have to worry about the dam breaking anymore.

At half past four, thunder crackled above the hills and the work crew called it a day. Monty escorted Mrs. Rollins and Mrs. Bixby safely home before the storm unleashed. They promised to come back tomorrow, and Monty tracked the short distance to his newly built home.

The earthy scent of fresh lumber welcomed him. His boots thumped on the plank floor and echoed in the hollow space, save for a small table and two matching chairs. The window glass sparkled, and the rooms were divided by walls, but the detail work had yet to be finished. The one-story structure sat on a stone foundation much taller than his previous home. It had a small attic, and multiple steps led to the front door under a covered porch. Job had already made himself at home by curling into a ball on the hearth.

Lightning flashed, bringing momentary light into the dim space. Annamae was supposed to meet him at the church at five, but the Red Cross would be busy securing the tents from the wind. It was doubtful she'd come now. Just as well. He didn't know how to best handle the situation.

Monty scooted a chair in front of the barren fireplace, sat in the growing darkness, and prayed.

Sometime later, frantic knocks beat against his door. Annamae's muffled voice called his name from the other side. He crossed the room and opened it as a bolt of lightning streaked across the sky. Rain slapped against the roof and blew across the porch. The dirt roads had turned to mud. Annamae's hair was in disarray, the wind having fought against it on her walk. Cheeks flushed and appearance imperfect, she'd never looked more beautiful.

His heart had never throbbed so painfully.

He stepped aside and let her in. Her skirt brushed his leg as she passed, stoking his indignation. What he wanted to do right now was far from confronting her about her actions, which made the situation more precarious.

"I thought we were meeting at the church, so I went there first." She smoothed her hands over her hair. "I'm glad I found you here. I was about to give up and go back to my tent, but I would've been soaked through by the time I got there."

Monty didn't respond. Only struck a match and lit the lone lantern resting on the countertop by the sink. A well pump mounted to one side had yet to be connected to the town's water supply.

The raising of the wick must have illuminated the stern lines he could feel slashing his face.

"What's wrong?" She reached for his arm, and it took everything in him not to pull away.

"I read something very interesting in the newspaper this morning."

Large, doleful eyes that usually held him captive widened. Her lips parted in shock before twisting. She released his arm and hung her head.

"It *was* you." He sighed. Of course it was. How foolish he'd been to hang on to the hope it was someone else.

"I…" She pulled out the other chair and dropped onto it. "You're angry."

A snide and unkind comment almost slipped from his lips, but he swallowed it down. "I told you that information in confidence. Then you assured me you would put your trust in me and let the courts handle it."

"And *then* I saw what they did to you!"

"Which should make you afraid of what they'll do to *you*, should they discover you're the source."

Lightning struck again, followed by a booming crack of thunder. Job startled and weaved between Monty's legs.

"If justice is served and those men are forced to pay for their crimes, then they won't be able to harm anyone again."

"Stop being naive, Annamae." Monty paced the room, fingers running tracks through his hair. "Men like Carnegie and Frick, they have people placed strategically all over the globe, willing to do their bidding. Even from jail. Don't think for a second your crusade for revenge will stop theirs."

The pounding of rain filled their silence.

She cleared her throat and lifted her chin. "My crusade isn't a quest for revenge. It's a quest to see corruption exposed and the common man not lorded over by tyrants who can silence them permanently if they so wish."

"Then betraying my trust is all right as long as it falls in line with your crusade?"

The chair legs scraped against the floor as she stood. "It wasn't long ago we celebrated the one hundredth anniversary of this country. A country that never would be if it weren't for men and women willing to stand up for what's right."

Monty opened his mouth to speak, but she cut him off.

"Here we are, a hundred and thirteen years after the revolution, ruled by a different tyrant. The tyrant of greed and monopoly, where payment for backbreaking work is given in company scrip that can only be used at the company stores where prices are higher than anywhere else. After years of sacrificing health and family, the reward is death."

She stopped to take a breath. Tears rolled down her cheeks. "And upon that death, they give your only family, a sixteen-year-old girl, three days to vacate the only home she's ever known.

"Someone must fight against them, Monty. Someone must make them pay for what they did to my father. For what they've done to the innocent people of this town. For what they've done to you."

Voice cracking, she flopped back onto the chair, plunked her elbows on the table, buried her face in her hands, and wept.

Monty watched the rain blur the view from his window. His chest burned as the answer to his prayer uttered before she'd arrived settled inside his heart. He scrubbed a hand over his face. Saying it would be hard, but as a pastor, he had to put the spiritual needs of others before his own comfort and desires. If she was ever going to have peace and joy in her life, she had to relinquish her bitterness. Only then could she be the woman he needed by his side, the woman to work beside him with his congregation. The woman with a full and open heart for God to bless the rest of her days.

He moved his chair away from the fireplace and carried it to the table. It didn't creak with his weight like his former ones did. These were new and sturdy, all the joints secured. Like their courtship needed to be before they committed themselves in marriage.

"Annamae," he said softly, "I'm truly sorry for what happened to your father and for the hardships you've endured because of it."

She lifted her head, her face a mottled red in the flicker of lantern light.

"But it doesn't excuse betraying the confidence of a friend. You've let old emotions you've never resolved return to haunt you." He placed his hand over her wrist to soften the blow of his next statement. "You're telling yourself you did it for the good of mankind, but you really did it because you think that if those men are made to pay, all the anger and bitterness you hold inside will magically evaporate and you can have peace. But it doesn't work that way. It won't work, because it won't bring your father back."

"That isn't true." She pulled her arm away.

"It is. Even if they're convicted and sentenced, you'll always burn with hatred for them every time you think of your father, if you don't learn to forgive."

Her lips pursed, and her chin wobbled. "I know hatred is wrong, and I'm not only doing this to avenge my father. You're a smart man, Monty, but you don't know everything. You can't see inside my heart."

He swallowed, hating what he was about to say. "I can see into your heart enough to know that if you don't give this to God and let go of the hostility breeding inside you, there will never be enough room in there for me."

For ten solid seconds, she simply stared at him. "I see."

With the grace of a queen, she wiped her cheeks as she rose from her seat, walked to the door, and closed it softly behind her.

Chapter Twenty-Seven

"God never did make a more calm, quiet, innocent recreation than angling."

~Izaak Walton, author of *The Complete Angler*, published in 1653

TUESDAY, JULY 30

"I want my daddy." Blood smeared the girl's skinned arms and legs as Annamae attempted to clean the scrapes.

I do too, echoed in the chambers of Annamae's heart. Over the past week, a loneliness had settled in her bones like she'd never experienced before.

After her father's funeral, seclusion had become her constant companion. Spite, her motivation to succeed. She'd kept a respectable distance from everyone in every capacity in her life to keep from feeling the agony of loss again.

Until Monty.

Foolishly, she'd let him in. And now she was hurting.

"You're being very brave, Katie Lynn." Annamae had seen the girl more than once since she'd tripped over a pipe the day of the three-legged race. It seemed as if the rough-and-tumble child was always getting hurt. Thankfully, a local couple had chosen to adopt her, and she'd have someone to offer comfort and look after her.

Annamae squirted iodine on a cotton round and dabbed it on Katie Lynn's kneecap. She'd already flushed the dirt and gravel from it, which made the girl howl as loudly as the Cambria Iron Works' noon whistle. "After we're finished, I'll give you a peppermint stick for being such a good patient."

The sobs stuttered. "Really?"

Annamae smiled. "Really."

Katie Lynn hiccupped and squirmed but didn't issue any more protests.

Finished, Annamae replaced the cork on the iodine bottle and helped the girl sit up. "While that's drying, I'm going to wash my hands and then fetch your peppermint stick. Stay here, please."

Katie Lynn nodded, wiping the clean tracks her tears had made on her dirty cheeks.

Her older brother had brought her in, claiming she'd fallen from the top of a giant pile of stones collected from all over town while clearing debris. Annamae had reminded the girl that the stone piles were there for folks needing them during the reconstruction or for areas that had been washed away and needed reinforcement. Not for entertaining children.

That had earned her a scowl and the beginning of a long wave of tears.

Annamae returned with a peppermint stick wrapped in a strip of brown paper. Katie Lynn held her filthy hand out. Annamae handed her a cake of soap. "First, you must wash all that grime from your hands and fingernails. It will help keep germs out of your body and keep your candy from tasting like dirt."

Katie Lynn hopped down from the bed, inspecting her palms. "My new pa says dirt never killed nobody."

"If that dirt contains a harmful germ, it could."

"I don't see nothing that looks harmful." Her little hands fell to her sides, and she lifted her chin. "I'll take that candy now."

Annamae held it farther away. She would win this battle, even if she couldn't win any others in her life. "That's because germs are invisible to the naked eye. Now, wash."

Wiping her hand against her dripping nose, Katie Lynn went to the washbasin and obeyed. "Whatcha mean about eyes being naked?"

Holding in a chuckle, Annamae explained how scientists had recently used microscopes to discover germs swimming in water droplets and uncooked foods. Those types of germs could make a person very sick and even prove fatal. She also explained that the term "naked eye" meant what a person could see using normal vision. That got Katie Lynn's attention, and she scrubbed her hands and fingernails until Annamae feared she'd claw her skin open.

"You've done a sufficient job killing the germs." Annamae instructed the girl to pat her hands dry on the towel, and then she passed over the candy. Katie Lynn swiped it and ran out of the tent faster than a scared deer when startled.

Annamae looked after the girl, shaking her head and smiling.

A light touch brushed her elbow. Hetty's eyes, a blend of brown and gold, blinked at Annamae behind thick spectacles. "I didn't want to disturb you until you'd finished with your patient, but there's a man been waiting to see you."

Annamae's heart buoyed. Monty had kept distant over the past week. When they had seen each other in passing, their conversations consisted only of paltry things that wouldn't start any arguments. Had he finally come to see that her actions were justified? Maybe his affection for her was growing stronger than his judgment.

"Thanks, Hetty. I'm going to step out for a bit, but I'll be back by two o'clock."

"No need to rush." Hetty clasped her hands, a dreamy grin on her face. "If a man that handsome was waiting for me, I'd take all day."

Annamae giggled, removed her apron, and left, excited to see Monty. As she approached Red Cross headquarters, her disappointment cut deep when she saw that the man sitting in the chair waiting wasn't the one she'd expected.

"Miss Worthington. Thank you for agreeing to see me." Mr. Colt rose. His tall frame dwarfed her.

He was the man Hetty found handsome. True, Mr. Colt could be described as such, but he paled in comparison to Monty.

"What can I do for you?"

The initial pleasantries in Mr. Colt's features turned grim. He handed her the folded newspaper she hadn't noticed him holding. "I'm truly sorry, Miss Worthington. We gave it valiant effort."

Confusion fogged Annamae's brain. She opened the newspaper, and the headline shifted the ground beneath her feet. JURIES DECLARE AN ACT OF GOD. Her vision grew fuzzy at the edges. Blinking, she skimmed the article, fury building in her veins so fierce she expected it to flow from her fingertips and singe the page.

The entire article could be summed up in one sentence—the South Fork Fishing and Hunting Club wouldn't be held responsible for the destruction of Johnstown.

"I think we were too late." The sympathy vibrating from his voice made her want to weep. "Maybe if we'd printed the information sooner..."

They wouldn't have been too late if she'd handled the matter on her own from the start instead of letting Monty handle it his own way. Not only would there have been a greater chance for justice, but she and Monty wouldn't be at odds with one another now.

She swallowed every response rising to her lips and instead said, "Thank you for trying."

His forehead creased with regret and disappointment. He started to say more but stopped and gave her arm a gentle squeeze. "If I can do anything else for you, Miss Worthington, you need only ask."

Through blurry vision, she watched him take several large strides toward the newspaper office before disappearing into her tears completely.

Clutching the paper in her fist, she plunked down in the chair he had vacated. The summer heat made the rage in her body hotter. They'd gotten away with murder.

Again.

"I'm sorry, Daddy," she whispered.

"Miss Worthington, are you alright?" Doctor Hubbell knelt beside her, assessing her face.

"I'm fine. I just..." She let the sentence taper and fanned herself with the crinkled, folded paper.

Her cap blocked air from circulating around her face. She untied the strings and placed it on the chair beside her.

"Are you dizzy?" he asked.

"I need to take a walk." She stood but wavered.

Doctor Hubbell steadied her. "I don't think that's wise. You may be overheated."

She was already walking away and didn't listen to what else he had to say. She was never rude to people, especially those with whom she worked, but if she didn't walk and think and burn some of the agonizing energy surging through her veins, she might collapse and become their next patient.

Without thinking about where she was going, she walked in a daze until she lost track of time. When her legs grew tired and sore, she focused on her surroundings and discovered she was just outside of Monty's church.

It made sense that she would come here. She wanted to fall into his arms and weep and rail against injustice. She also wanted to throttle him for convincing her to wait on God's timing and for making her feel as if her desire to see the club members held accountable was wrong. Fighting for the lives of others was never wrong.

The church door opened easily, and she stepped inside. The scent of freshly planed wood and dusting polish filled her senses. Light spilled from the stained-glass window and reflected its colors on the wooden cross behind the massive pulpit. The new pews were lined in perfect order along both sides of the sanctuary, leaving a path straight down the middle.

The sanctuary was empty. She felt a pull to the center aisle, a beckoning to the altar where she could unleash her troubles to the Lord, but He already knew what plagued her and had let them win, so she returned to the summer heat. Monty's new house was only half a block's length from the church. If he wasn't there, she didn't know where she'd go next.

Ten steps led to his open front door. She barged in to find Mr. Breslin and Mr. McDonough moving furniture. "I'm looking for Mon—uh, Pastor Childs."

Mr. McDonough lowered the end of the settee he'd been holding. Sweat rolled down his ruddy face and threatened to drip onto the brushed upholstery. "He's in the back rooms, Miss Worthington, setting in his new furniture. Let me get him for ya."

"Thank you, but I know the way." She wanted to slap herself for relaying that. "I mean, it's a one-level home with limited rooms, so I'm capable of finding him myself without interrupting your day."

Mr. Breslin, still holding on to his end of the settee, had difficulty hiding his amusement. Job rose from his curled position on the hearth to greet her.

"Annamae?" Monty traveled the length of the hallway and into the room where they stood. "I thought I heard your voice. What's wrong?"

She had the newspaper clutched in her fist so tightly her fingers hurt. Her breath came fast, and she couldn't answer his question.

"Guys, could you give us a few minutes, please?" Monty ushered them out. On the porch, he mumbled something to the men then closed the door, blocking what little breeze stirred the room.

He came and stood before her, hands buried in his pockets, and waited for her to speak.

That was when her sobs broke loose.

"What is it, sweetheart?" He stepped toward her, but instead of letting him console her, she held out the newspaper.

Warily, he took it and opened the folds. She knew when he spotted the headline, because he blew out a loud breath.

"They got away with it." Her chest heaved faster than her lungs could keep up. The air became thinner.

"Calm down." Monty hugged her close and rubbed circles on her back. "Shh. It's going to be okay."

She shook her head against his chest, soaking his shirt, her tears melding with the sweat already dampening the fabric.

"Shh," he repeated, rocking her until her sobs quieted.

She lifted her head, and he wiped her tears with his thumbs. "Why does God keep allowing them to get away with murder?"

He winced. "None of our sin goes unpunished. There are always consequences, whether they happen right away or later in life. Either way, those sins can be forgiven if the person asks. We must remember that

Jesus died for their sins too."

Annamae pulled away and paced the new rug covering the floor. That thought didn't sit parallel with her feelings toward them. "What if those men don't want forgiveness? Then what?"

"Then the Lord will deal with them on Judgment Day."

"I know that. I mean... You keep telling me to forgive them for what they did to my father, but they've never asked me for forgiveness. How do I forgive someone who doesn't believe what they did was wrong and doesn't even care about being forgiven?"

Monty tested the new love seat, calculating the precise measurement of each thought, she could tell. He patted the spot beside him, and she perched on the edge, suddenly exhausted from her emotional rush. She folded her arms around her middle and waited for the wisdom she hoped would set her free.

"Everyone's sins nailed Jesus to the cross. He wrote each of our names in His wounds. Even the ones of those He knew would never ask for forgiveness. That way, everyone would have a fair chance at Heaven if they chose to accept Him. He forgave out of *love*."

His words pricked her heart. "I'm not Jesus," she whispered, more tears spilling down her cheeks. "I don't love those men like He does."

Monty reached for her hand, holding it tenderly between his. "None of us loves like Jesus. But it's something we should constantly strive for."

A groan escaped her throat, followed by more sobs. His words might be true and wise, but they did not set her free.

Face shielded by her hands, she cried for her father. She cried for the memories gained and lost. She cried for all the grieving she'd wanted to do in the past but couldn't because she'd been too busy surviving.

Alone.

She cried for Johnstown and the surrounding communities and the lives lost unnecessarily. She wept for the survivors whose lives, like hers, would never be the same. She wept because, at the moment, that was all she was capable of doing.

Chapter Twenty-Eight

"The man who dies thus rich dies disgraced."
~Andrew Carnegie, *The Gospel of Wealth*, May 1889

FRIDAY, AUGUST 2

Monty stretched, well rested from his first night's sleep in his new bed in his new house. He'd been more than grateful for any safe place to rest his head after the flood, but there was no place like home.

He dressed and visited the outhouse before slipping on his boots and making his way to the commissary for breakfast. Stocking his pantry was a task he needed to add to his list. He greeted friends and neighbors, all the while wondering if Annamae was safe and wishing she were by his side.

Quiet and distant since their talk a few days earlier, she was working through her turmoil. He could sense it. He hated to see her struggling but knew if she'd let God finish the work He'd started within her, it would enrich the rest of her life.

After a quick meal of bacon, eggs, and oatmeal, Monty mailed his latest letter to Joanna and went to the bank to inquire about the status of his frozen account in Pittsburgh. He chatted with Mrs. Rodriguez about her husband's job at the new livery until the proprietors unlocked the front doors.

The institution smelled of disinfectant and damp currency. The ping of coins sounded as Mr. Kohl counted the money in his tray. Two long lines had already formed with folks collecting their portion of the disaster relief funds donated from across the country. After purchasing supplies, the financial committee, spearheaded by George Swank and Cyrus Elder, had an abundance of cash left over to distribute among the survivors.

An abundance that had left the committee in a quandary, according to the town council meeting last evening. No one could decide on the best course of distribution. Some survivors argued they should get more than others because they'd owned a business or were wealthy before the flood and, therefore, had lost more than those who'd lived in tenements. Others argued the flood forced everyone into the poor class, so the funds should be distributed evenly as everyone started anew.

No matter how the funds got dispersed, some would be unhappy. Monty was glad he wasn't in charge of the job.

"Next customer, please." Mr. Porter, a short, thin gentleman with gold spectacles and a limp in his gait, waved Monty forward.

"A hold was placed on my account at the Pittsburgh Savings Bank after the flood to prepare for its transfer to my next of kin had I not survived. I filled out the paperwork a few weeks ago to prove my existence and request access to my account once again. I was wondering if you'd received any update on the situation."

"Let me check, Mr. Childs." Mr. Porter adjusted his glasses and shuffled into an adjoining room behind the long counter.

Several minutes passed. Customers at the back of the line complained. Finally, Mr. Porter returned, holding an envelope. "Sorry for the delay, Mr. Childs." He adjusted his glasses once again. "The postman delivered this notation last week. You should find the information inside sufficient for answering your question."

"Thank you."

Monty slipped a finger beneath the flap of the envelope, wanting to read the contents before leaving the line in case he had more questions, but a man bumped him out of the way and took his place at the barred counter.

Swallowing his frustration, Monty exited the building, needing fresh air.

The bright sun made the paper hard to read. He moved to the west side of the building, shaded this time of the morning. The notation, as Mr. Porter had called it, stated that the bank had received his paperwork, had unfrozen his account, and that his account balance was now three hundred and eight dollars.

Monty blinked.

He scanned the paper again, reading carefully. He had tried to withdraw fifteen thousand dollars on July 2 and couldn't because his account had been frozen. His inheritance money was gone. And there was only one person on earth who would have the clout to withdraw money from Monty's account despite it being illegal. What a coincidence that the amount withdrawn was the exact amount "donated" to rebuild his church.

Fuming, Monty crinkled the paper in his fist then shoved it into his pocket. As he stomped off, he could hear Annamae's voice ringing in the back of his mind, reminding him that this was yet another instance where too much power yielded injustice. She was right. Men like his uncle needed to be accountable for their actions.

Then the Holy Spirit pricked his heart and he suddenly stopped, wiped a hand over his brow, and took a deep breath. Justice must be served in the right manner. Not in hate and malice, despite how his flesh wanted to react right now.

He walked back, prepared to reenter the bank and stand at the end of one of the long lines, when he plowed into the formidable man himself. Monty's eye twitched from the zing of pain, but he schooled his features. He was glad his broken nose and the bruises on his face had healed, all except for two small areas that were a pale yellow. When he faced his uncle, he wanted to do it as a whole man.

Amusement played on Uncle Henry's face. Thin lips upturned beneath his mustache that curled at the edges and blended into a beard that held as much gray as brown. "You look mighty angry, son. Haven't I taught you a cool head keeps the mind clear? You can't possibly strategize against the enemy if your emotions cloud your thinking."

Monty stood to full height. "I haven't the luxury of hiring someone to act out my emotions for me."

Monty reached into his pocket and produced the banknote.

The dark bags beneath his uncle's eyes puffed as he smiled. "If you'd have stayed with me where you belonged, money would be of no consequence."

"And what about withdrawing money from an account that isn't yours? Does that hold any consequence?"

"You requested that money yourself days earlier. I simply persuaded the bank manager to let me send it to you personally."

Monty hadn't intended to use the entire fifteen thousand dollars to rebuild his house and the church. Losing Joanna to an orphanage so far away had made him realize how important such an institution would be to Johnstown. If they'd had one from the start, Joanna and the others wouldn't have had to leave their community. Monty had decided to use part of his funds to fill that need.

"How nice of you to deliver it with a personal *touch*." Monty rubbed his sore ribs.

Uncle Henry nodded. "My employees are loyal to me and don't take kindly to threats."

"And I don't take kindly to you destroying my town. Or interfering in my business."

His uncle's stern frown might have once intimidated him, but not anymore. "You'd better watch your tongue, son."

"I'm not your son." Monty delivered the words with a calmness he didn't feel. Turned out he had more of Annamae's crusading spirit lying dormant inside than he'd thought.

Uncle Henry rotated the crystal top of his cane. The thing served no purpose other than to remind others of his wealth and status. "You lived off the bounty of my fortune as if you were my child, without complaint. Until you abandoned your birthright and left to wallow among common men."

Times like this made it hard for Monty to act honorably. He understood Annamae's fury, though he couldn't act on it. "What do you have against the common man? If it weren't for them running your factories, you wouldn't have your fortune."

"True, but you see, there's something that sets us apart. It's called ambition. We all have it, but they capped theirs at mere survival. I plan to leave a legacy that will transcend the ages."

"You'll leave your legacy, but it won't be the kind you think."

His uncle laughed. "Says the orphan who threw away his shares in the greatest coke company in the world to live in a town so dirty the trees can't breathe."

He reached inside his tailored coat and pulled out a book. "Whitney asked me to give this to you. She figured your original copy was destroyed in the flood and it might bring you comfort."

Great Expectations. Monty tucked the tome to his side. "Thank her for me, will you? I'm touched that she would think of me in such dire circumstances."

Uncle Henry glanced around. "Do they even know who you are around here?"

Monty tried to view the scene from his uncle's point of view as shame spun in his gut like a cyclone. No. His congregation did not know he was a nephew of the Coke King.

He'd wrestled with his omission many a night since the flood and had concluded he needed to confess. It was only fair he come clean. These were his friends, and they deserved no less.

His introspection was cut short when he spotted Annamae exiting the newspaper office across the street, a young, tall reporter way too comfortable by her side.

Through the haze of dust clouds and people crossing between them, Annamae's gaze locked with his. The reporter's smile fell, and he blinked. He said something to Annamae and pointed at the man standing beside Monty.

Her face went pale.

"Ah, the very woman I came to see." Uncle Henry stilled his cane and stood erect.

Monty's heart thumped hard. "What do you want with Annamae?"

"Annamae, is it? I came to thank Miss Worthington for informing the world of my membership in the club as well as the exact location of our charter. What she meant for the club's detriment, I'm certain, came to our benefit."

A warning bell sounded in Monty's ears. "What makes you think Annamae was the source?"

Uncle Henry huffed. "Come now, boy. You're foolish, not suicidal. But once again, you allowed your bleeding heart to loosen your tongue, and she betrayed you."

With a determined set of her mouth and a raised chin, Annamae lifted her skirt and marched toward her enemy.

———— ••◦ ————

Seeing Henry Clay Frick before her eyes was like seeing a mirage in the desert after many years of wandering in circles. Was Mr. Colt correct in recognizing the man? He looked like Mr. Frick's picture in the paper. Why was he talking to Monty? Had Monty recognized him and confronted him for her? For the town?

Questions raced through her mind in the quick seconds it took her to cross the street to them.

Mr. Frick's lip curled at her approach.

Monty didn't appear incensed with the man wearing a perfectly tailored suit and silk tie. In fact, he looked...sick. Had Mr. Frick threatened him? Or her?

She swallowed her fear and plowed ahead. "Monty."

Monty's fingers grazed her elbow. "Annamae, now's not a good—"

"Are you Mr. Henry Clay Frick?" She stared at the man before her, observing his thin hair slicked to the side and the way the tops of his ears pointed away from his head.

"I am. Lovely to make your acquaintance, Miss Annamae Worthington."

Shock stole her next words. Had Monty told him her name?

"As I was saying before you crossed the street," Mr. Frick continued, "I came to thank you for leaking such tantalizing details to the *Pittsburgh Post*. How unfortunate your scheme didn't result in the ending you'd hoped for."

The viper refused to look her in the eyes, as if she wasn't worthy of the gesture.

Her hands shook with animosity. "How fortunate for you to get away with murder yet again."

Monty gripped her arm and attempted to steer her away from the man. "Careful, Annamae."

She wrenched her arm from his grip and swung around. "Does the name Abraham Worthington sound familiar?"

Monty lowered his head into his hand.

Mr. Frick acknowledged her then. "Should it?"

Tears pricked the back of her eyes at his callous tone. "He was a puddler at the Edgar Thomson steel mill. He died falling into a vat of molten iron after *you* refused to improve working conditions, citing that unions have no business in your factories."

Cold, uncaring eyes calculated her. "The name is of no significance to me. Accidents happen in places that employ thousands of workers. Surely a Red Cross nurse understands that."

Her fingers curled into fists against her thighs. She'd never wanted to inflict harm on another human being the way she did right now. "How convenient for you that the deaths of two thousand people living below your precious lake were also deemed as 'accidents.'"

The sardonic twist of Mr. Frick's mouth sent a chill down her spine. Monty angled his body in front of hers.

"Well done, Montgomery. Every time I sent you the most beautiful women in the country only for you to refuse them, I thought you were mad. You were simply waiting on a filly with spirit."

Lasciviousness snaked around his statement.

Monty. . . Mr. Frick sending him the most beautiful women in the country? How well did he know Mr. Frick?

"I see I've taken you completely by surprise, Miss Worthington." Mr. Frick chuckled then turned to Monty. "Have you not shared with your intended that you were once the most eligible bachelor in Pittsburgh?"

A chill shot down her spine. She studied Monty. The blue eyes she'd dreamed of waking up to every morning narrowed in regretful apology.

She faced Mr. Frick. "What do you mean?"

The tip of Mr. Frick's cane sparkled in the sunlight as he rotated it in his fingers. "Only that my nephew is quite taken with you."

She sucked in a breath.

Monty turned away.

The world around her grew fuzzy at the edges.

Her legs went weak. Why wasn't Monty correcting this horrible man? Shouting that he was a liar?

Why did she know her life was about to change in a horrible way she didn't want it to?

Mr. Frick's chagrin looked anything but genuine. "I apologize, my dear. I see I've surprised you once again by revealing that Montgomery is my nephew. Sad tale, really. He is the only child of my wife's brother, Thaddeus Childs. His parents and siblings were killed in a storm crossing the Atlantic. We raised Montgomery as our own. We gave him the best of everything, including a position running the family business, but, unfortunately, he thinks his purpose is here."

He spat the last word as if it were rotten food.

Monty's reluctant gaze found hers. It was true, all of it.

She was going to be sick.

Covering her mouth with a shaky hand, she spun and walked as fast as she could away from the man who'd killed her father and the man who'd shattered her heart.

Sounds ricocheted in her ears, bouncing from loud to soft and back again. Her cotton blouse stuck to her clammy skin, offering no relief from the heat. Bile worked up her throat, but she swallowed it down, determined not to make a spectacle of herself in front of the whole town.

She thought she heard someone calling her name, but she kept walking as fast as she could to the edge of town. Without a clue where she was going, she kept moving, kept attempting to flee the reality that had upended everything she'd thought was real.

When she went until she couldn't take another step, she covered her face and let the tears fall. Monty was Henry Clay Frick's nephew. He'd listened to her story about her father, held her, and encouraged her to forgive that wicked man, all the while concealing that he was one of them.

Of course he wanted her to forgive. Her vendetta was against his family, and blood was thicker than water, as the saying went.

She startled at the shuffle beside her. Monty reached out.

"Don't touch me."

He stepped back. "I didn't mean for you to find out that way."

"I'm sure you didn't." Tears blocked her vision of him. "You didn't intend for me to find out at all."

"That's not true."

"Then why? Why didn't you tell me? When were you going to tell me?"

He faced the stone bridge below them and the repairs nearing an end. "Everything I've told you is the truth. I walked away from my family when it became clear that men like my uncle were their own gods. I didn't want any part of it. I wanted to follow a God who was infallible. One who wasn't limited to a finite mind. One who couldn't make mistakes like the flesh can. God called me here, and I haven't seen or spoken to my uncle since. He banished me from Clayton and the family the day I announced I'd chosen God over what he offered. As far as I'm concerned, I'm just Monty."

Her chest heaved. "That doesn't explain why you didn't tell me. Especially after knowing that evil man killed my father."

He inhaled and exhaled loudly. "When I came here and saw the state of this town, the success and the detriment, I realized right away that no one would listen to what I had to say if they knew where I came from. A starving man won't listen to the message of one who's never experienced the pangs of hunger."

"That's as ridiculous as saying a wounded patient won't listen to my counsel if I'm not bleeding as well. The fact is, you took the coward's way out, afraid no one would accept you if they knew who you were. You didn't want to be rejected, because you'd already lost everything."

She threw daggers as fast as she could and didn't care where they landed. "In your quest to spread the truth, you hid it. You stole our chance to judge you for ourselves. You're no different from your uncle, parading around like you're one person when you're really another."

Monty tipped his face to the sky. "I suppose I deserve that."

Annamae dabbed at her nose with her handkerchief. "Now I know why you didn't want me to expose the club member list. You wanted to protect your uncle and your reputation."

"No, I did it to protect *you*." He gripped her elbows, eyes intense. "Do you remember what I looked like the day Jim found me in the church? I was half-dead, Annamae. My uncle sent his henchman to silence me after I wrote to him and threatened to expose his involvement. He did that to his own *nephew*. I know what my uncle is capable of, and I didn't want his corruption to taint you."

Flashes of him lying on the bed with oozing cuts and a broken nose flashed through her memory. So did her agony over the possibility of internal wounds that might take his life. "You've encouraged me to forgive that man."

Her voice broke.

"I only encouraged you to do what I had to learn to do myself. Believe me, I understand how hard it is to forgive that man."

The ice in Mr. Frick's tone when he'd informed her that Abraham Worthington's life was of no value to him was something she didn't think she could ever forgive. A pastor's wife must be capable of forgiveness, which made her unworthy of Monty. His omission made him unworthy of her. Which meant they had no future together.

She pressed her fingertips to her swollen eyes, and her next steps became clear. She dried her cheeks with her sleeve and smoothed her hair and blouse. She placed careful steps on the uneven path to leave in search of Clara.

"Now I'm going to ask you to forgive me," Monty called from behind her.

She halted and closed her eyes. Words pressed against her lips, but she clamped them together.

"We're both guilty of sin. We're both guilty of poor choices." Agony carried his voice. "Please don't abandon us. We can spend our future overcoming and striving to be better people, together."

Or she could return to Washington to her quiet, solitary life where she could protect her heart.

"The beauty of being set free from bondage is that we don't have to let the anger and bitterness of our pasts hold us back anymore. We can drop the chains and walk away."

She let his statement penetrate her mind. Then she dropped the chains of hope she'd carried for so long—hope that she would someday find companionship—and walked away.

Chapter Twenty-Nine

*"I defy the tyranny of precedent. I go for anything
new that might improve the past."*

~Clara Barton

MONDAY, AUGUST 5

Annamae waited three full days before she went in search of Clara. She wanted to make certain of her decision first. With each day that passed, she grew more confident of her choice. She couldn't face Monty right now. Not when they were both right and wrong. Not when insecurity wrapped around her like an invasive vine. She needed clarity, and she wasn't going to find it in Johnstown.

She stepped into the Red Cross headquarters, which had moved from the tent to a simple building erected from spare lumber. The building was more efficient, protecting the paperwork and the bookkeepers from the wind and rain. Unfortunately, it did nothing to ease the heat. A bead of sweat dropped between her shoulder blades and raced down her spine.

Clara was bent over the desk, flipping through a stack of papers in disarray.

"Miss Barton—Clara—I'd like to speak with you about something if you can spare a moment."

"Have a seat." Clara didn't stutter in her task. She must have found what she was looking for, because she yanked a paper from the stack, sending the ones on top of it knocking into her bosom. Clara caught them and huffed. Her stern expression fixed on Annamae.

The chair creaked as Annamae perched on the edge. Folding her nervous hands in her lap, she said, "After much consideration, I've come to ask you to relieve me of my Red Cross duties so I may return to the hospital in Washington."

Clara frowned. "We are always the last to leave the field, Miss Worthington."

Using her surname meant Clara was displeased. "Indeed, but the residents of Johnstown need our services less every day. The county commissioners, as well as the town board, have declared that most Johnstown residents are now self-sufficient, both physically and financially. With other Red Cross committees from other cities volunteering and donations still pouring in, I thought perhaps you could spare me."

Clara tipped her head to the side. "For what purpose, Miss Worthington?"

Against her will, Annamae broke eye contact to study her fidgeting fingers. "I've been gone from my position for over two months now. When Doctor Martin came to volunteer, he mentioned the strain on the hospital staff because of my absence. I thought—"

"Does this have anything to do with spoon-feeding confidential information to a Mr. Colt White at the *Pittsburgh Post*?"

Annamae's face flamed like a lightning strike on parched prairie grass.

Clara reached into her desk drawer and pulled out an envelope. "It is convenient for me that you asked for your release. I'd planned to seek you out later today to dismiss you myself. Effective immediately."

She was being fired?

Annamae opened and closed her mouth, unsure what to say.

"Why are you shocked, Miss Worthington? This is what you wanted when you came here."

"Yes, but I didn't expect that you'd already planned to let me go."

Clara sat back in her chair. "Miss Worthington, you are one of the most skilled and dedicated nurses I've ever known besides myself. Your addition to the Red Cross was refreshing and most welcome. But ever since our arrival, I've noticed traits that are hindering you from blossoming into the skilled professional you're capable of being."

Everywhere Annamae turned, she felt as if someone told her to act differently. She licked her lips. "Can you be more specific, please?"

"You've always closed yourself off from others. Risen in defense of your actions. Then when we arrived in Johnstown, something swept over you. An unstoppable energy. A bursting from your shell. A force to be reckoned with. You opened your heart to others and found a purpose to fight for. But even good qualities need to be kept under control. You failed to maintain composure and professionalism the day you spoke with that reporter."

"I've lived by your example, Miss Barton. The crusader, the woman who defied all odds and infiltrated a man's world to make it a better place than she found it. Your work has not only saved lives but has given them purpose. Your work may very well change the medical field for future generations."

"Yes, Miss Worthington, but there also needs to be a balance. Crusading isn't just about invoking emotions in others. It's about rallying a response from them to support your cause. Not exhibiting your emotions to reach a desired end."

"I don't understand the difference."

"I know. That's why I'm letting you go. That and because I had a visit from Mr. Henry Clay Frick before he left Johnstown yesterday. He told me of your aggressive behavior regarding his reputation and made it clear in no uncertain terms that if I allowed you to continue your work here, he would file a complaint with every politician in the country. I've worked hard for many years to keep a stellar reputation. I cannot allow your actions to sully it or the organization I fought so hard to establish."

So this was how Mr. Frick planned to destroy her. Instead of commanding one of his goons to make her disappear, he'd wielded his power to inflict a wound deep enough to make her bleed out. He'd likely file those complaints with his lawyer to see she lost her position at Jericho Square Hospital too. Without the affection of his nephew, her work with the Red Cross, and her position in Washington, she had nothing. No one.

How Annamae's tear ducts continued to produce liquid after already crying enough tears over Monty to refill Lake Conemaugh, she didn't know. She stood, but Clara reseated her with a raised finger.

"Miss Worthington, when I saw a desperate need for nurses on the battlefield, I didn't convince the men of Washington to allow me the privilege of first passage using threats and shaking my fists. I kept control of my emotions and presented facts and statistics in a way they themselves would do in my position. Men have no patience for a simpering female. You must think like *them*. Act like *them*. While still being a lady, of course.

"You see, the crusade itself and the changes that can result from it have always been more important to me than my feelings about the men making the rules."

Clara handed Annamae the envelope. "Your work here is appreciated and commendable. So is your desire to see the members of the South Fork Fishing and Hunting Club held responsible for their actions. It's despicable how they let their negligence steal the lives of over two thousand people. I told Mr. Frick as much."

Annamae swallowed. "If you approve, then why are you angry with me?"

"I'm not angry with you, dear. I'm angry with the way you chose to fight. It compromised our work here. I'm forced to let you go."

Pressure built in Annamae's chest. "I'm grateful for the opportunity to work beside you, Miss Barton. I'll clear out my things and return to Washington posthaste."

She rose, and her skirt sent the chair teetering as she brushed against it. The legs steadied with a loud *thwack*.

"Miss Worthington?"

Annamae froze, unable to turn and face Clara again.

"According to the papers, Mr. Andrew Carnegie has returned from Scotland and will visit Johnstown to see the damage for himself and assess how he can help. If he dares say anything about your behavior, I will tell him the same thing I told his business partner, Mr. Frick. Reporting the truth in a newspaper isn't defaming anyone's reputation, and I don't appreciate threats wrapped in polite niceties.

"Annamae, I'm only giving you time to consider what I've said, to get yourself in the proper order, and allow enough time for this to blow over. Then I expect your return to the Red Cross *posthaste*."

How Annamae would have loved to see the little warrior stand up to the Coke King. She pivoted enough to look her in the eyes. "Thank you, Clara."

Annamae went to her tent and packed her meager belongings, all the while grateful for the mercy shown to her by Miss Barton. She scribbled a quick note to Monty, paid a courier boy to deliver it to the church, and headed for the train station without informing anyone at the Red Cross of her leaving. At five o'clock that evening, she'd travel east, away from the town—and the man—who had changed the course of her life.

Chapter Thirty

"To her timely and heroic work, more than to that of any other human being, are the people of the Conemaugh Valley indebted."

~ Editorial written about Clara Barton and her Red Cross

With the last train whistle and the puff-and-chug of the engine, Annamae was gone. She'd swept in and out of his life as quickly as the water out of the dam. She'd sent a note by courier, letting him know she was returning to Washington. Heart protesting, he'd sprinted to the train station to change her mind, but as he saw her board the railcar, sluggish and dejected, a force stronger than himself stopped him in his tracks.

The invisible hand holding him in place was firm. Absolute.

God couldn't have spoken more clearly.

If there was one thing Monty had learned about the Almighty, it was that His timing was perfect. He wanted Monty to let her go.

But Monty hadn't wanted to let her go. He'd wanted to jump onto that train, beg her forgiveness, and kiss her senseless. Impatience had never gained him a thing, however. If God was going to work this out for his good, he didn't want to ruin it by plowing ahead in his own power.

Annamae needed to go home. Losing her battle against the club, meeting his uncle Henry face-to-face, and discovering that the man she courted didn't spawn from the humble beginnings she believed he had dealt cruelly with her pride. She needed time to heal. To discover what God had created her to do and strengthen her walk with Him.

Monty needed to do the same. One must never grow complacent in their position but should desire and strive to grow taller in Christ. Since his arrival in Johnstown, he thought he'd been doing that by settling into the person most akin to his core instead of what society expected him to become. Through the flood, Annamae, and Uncle Henry, God had shown Monty how blind he was in his thinking. His congregation didn't know him. Not really. They only knew the parts Monty had wanted them to know.

His first attempt to lead a congregation had failed.

He'd also failed his first attempt to convince a woman he was worth marrying.

WASHINGTON, D.C.
TUESDAY, AUGUST 6

Annamae yawned as she unlocked her apartment door. The hallway was empty this early in the morning, the building silent. Seclusion had never felt this unbearable before. It was her companion anyway, waiting for her in the stale air of her room.

She curled her nose at the dust that greeted her as she padded inside and set down her bags. The light revealed every item neatly in its place, just as she'd left them. The chaos of Johnstown had her craving reticence in those first few weeks. Now, she wished for the sound of a streetcar bell, the clop of horse hooves, or a mouse scurrying in the wall—anything to distract her from her loneliness.

Her bed squeaked as she sat upon it. "What now, God?" she whispered.

Not only did she not have her former life intact, but she didn't have the one she'd imagined with Monty either.

Shoes and all, she curled in a ball on top of her covers and grieved over all she'd lost.

Chapter Thirty-One

"There is no fear in love; but perfect love casteth out fear: because fear hath torment. He that feareth is not made perfect in love."

~I John 4:18

JOHNSTOWN, PENNSYLVANIA
SUNDAY, AUGUST 11

"And that, folks, is who I am."

Monty's grip on the pulpit relaxed. Though shame swirled around him like dust in a wind tunnel, peace settled on his shoulders after confessing his omission. Annamae had been correct in accusing him of being a fraud and telling him he'd needed to come clean.

Stanley Bell stood from a center pew. "Why didn't you tell us sooner, Pastor?"

"I suppose part of me was ashamed to be associated with my uncle's evil deeds. Another part of me was afraid you all would never accept me if you knew I was born into the Frick-Childs family."

Monty cleared his throat. "But the biggest part of me felt I needed to prove to *myself* I could follow God's calling with no aid or acknowledgment of my family. Like when the apostle Paul had to prove his conversion from a persecutor to an apostle. I now realize it was nothing but a lack of faith on my part."

A breeze from the open windows stirred the silent congregation. All night, Monty had prayed for understanding from his friends. He'd either get it, or they'd send him packing on the next train.

Mr. Breslin leaned forward in the front pew, elbows on his knees. "I won't deny that I wish you'd been honest from the start, but I also can't deny that a man shouldn't be defined by his family. A man's got to prove himself, and in the last three years you've certainly done that."

Murmurs of agreement rippled through the room. Monty's three-year anniversary in Johnstown had passed, and he hadn't even realized it.

Hope buoyed Monty's spirit. "I'd love to stay and continue as your pastor if you'll allow me the privilege."

Men and women around the room looked at one another. Within a matter of minutes, they declared their approval.

Silently thanking the Lord, Monty closed in prayer then personally thanked every member as they left to enjoy their afternoon. Ernie was the last to go through the doors. "Thank you for your support," Monty said, shaking the man's feeble hand. "You're a good friend."

Ernie blinked at him. " 'Taint nothin', Pastor. You've overlooked my shortcomings. I can do the same for you."

His eyes were clear without the booze, but they filled with emotion easy enough nowadays. The cravings rode Ernie like a tick on a dog, whispering their demonic promises in his ears.

One day at a time. In reality, it was all any of them could do.

"If you need anything, my door is always open." Monty slapped a farewell on the man's back.

Ernie nodded and concentrated on his steps as he transitioned onto the lawn.

Annamae would be pleased with Ernie's progress.

Maybe Monty's too.

An ache started at his center and radiated outward the way it did every time he thought of her. He'd hadn't ceased praying that she'd allow the

Lord to finish His work in her and that she'd find her way back to him.

Job's meow rose from Monty's ankles. The tabby rubbed his face on Monty's pant leg then released a yawn. Monty bent and scratched the cat's spine. Job's purr vibrated through his fingers.

Monty stretched and gazed at the town, amazed at the progress made in the twelve short weeks since the flood. Johnstown would thrive again. With God's help, he and Annamae would too.

———◆◆◆———

WASHINGTON, D.C.
MONDAY, SEPTEMBER 2

This apartment no longer gave her independence and satisfaction but hit her with isolation and regret every time she entered it. Annamae swallowed a growl as the room shrouded her in darkness save for the glow of gaslight from the streetlamp outside her window. Her work at the hospital no longer fulfilled her. She craved companionship. The noise and the crowded streets.

She missed Monty desperately.

Her anger toward him had fizzled with time, though it hadn't faded entirely. It still hurt that he hadn't trusted her with the knowledge of his family's identity, even if he had cut ties with them years before. He should have told her that night they stood beneath the moon, after she'd confessed the details of her father's death. Then she would have. . .

What would she have done?

She'd like to think she would have been understanding and not held him responsible for his uncle's actions, but wasn't that what she was doing now?

Guided by the glimmer of the streetlight through her window, she stalked toward the bed. No, she was angry with him for hiding it from her. Or was she holding him responsible? His claim of protecting her was valid. After all, she'd seen what Mr. Frick's henchman had done to him. It had bruised her pride to find out his secret the way she had, but was she secretly punishing him because she couldn't punish his uncle?

As Clara had pointed out, Annamae tended to let her passion cloud her thinking. A characteristic she hadn't realized she possessed until the reticent, solitary nights had given her ample time to examine herself. The truth was, she could try to fight against the injustice of men like Mr. Carnegie and Mr. Frick for the rest of her days and never succeed. Men like that would likely always win.

She'd given up a good man who'd only tried to help her overcome her faults and live up to her potential. She'd also jeopardized the greatest opportunity to serve her fellow man with the greatest medical organization in the nation, all because she couldn't let go of her hatred. Now she had no justice, no husband, and no future.

Unable to stay in the desolate confines of her room, she removed her apron and cap, tossed them on the floor, and went for an evening stroll. The air was cool but comfortable. The scent of rain clung to the atmosphere. Would she ever see rain again without thinking of Monty and the friends she'd made in Johnstown?

She wrapped her arms around herself and stared up at the sky, wishing her father were there to tell her what to do next. She'd give everything she had to spend one more day with him. To feel his large, muscular arms embrace her in a gentle circle. To hear his laugh, smell the metallic scent of smoke in the fibers of his clothes.

Monty was right. Hating the men responsible for her father's death wouldn't bring him back. Neither would justice. She knew this. She needed to forgive and move forward with her life, but she didn't know how to forgive someone who wasn't remorseful for their actions. She felt she shouldn't have to.

Forgiving them seemed as if she was saying she was okay with what they'd done to her father, and she wasn't. But the bitterness and anger, the pulsing need to make them pay, prevented her from truly living.

She knew she shouldn't walk far without a chaperone, and yet she found herself on the grass stretching hundreds of yards to the Washington Monument. The moon was full and bright with peace and promise. *How do I forgive, Lord? Help me to forgive.*

Crickets serenaded her prayer.

Was Monty staring up at this same moon, missing her too? Did he miss their afternoon walks, their evening strolls, the barest of touches that shook her to her core?

When the night sky grew darker, she walked back to her apartment, dreading the long night ahead.

She rounded the corner of her building to find Matthew standing beneath a streetlamp, staring up at her window. Annamae had only seen him twice since her return, as her long absence with the Red Cross had forced her to a different shift. She also suspected he did what he could to ensure they didn't work together.

Her footsteps caught his attention, and he jumped. Their gazes locked. Shock turned to mortification, and he attempted to mask it with a sheepish grin. Her stomach knotted with the awkward conversation sure to follow.

"Good evening," she offered.

Matthew concentrated on his shuffling feet. "You're probably wondering what I'm doing here."

A light breeze blew strands of her hair, and she shivered, wishing she had her shawl. She rubbed her arms. "Is everything all right?"

He craned his neck toward the sky. "It is."

She studied him. Waiting.

Matthew sighed. "When I returned from Pennsylvania without you, I couldn't sleep. I started taking nightly walks to clear my head. Somehow, I always found myself walking past your building. I'd stop beneath this lamppost and say a prayer for you. For your health and happiness."

Her heart throbbed with sadness for him. Matthew was a good man. He deserved a woman better than her.

As did Monty.

"Those walks have become habit. I tried to make myself stop coming to this end of town after you returned, yet I still find myself outside your apartment every night. I mean no harm. And I've never meant it to be a burden to you."

He moved to walk away, but she stopped him. "You've never been a burden, Matthew."

His back to her, he hung his head.

"I'm sorry I've hurt you so deeply you find yourself here every night."

Matthew faced her. "I never came out of hurt. I came to heal."

"I don't understand."

"True healing is feeling peace in situations that once stirred a reaction from you. For example, visiting my wife's grave, though never easy, no longer keeps me indoors, ignoring my responsibilities for days. Once I'm able to pass by you and not feel the sting of rejection anymore, I'll know I've moved on."

She wanted to weep. She swallowed to erase any agony from her tone. "Is it getting any easier?"

"I think so." He moved closer. "Now, more than concentrating on my pain, I'm more concerned about yours. Forgive my saying this, but you don't look well, Annamae. That spark of life I saw in you in Johnstown is gone. Am I correct in assuming you have a broken heart too?"

She wilted against the streetlamp. "I misjudged some things. Myself, mostly. Instead of confronting my actions, I ran home with my tail between my legs."

Beneath the shadow of the glowing light, she told him about her father, her attempt to bring the club members to justice, and the last harsh but true conversations she'd had with Monty and Clara.

"We all make mistakes, Annamae. If this Monty fellow truly loves you, he'll acknowledge that and accept your apology."

"I don't think I can go back. Without Monty, and with the Red Cross work nearly completed, I've no excuse to return."

Silence fell between them for so long she wondered if Matthew would respond.

"Love never needs an excuse," he mumbled. "But if you must have one, they're building a new hospital in Cambria. It'll be used mostly by the men and their families at the iron works but will also serve as a public hospital as well. With your skills and talent, I'm sure you'd prove most useful."

She smiled her thanks, wishing things could have gone differently between them. "I'll be praying God sends the best of women to you, as you deserve no less."

"I wish you the best as well, Annamae, in whatever you choose to do."

She bade him good night and opened the main door to her building when his voice made her pivot.

"Thank you," he said.

"For what?"

He grinned. "This conversation wasn't as hard as I'd imagined it being when I saw you come around the corner."

Perhaps he'd stepped onto the other side of healing.

She raised a hand in farewell, walked to her apartment, and stepped into the shadows. This time, the darkness didn't threaten to swallow her whole. As she readied for bed, then slipped beneath the covers, she thought about what Matthew told her regarding the new hospital.

Cambria, huh? It would be a good excuse to stay close to Monty as they repaired their rocky courtship. If he was willing to forgive her.

Knowing what she knew of the handsome but reserved pastor, she supposed he would.

Chapter Thirty-Two

"I think it is better to know the worst, rather than trying to imagine it."
~Ellen Emerson White

JOHNSTOWN, PENNSYLVANIA
TUESDAY, OCTOBER 1

Annamae stepped off the train, greeted by the acrid smell she'd come to know as Johnstown. From her vantage point, the town looked as if it had grown twice in size since she'd left two months ago. New construction was still progressing, and gaping holes where buildings used to stand remained, but it was a beautiful sight to behold. With a little hope, lots of determination, and kindness from others, this town would thrive again to usher in the twentieth century. She just hoped she'd be there when it did.

Gripping her bags more securely, she moved down the platform, prepared for the long walk ahead. The hills were afire with red and gold leaves. The valley was chilly, and she was grateful for the sun warming her shoulders. Streetcars were running. The opera house sign boasted a performance of *Macbeth* at year's end. Annamae recognized faces here and there, but there were plenty of faces she'd never seen as well. More businesses had moved in, and the woolen mill appeared to be back in operation.

A whistle blasted and echoed through the hills, the Cambria Iron Works' reminder that it was the noon hour.

The acreage below that once flowed with white tents was open ground now that the hospital had opened. Only the Red Cross warehouse remained, as well as the flag waving above the building. On the stop in Sang Hollow, she'd heard the Red Cross had dismantled and the workers had gone home. Annamae hoped her benefactress was still in town.

According to the papers, the people of Johnstown had presented Clara Barton with a diamond locket to show their appreciation for all her Red Cross had done to help them. Once she returned to Washington, President and Mrs. Harrison planned a grand feast at the Willard in her honor.

Twenty minutes later, Annamae arrived at headquarters, out of breath and arm muscles burning. Hetty was packing papers and record books into boxes, while a man Annamae didn't know carried out the furniture. Annamae set her bags on a nearby chair. Relief flowed into her appendages. "Is Miss Barton still here?"

Hetty turned in surprise. "Annamae! Goodness, you're back. Yes, she's in the warehouse, taking stock of what remains so she can gift it to the supplies committee." She looked at Annamae's luggage, and her elated expression fell. "I'm sorry, but our work here is finished. Only a few of us remain, and we'll be going home in the next day or two."

"I understand. I'm here for a different purpose but wanted to see Miss Barton before she leaves." Annamae lifted her burdens again. "It's good to see you, Hetty. Take care of yourself."

"You too."

Hetty went back to work, and Annamae went in search of Clara.

She found her at the rear of the warehouse, counting blankets stacked on top of a crate. One eyebrow raised when she spotted Annamae. She finished counting and notated the number before speaking. "You're the last person I expected to see as we prepare to leave."

Annamae shifted the weight of her bags. "I've been hired as a nurse at the Cambria hospital."

"You're leaving Washington?"

"For now."

"Did you not find what you were seeking then?" Clara's eyebrows pulled together.

Unable to hold on any longer, Annamae plunked her bags on the lid of a nearby crate. "In one way, I did."

"And?" Clara put down the pencil and waited. She wasn't going to let Annamae off easily.

"I realized that the actions of man will frustrate me the rest of my life if I allow them to. I won't stop praying and doing my part to see a positive difference made, but I also won't let the outcome rule my life anymore. It's time to see what I can do for others instead of fixating on what I can do for myself."

Satisfaction lifted the corners of Clara's mouth. "Are you ready to rejoin the Red Cross? I can write a letter of recommendation to the Pittsburgh or Philadelphia chapters."

"While I've adored working with you and appreciate every opportunity that afforded, I believe the Lord is calling me into a different kind of servanthood."

A pastor's wife, if Monty would have her.

Clara picked up her pencil and clipboard. "Well, you know my address and how much I enjoy catching up on my correspondence when time allows. I'll look forward to hearing about this new venture."

With a two-finger salute, Annamae reclaimed her luggage and continued her walk of humility up the hill to Monty's house.

Proprietors swept their porches. Children played outside their homes, some barefoot with sprigs of grass tickling their toes. She'd read in the newspapers that several families who'd left after the flood had returned to Johnstown now that school was in session and the town was stable again. The city burst with life.

She'd never get to the top of Monty's porch steps carrying her bags, so she left them sitting on the third step and finished the journey to his front door. Would he be happy to see her? Angry at her for leaving? Had he moved forward with his future and started courting someone else?

He hadn't come to the train station to ask her to stay, nor had he written. Maybe this wasn't a wise idea after all. Another case of her emotions overshadowing her good sense.

Mustering her courage, she rapped her knuckles against the door. A few seconds later, footsteps thumped closer. Her stomach knotted.

She hadn't realized how much she'd missed him until he stood on the other side of the open doorway.

He blinked. "Annamae."

The entire ride from Washington to Johnstown, she'd thought about what she wanted to say when the moment came. Now she couldn't remember one thought.

He glanced at her bags waiting on his steps and frowned. "Would you like to come in?"

She took a step forward, and he moved out of her way. He pointed to her luggage.

"They're fine," she croaked. "I can't stay long."

He closed the door behind them. "Are you only passing through?"

Job napped in the curve of the settee. The room smelled like meaty stew. Steam rose from a bowl at the table. A muffin—peach?—rested on a napkin beside the stew. She'd interrupted his lunch.

How she longed to see two bowls there. Every night. Forever.

"I. . ." She shoved away the image of what a future with him might look like. "I've been hired as a nurse at the new Cambria hospital."

His brows rose. "What about Washington?"

"It doesn't feel like home anymore." As soon as she'd come to that conclusion, she'd made plans to vacate her apartment and given the hospital administration sufficient notice of her leaving.

"Does Johnstown feel like home?" He crossed his arms and leaned against the counter.

My, he looked glorious. Bruises healed, his confident stance and the slightly arrogant curve of his lips stirred her blood.

"You feel like home, Monty," she whispered.

The end of her nose burned, and she sniffed. "An unexpected person in the most unexpected of ways showed me I owe you a great apology for my behavior. I'm sorry. I hope you can forgive me, as I've been working very hard to forgive."

She swiped the blasted tear she'd tried to keep from escaping. "I'm stubborn and fiery and imperfect, and forgiving the wrong done to my father will be a choice I'll have to make every single day for the rest of my life, but a future with you is something I want more than revenge. If you still want me."

He said nothing in return, simply stared at her. She squirmed beneath his scrutiny. When she decided she couldn't bear another awkward moment, he opened the front door and left.

If a heart could physically split apart, hers had.

She squeezed her eyes closed, letting the tears come. He was too kind a man to voice what he really thought of her, so he'd left instead. She'd been foolish to come back.

Footsteps sounded again, and when she opened her eyes, he filled the open doorway, luggage in both hands. Kicking the door closed behind him, he moved to the settee and dropped the bags, scaring Job.

"Even though I'm a preacher, I'm not allowed to perform our own ceremony, so we'll have to find another. Reverend Beale is gone. Had a disagreement with his congregation for using the church as a morgue without the elders' permission. But I'm sure Reverend Palmer or Father Cline will agree as long as they're available."

She slapped a hand over her mouth to keep from melting into a simpering mess.

"That is, if you're willing to accept a once-spoiled, pretentious, and imperfect man."

She laughed, dropping her hand and nodding.

Through her haze of happy tears, he moved toward her with purpose and placed his palms against her cheeks. He lowered his mouth to hers and showed her just what a future with him would be like.

Her salty tears mingled with the savory taste of man and peaches. His lips were soft and commanding. Powerful yet controlled in that special way that made him Monty. A quiet moan vibrated in her throat.

He drew her closer, deepening the kiss. She wrapped her arms around his neck, losing all sense of space and time. When her brain went fuzzy and every inch of her body was languid, he pulled away.

"Let's go find that preacher."

Epilogue

❧

"It may be well to consider that the flood, with all its train of horrors, is behind us, and that we have henceforth to do with the future alone."
~George Swank, as quoted in the *Johnstown Daily Tribune* on June 1, 1892

MAY 31, 1892

The day dawned warm and bright. Unlike that fateful day three years before when the South Fork dam collapsed and the waters raged down the mountain. The day everything had changed. Not only for the residents of Johnstown but for Monty.

Silence fell over the Grandview Cemetery in anticipation of the unveiling of the Monument to the Unknown Dead. The Pennsylvania Flood Commission had purchased a plot of twenty-thousand square feet and sunk seven hundred and seventy-seven marble grave markers into the ground. Thousands of people attended the ceremony, all to honor the victims of the great disaster.

Faces old and new surrounded them. Gertrude Quinn, tall and slender for a girl of nine, stood ten feet away, gripping her father's hand. When she recognized Monty, she started to wave but caught Mr. Quinn's silent reprimand and lowered her arm. Monty winked to acknowledge her gesture, and she smiled.

Robert Pitcairn, Tom L. Johnson, John Fulton, and many other pillars of Johnstown were in attendance. Sadly, not one of the other club members had come. As the months passed, the newspapers mentioned less of their involvement and started reporting other news. In a decade, Johnstown would be forgotten.

Annamae entwined her fingers in his, looking up at him. Her large brown eyes radiated empathy. Though she hadn't experienced the flood personally, she'd lain with him many a night while he voiced the horrors he'd stuffed deep inside. Many in the community had shared their experiences with her as well while she ministered alongside him. Her many talents complemented his, and together they'd made a wonderful life and a wonderful church family.

The sun reflected off her hair, giving it an almost reddish hue. The long procession from town to the cemetery had put pink into her cheeks. A small mound peeked beneath the waistline of her skirt. The one only he was privy to for now. Pregnancy had filled out her thin figure, making her even more desirable. She was a wonderful mother to Joanna, and he couldn't wait to see the life they'd created together swaddled in her arms.

Even amid disaster, time marched on. The day he'd stood on his rooftop and watched life after life pass by, he never would have believed God had set the bigger plan of his future into motion.

At the foot of the covered statue stood their former governor, James Beaver, and their current governor, Robert Pattison. In perfect synchronization, they tugged on the ripcords, revealing the twenty-one-foot sarcophagus topped with three life-sized figures of Faith, Hope, and Charity. Heads bowed. The band began playing a melancholy tune, drawing out the sobs of the women. The men who'd lost wives and children let their grief fall down their faces.

Monty wrapped his arm around his wife and pulled her close. To his dying day, he would hear the echoes of their screaming, see the sheer terror on their faces. Smell the stench of burning flesh, oil, and contaminated water. But he would also remember the joy of reunited loved ones, the relief of lost items found, and, most of all, the knowledge that God always keeps His promises.

The choir began singing "God Moves in a Mysterious Way." Boy, did God ever.

With one palm against her stomach, Annamae rested her head on Monty's shoulder. At the end of the song, Governor Pattison raised his voice to be heard among the crowd.

"We who have to do with the concentrated forces of nature, the powers of air, electricity, water, steam, by careful forethought must leave nothing undone for the preservation and protection of the lives of our brother men.

"To God, to country, and to Johnstown."

Dismissed, the mass dispersed down the curvy road that led back to town. Some lingered at the monument, working through their farewells. Joanna ran up to them. "Thank you for letting me stand with the Murphys. They've invited me to their house for dinner. May I go? Please?"

Petite for fourteen, the horrors she'd gone through caused her to think and act like a girl much younger. Annamae was the epitome of patience and kindness to the girl, and she was blossoming beneath Annamae's care.

Annamae smiled her approval at him.

"All right. Mind your manners, and be home by eight."

"Thank you, thank you." In a flash, she was gone again, leaving them alone and laughing.

Holding on to his wife's hand, Monty led her behind the group, down the hill toward home. It had been a long, emotional day, and a lazy afternoon nap in a quiet house would do them both good.

"I remember when you first brought me up here," Annamae said.

"Me too. I'd heard it was the best place around to spark a woman, but I'd never visited before you."

Her eyes grew wide, and she glanced around then swatted his arm.

He chuckled. "No one is close enough to hear. They walk faster than we do. In fact, we'd better pick up the pace if we want to make it home before Joanna does."

She rolled her eyes at his teasing. "I'm tired. I think I could sleep for weeks."

As if on cue, she yawned.

He pulled her closer to his side and kissed her temple. "I'll tuck you in as soon as we get home."

Annamae grinned. "After I make us dinner."

"No need. You rest, and I'll grab us something at the café."

"Meat loaf sounds wonderful. With mashed potatoes, green beans, corn, and yeast rolls with a large dollop of butter."

"Is that all?"

"And cherry pie. Ooh, and fried chicken."

He stopped and faced her. "Darling, I don't think that tiny babe can handle that much food."

She clasped her bottom lip between her teeth. "But two of them can."

"What?"

"Doctor Thayer said he hears two heartbeats besides my own."

Monty's pulse kicked up its pace. "Twins?"

She laughed. "Yes, that's what that means."

A long breath escaped him. Bringing one babe into the world scared him enough, but two?

Annamae looped her arm through his and tugged them closer to home. "God is good, Monty. He'll provide."

He couldn't argue with that.

Author's Note

The accounts of the Johnstown Flood of 1889 caught my attention several years ago when I was watching the History Channel documentary *The Men Who Built America*. The tragedies, the survivor accounts, and the outpouring of charity from across America and beyond amazed me. What stuck with me the most and has never let go is that not one charge was ever brought against the South Fork Fishing and Hunting Club nor any of its members. Despite proof of negligence, no one was ever held accountable.

This broke my heart, and I knew someday I would write a story based on this disaster to not only educate readers about the events but also to honor those who experienced that terrible day.

As in the story, the day before the flood was full of celebration, as Johnstown observed Memorial Day. Many sources I studied revealed that it was such a grand day, no one would have guessed that for many it would be their last night on earth.

While the main characters and basic storyline of *When the Waters Came* are completely fictional, real survivors waltz across the pages throughout the story. There were so many details and accounts I wanted to add, but I had to limit what I used to avoid writing a story that was too lengthy. I used exact quotes as dialogue in every place I could, only making small grammatical changes so it flowed easier. The legendary horse rider in chapter two who warns the folks of Johnstown about the oncoming wave has been deemed by experts as fiction, but the following true events were used in my story and spotlight real-life survivors.

James and Rosina Quinn owned Quinn's Dry Goods. Their six-year-old daughter, Gertrude, was thrown from their house when the wave hit, ripping off everything but her underclothes. While riding the water toward the burning stone bridge, she was rescued by Max McCachren, a painter and paperhanger, "a beast of a man" with the gentlest of hearts. He'd been separated from his wife and fifteen children during the flood and joined several others on a raft. When he spotted Gertrude kneeling on the mattress, hands clasped and raised to the sky in prayer, his heart broke. He swam to her and later pitched her to two men on a rooftop. He continued toward the bridge. By the grace of God, Max survived the flood, but he and Gertrude never saw each other again. The man who caught Gertrude that night was Mr. Henry Koch, who owned Koch House, a hotel and saloon in Johnstown.

The scene where Monty takes Gertrude to the apartment where she was recognized by the Bowser sisters is a true account and detailed beautifully in David G. McCullough's *The Johnstown Flood*.

In chapter five, Ernie Dickenson says to Monty, "You've always told me that the Lord would care for me. Will He look after me now?" This line was actually spoken by a child to his mother, Mrs. Fenn (who's quoted at the beginning of chapter three), when she placed him on driftwood and raised the attic window to release him in hopes he'd survive somehow versus certain drowning in their attic. He drifted away, and she never saw her little boy again. As a mother, that account shredded my heart, and I felt it was too heavy to portray the details in the story using its exact form. I mention it now to honor the story of Mrs. Fenn's son.

Looters almost immediately preyed upon Johnstown; however, the number of such cases and many of the details were sensationalized to sell papers. This made things even more difficult for immigrants in the area, causing many to fear for their lives.

Folks from all over the country poured into Johnstown to witness the wreckage. As mentioned in the story, some weren't above taking a meal at the commissary while visiting (limiting food for the survivors and volunteers), swiping trinkets they found in the wreckage for keepsakes, or purchasing keepsakes from hawkers attempting to capitalize on the disaster.

Many factors contributed to the dam's collapse, though none ranked higher than the negligence of the South Fork Fishing and Hunting Club. The growing town needed lumber, and the deforestation caused erosion that contributed to much of the town's spring flooding. Slag from the mills was dumped into the nearby rivers, narrowing the riverbeds and causing the water to rush at a faster speed. When Benjamin Ruff purchased the club's property from the Pennsylvania Railroad, one of the first things he did was remove the sluice pipes and sell them for scrap. The control tower to raise and lower the water burned, and parts of the concrete culvert were removed and packed with mud and hay and other substances. This caused the dam to sag in the middle and was made worse when the carriage road that ran the length of the dam was lowered and widened to allow two carriages to pass. For nearly a decade, folks had expressed their concern about the dam, but Ruff and the club members ignored the pleas to strengthen it.

Colonel Elias J. Unger worked to prevent the dam's collapse, but his efforts were too little, too late. After watching the water shoot from the dam with the force of Niagara, he collapsed and had to be carried to his home. His health never fully recovered. Years after the flood, a Civil War military record was found for him (unlike in the story), but it appears as if he never saw combat.

General Hastings, Doctor Hubbell, Cyrus Elder, Tom L. Johnson, John Fulton, Clara Barton, Doctor Hamilton (Surgeon General of the United States), Henry Clay Frick, and several others were real and vital characters in Johnstown.

The Red Cross arrived in Johnstown five days after the flood. The accounts of injuries, typhoid, and distribution of supplies and disinfectants I used in the story are accurate according to my research.

Clara Barton was a fascinating woman to learn about, and I thoroughly enjoyed making her part of the story. I detailed her quirks and personality to the best of my ability, according to the information I found in her biographies. The account of her brother's injury when she was eleven is true, and most of the dialogue used in that scene are her exact words.

John Fulton's speech regarding the Cambria Iron Works building their business back better and stronger actually happened. His speech is almost verbatim.

Monty's scene with Cyrus Elder reflects Elder's true statements on the matter of the South Fork Fishing and Hunting Club's responsibility for the dam's collapse.

Many of the newspaper headlines and articles in the story were pulled from actual periodicals. All quotes that begin each chapter are cited from authentic sources.

Sadly, Henry Clay Frick never visited Johnstown, which shows his callous attitude regarding the club's responsibility, but the story called for a confrontation between Frick and Monty, so I wrote Frick's visit for the sake of storytelling. Frick did not have a nephew named Monty.

Andrew Carnegie did visit Johnstown when he returned from Scotland in the fall of 1889, and afterward donated thousands to aid in the reconstruction, including providing Johnstown with a new public library—one of over 1,600 he'd later establish across the United States. Since Carnegie was such a prominent member of the club, generations have believed that he owned a private cottage at the lake, but a discovery nearly a century after the flood showed that he never owned a cottage nor did he ever stay at the South Fork Fishing and Hunting Club's clubhouse on Lake Conemaugh. Carnegie owned his own mountain home in Cresson where he recreated. He likely joined the club merely to associate his name with other important men in the country.

In the story, I mention that the club's charter was filed in the Court of Common Pleas in Allegheny County instead of the Cambria County courthouse as it should have been. This happened to keep the club membership secretive. However, this wasn't discovered until many years later. I used it in my story to give Annamae something to reveal to the reporter that would provoke Mr. Frick to confront her.

Sadly, the Johnstown Flood of 1889 isn't the only time the town has been inundated by floodwaters. It flooded again in 1936, killing two dozen, and again in 1977, killing eighty-five.

If you would like to learn more about the Johnstown Flood of 1889, the South Fork Fishing and Hunting Club, or the Red Cross, I recommend visiting the Johnstown Flood National Memorial, the Johnstown Flood Museum, and Grandview Cemetery. I also recommend the following books and websites:

The Johnstown Flood by David G. McCullough,
Simon & Schuster, 1968

Johnstown and Its Flood by Gertrude Quinn
Slattery, Wilkes-Barre, 1936

*_History of the Johnstown Flood, Illustrated_ by Willis
Fletcher Johnson, Edgewood Publishing Co., 1889

*_The Life of Clara Barton_ by Percy H. Epler, The
Macmillan Company, 1919 (this book includes transcripts
of her journals and personal correspondence)

*The Johnstown Flood documentary, narrated by Richard Dreyfuss

*_Ruthless Tide_ by Al Roker, William Morrow, 2018

*Johnstown Area Heritage Association and
Johnstown Flood Museum (Jaha.org)

*Flood map of Washington, D.C., in June 1889 (mallhistory.org)

*National Parks Service, Johnstown
Flood, National Memorial Pennsylvania
(https://www.nps.gov/jofl/learn/historyculture/cyrus-elder.htm)

*Johnstown National Flood Museum Facebook page

Acknowledgments

I hope you've enjoyed learning about the Johnstown, Pennsylvania flood of 1889. The accounts, the places, and the people have come to feel like family to me. I shed many tears over their suffering while researching and writing this story. It is my deepest wish that I've not only written a novel that will stay with you long after you turn the last page but that I've honored the victims, survivors, and descendants of the flood.

Huge thanks to Ranger Elizabeth Shope for being such a wonderful tour guide at the former South Fork Fishing and Hunting Club clubhouse and cottage row tours through the National Park Service. Thanks for bringing history to life for geeks like me!

To David G. McCullough for making it your life's passion to compile the accounts of that fateful day in your wonderfully written book. Your book was vital to the life of mine, and I'm grateful.

This book would not exist without my agent, Linda S. Glaz of the Linda S. Glaz Literary Agency. I'm blessed to take this journey with you.

None of my books would be complete without the "sisters of my heart"—the Quid Pro Quills. Thank you for critiquing my manuscripts and offering your friendships. Pegg Thomas, Robin Patchen, Jericha Kingston, Kara Hunt, and Susan Crawford—I couldn't survive my fictional worlds without you.

For Becky Germany, my editor, Ellen Tarver, and the rest of the Barbour team for the beautiful cover and fantastic editing skills. I love being a part of the Barbour family.

To my husband, Adam, for walking beside me every step of the way. Your patience during deadlines, your comic relief, and your willingness to help me succeed are priceless. Thank you for loving me no matter what.

To Levi, Silas, and Hudson—no matter how many books I write or what else I do in life, you are my greatest accomplishments. Thanks for supporting my dreams all these years. Now go chase yours!

Above all, I thank my Lord and Savior, Jesus Christ. All honor and glory are His.

Thank you, dear reader, for taking the time out of your busy lives to spend it with my characters. Until next time. . .

Candice Sue Patterson studied at The Institute of Children's Literature and is an elementary librarian. She lives in Indiana with her husband and three sons in a restored farmhouse overtaken by books. When she's not tending to her chickens, snuggling with her Great Pyrenees, or helping children discover books they love, she's working on a new story. Candice writes Modern Vintage Romance—where the past and present collide with faith. For more on Candice and her books, visit www.candicesuepatterson.com.

A Day to Remember

A new series of exciting novels featuring historic American disasters that changed landscapes and multiple lives. Whether by nature or by man, these disasters changed history and were a day to be remembered.

When the Flames Ravaged
By Rhonda Dragomir
July 6, 1944

World War II Gold Star widow, Evelyn Benson, is taken in by her brother and soothed by the love of his wife and children. Evelyn refuses to cower in grief, so on a sweltering July day in 1944, the family attends the Ringling Bros. and Barnum & Bailey Circus in Hartford. When a blaze ignites the big top, Evelyn fears she will lose all that remains of her life, while Hank Webb, who hides from his murky past behind grease paint as Fraidy Freddie the clown, steps out of the shadows to help save lives and return hope to Evelyn.

Paperback / 978–1–63609–786–2

When Hope Sank
By Denise Weimer
April 27, 1865

The Civil War has taken everything from Lily Livingston, leaving her to work for her uncle at a squalid inn along the Arkansas riverfront that is overrun by spies and bushwhackers. Her only hope of escape is a marriage promise she is uncertain will be fulfilled. When on April 27, 1865, the steamboat *Sultana*, overloaded with soldiers, explodes and sinks, Lily does all she can to help the victims, including Lieutenant Cade Palmer. But what would the wounded surgeon think of her if he knew she could have prevented the disaster—and may have knowledge of another in the making?

Paperback / 978–1–63609–829–6

Books by Candice Sue Patterson

Modern Vintage Romance—where the past and present collide with faith.

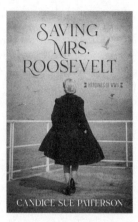

Saving Mrs. Roosevelt
(Heroines of WWII series)

Shirley Davenport is as much a patriot as her four brothers. She, too, wants to aid her country in the war efforts and joins a new branch of the Coast Guard for single women called SPARs. At the end of basic training, Captain Webber commissions her back home in Maine under the ruse of a dishonorable discharge to help uncover a plot against the First Lady. Shirley soon discovers nothing is as it seems. Why do the people she loves want to harm the First Lady?

Paperback / 978-1-63609-089-4

The Keys to Gramercy Park
(Doors to the Past series)

Nothing unusual happens in lower Manhattan until the day aspiring investigative historical journalist Andrea Andrews discovers post–Civil War counterfeit bills hidden in her apartment wall. Here could be the story she needs to boost her career with the *Smithsonian Magazine*. Two centuries earlier, wounded Civil War veteran Franklin Davidson lost everything, only to gain a position with the newly formed Secret Service. His new life and home in Gramercy Park are the envy of his peers, but nothing is as it seems. Secrets are meant to be kept, and Franklin will take his to his grave.

Paperback / 978-1-63609-533-2